THE OUROBOROS WAVE

JYOUJI HAYASHI

THE OUROBOROS WAVE

JYOUJI HAYASHI

TRANSLATED BY JIM HUBBERT

HAIKA SORU

SAN FRANCISCO

The Ouroboros Wave
© 2002 Jyouji Hayashi
Originally published in Japan
by Hayakawa Publishing, Inc.

English translation © 2010 VIZ Media, LLC

Cover illustration by Tomoyuki Fukutome

HAIKASORU
Published by
VIZ Media, LLC
295 Bay Street
San Francisco, CA 94133

www.haikasoru.com

Library of Congress Cataloging in Publication Data

Hayashi, Jyouji.
  [Ouroboros wave. English]
  The Ouroboros wave / Jyouji Hayashi ; translated by Jim
Hubbert.
     p. cm.
"Originally published in Japan by Hayakawa Publishing, 2002."
  ISBN 978-1-4215-3645-3
I. Hubbert, Jim. II. Title.   PL871.A93O9713 2010
  895.6'35—dc22
                    2010037419

The rights of the author of the work in this publication to be so
identified have been asserted in accordance with the Copyright,
Designs and Patents Act 1988. A CIP catalogue record for this
book is available from the British Library.

Printed in the U.S.A.
First printing, November 2010

CONTENTS

HAPPENSTANCE is necessity in disguise.

A proverb is often borne out by events, and the discovery of the black hole humankind would eventually name Kali was one of these events. If Dr. Ochiai hadn't entered erroneous coordinates for her X-ray observation satellite, its sensors would never have focused on a seemingly empty part of the heavens. Kali would have remained undiscovered, at least for the time being.

But happenstance was not content with fortuitous discovery. Kali was an astonishingly small black hole, about the same mass as Mars, emitting X-rays with clockwork regularity for reasons unknown. It was purest chance that the satellite turned its collimator toward Kali at the right moment to detect its emissions.

Kali may have been as old as the universe itself; the Big Bang gave birth to countless black holes. The smallest of these objects evaporated, and in the billions of years since the universe came into being, every black hole with less than a trillion kilograms of mass had disappeared. Kali, however, was six hundred billion times more massive.

At first it was just another object of interest for astronomers. But when those members of the human species who had already begun to make their home in space realized that this black hole was on a collision course with the Sun, they took action. Kali's orbit would be changed. Its energy would even be harnessed for humanity's benefit.

These actions sprang from necessity. Humans were not yet able to perceive meaning in the chance events that followed in necessity's wake.

THE OUROBOROS WAVE
A.D. 2123

1

THE FUNERAL BEGAN as the sun climbed above the ring's horizon. Moments earlier, East Platform had been in utter darkness. Now that smooth metallic surface, fifty meters broad, flashed into brilliance as light reflected from it. And the sun kept rising.

The shadows of the astronauts stabbed out across the platform's two hundred meters. As the sun climbed higher, each shadow withdrew into its owner like a living organism. Twelve minutes later the sun was at the zenith. For a few seconds the shadows disappeared. Then they began reaching out in the opposite direction.

This orientation kept solar energy distributed uniformly across Ouroboros, a revolving ring more than four thousand kilometers across. Still, this was a funeral, and the mourners took notice. The sun rose, fell, and rose again in less than an hour, whispering of death and resurrection.

"Yesterday—September 13, 2123—our friend and colleague, the brilliant astronomer Dr. Graham Chapman, was transformed into a celestial object."

Catherine Sinclaire had been a close associate of Dr. Chapman in System Control. As she finished speaking, a bright ring of gas floated into view over the heads of the mourners. At the same moment, the sun reached the zenith. The three-dimensional image dimmed in the sunlight.

The hologram showed the black hole at the center of Ring

Mega-Structure Ouroboros, over two thousand kilometers away. The accretion disk pulsed with energy as it spiraled into Kali, glowing with fission reactions. As Chapman fell toward the event horizon his mass was converted to energy.

Catherine's partner Tatsuya Kawanishi watched the hologram on his web, a multifunction computing and communications device. Kali was only a few millimeters across, but Chapman's disappearance into the singularity couldn't be viewed with the naked eye.

The ultimate goal of AADD—the Artificial Accretion Disk Development association—was to create an accretion disk around Kali as a source of harvestable energy. But this disk was different. It was Graham Chapman himself. Cosmic gravitational and tidal forces had transfigured him.

AADD had neither priests nor any need for them. Funerals did not comfort the spirits of the dead. They gave closure to the living. AADD funerals did not include religion, and AADD members did not stake their fate on a deity. Fate was something to be shaped with one's wits. The awe felt by a single human confronting the immensity of space far surpassed any religious teaching. No one here was arrogant enough to imagine that a deity would trouble itself with the affairs of humanity. Such a being might exist or it might not. It made little difference.

East Platform was the only place on the ring large enough for close to a hundred mourners. It was also the scene of the accident. Until yesterday, two cylindrical habitat modules had stood here, awaiting the start of full-scale construction. But the crews had not yet arrived, otherwise there would have been more casualties. Now only fragments of the modules remained on the expanse of bare metal.

Chapman's body, still in its space suit, had struck the modules, demolishing them. Luckily the structures on the inner side of the ring had escaped damage. But here on the outer surface, only the laser cannons standing guard against meteor strikes—each of the ring's four platforms had two—were unscathed. For now, the cannons were off-line.

All of the AADD division chiefs—men and women responsible for the construction of Ouroboros—were here, clad in hard-shell space suits. No one was recognizable; they communicated using their webs.

In spite of the anonymity imposed by the space suits, the somber mood on the platform was palpable. Chapman had been one of System Control's senior personnel, and most of those present had had at least some contact with him. Several mourners, including Catherine and Tatsuya, had been very close to him. Even those who hadn't known Chapman well were shocked by the accident. His death marked the first fatality on the Chandrasekhar Station construction project.

One after another, Chapman's friends shared their impressions of the deceased. He had hardly been a saint, but his virtues had outweighed his flaws. He had sometimes been hasty in judgment, but his achievements spoke for themselves. As the mourners recounted their memories, a shared sense emerged. Dr. Graham Chapman had been a human being, neither hero nor icon.

It was then that the mourners realized the funeral was over.

———◆———

AADD DID NOT FIT the usual image of a corporation. There were responsibilities and functions, but no rank or hierarchy. This alone made it difficult for Terrans to understand.

AADD was a collective of teams. Each team had a functional specialty and was independent, coming together with other teams as needed. Chandrasekhar Station—Ouroboros was only the first stage—was a typical example. The project teams were autonomous, but in the minds of their members, everything tied back to AADD. The picture was further blurred by the constant migration of specialists between teams. It wasn't unusual for teams to merge and divide again, amoebalike.

Dr. Chapman was typical of AADD's senior members. An astronomer by profession, he had also had deep expertise in data processing and artificial intelligence. He, Catherine, and Tatsuya had shared overall responsibility for System Control.

Of course, AADD operated this way for a reason, just as there were reasons for the distrust it had earned from the people of Earth.

The singularity around which Chandrasekhar Station was being constructed had come to be known as Kali. In 2100, an orbiting observatory had detected a source of bizarre X-ray emissions. Kali was a tremendous discovery: a tiny black hole with roughly the mass of Mars, only a few dozen AUs from Earth.

Soon after Kali was discovered, the Black Hole Reconnaissance Group of COSPAD, the UN's Cosmic Space Development Agency, was formed as a dedicated observation group. It was BHRG that first proposed the artificial accretion disk development plan. It then dissolved itself, only to immediately reemerge as AADD. That was in 2120.

BHRG quickly discovered something unusual about Kali: it had a high probability of colliding with the Sun in anywhere from a few hundred to a few thousand years. The lack of precision in the estimate was due to Kali's size. Calculating its orbital elements by standard methods was dauntingly difficult, but computer simulations confirmed that at some point the black hole was destined to fall into the Sun.

BHRG's proposal was to shift Kali out of its collision course and onto a trajectory that would make it a satellite of Uranus. At the same time, placing an artificial accretion disk around Kali would meet all of the solar system's energy requirements for as long as anyone was willing to guess.

The concept met with little interest at first; few considered it even feasible. Kali would not fall into the Sun for centuries, maybe even for thousands of years. It was hard to see it as an immediate threat. There was also little consensus concerning the physical effect of a tiny black hole colliding with the Sun. BHRG's proposal seemed dead on arrival.

Yet the scientists behind it were nothing if not determined. All of BHRG's original members were astronomers, but theoretical physicists and others soon began to join, forming a network that stretched throughout the solar system—a network of experts from the wide range of fields that would ultimately be needed for the construction of an artificial accretion disk. A development group quickly formed, with BHRG as its nucleus. Only a few of its members hailed from Earth, but they made up for their limited numbers in quality. As the group expanded across the solar system, membership expanded beyond the scientific and engineering community to include economists, psychologists, media specialists, and others. Ultimately AADD emerged as the official representative of this unofficial network.

This was the notion of AADD's foundation accepted by most Terrans. The reality was different.

Long before AADD was founded, Mars settlers were building a flexible, project-driven society starkly different from Earth's hierarchical class systems. Terrans tended to think the UN created BHRG, which then spawned AADD. In truth, the two groups were both born of United Nations decisions; the UN could be said to be the common ancestor of both. Colonists throughout the solar system had fused their individual development plans for each planet into a system-level agenda, and were coordinating to implement it. They created BHRG as one arm of this effort, used it to engage in a wide range of research, and finally created AADD as a concrete expression of that R & D network.

Given the nature of the project, most of AADD's members were from Mars or the asteroid belt. Many of its members from Earth eventually migrated offworld. Terran civilization had become extremely conservative. Preservation of established norms—and protection of established interests—was equated with virtue. The result was a kind of soft fascism that combined quasi–free market economies with authoritarian political control—not exactly an ideal environment for inquisitive scientists. Anything questioning the existing constellation of powers was a threat. The scientific community was strictly hierarchical, and research was allowed only in certain fields. The important thing was not productive science, but protection of the status quo.

For the promising young scientists and engineers who sensed the dangers of this system, the freedom offered by BHRG's philosophy was even more attractive than the prospect of working on accretion disk technology. Those who left Earth were seen as traitors. Other young researchers were branded as undesirable elements and forcibly deported offworld.

By the time AADD was established, plans were in place for what would become Ouroboros. From this point on, the artificial accretion disk and terraforming of the Martian surface were part of a single vision.

The accretion disk would be completed in thirty years, with another half century to terraform Mars. The eighty-year timeline kept the project within the lifetime of the investors. Once the accretion disk was producing energy, AADD would have its own source of revenue. The question was how to finance the project until then. AADD's solution was to entice investors with profits from rapid appreciation of real estate on Mars and the main asteroids, terraformed through energy provided by Kali. This incentive became the key to obtaining financing for the project. Chandrasekhar Station—beginning with the construction of Ouroboros—was the first step on a path that would continue for decades.

———

"WE WON'T HAVE TIME to mourn Graham after today, will we, Tatsuya?"

"That's how it is with any project like this."

Catherine and Tatsuya were on the ring's maglev, bound for South Platform. Nicknamed "the bullet" by the construction crews, the maglev provided rapid transportation between platforms. There were several other smaller vehicles, single-seaters dubbed "trucks." Both systems moved at satellite speed, covering the three-thousand-kilometer distance between platforms in under twenty minutes.

Viewed from the equinoctial point above Ouroboros, both bullet and ring would be revolving clockwise. Since they were traveling in the direction of rotation, Catherine and Tatsuya sat opposite each other at a table attached to the side of the train that was away from the ring. The train was pressurized and was often used as a temporary habitat as well as for transport. The door to the compartment was flanked with small lockers flush with the wall, with storage for emergency oxygen and coffee mugs labeled with the names of their owners.

Keeping the compartment clean was the responsibility of the users. While things were reasonably tidy, the walls were marked with stains from what might have been sauce that floated, weightless, through the compartment when the bullet had stopped while someone was eating.

"Okay, we're under the gun. But SysCon has more to do than just make up lost time. We've got to turn detective and find out why Graham was killed."

"Like in those whodunit softs you love to read? Figure out the killer from a speck of dust or some other microscopic bit of evidence?"

"Yes, but that's not enough. We can't just wait for suspects to get killed off one by one before we nail the culprit. We've got to work out a solution before someone else becomes a victim. Like Sherlock Holmes. Do you follow, Watson?"

"I don't know. Holmes was a genius who could run rings around the experts. But this is real. It's up to the Guardians—"

"It's up to us too. I've already briefed them, but they can't do anything about this on their own. There's an AI in the mix here. You sense it too, don't you? There's something very wrong about this accident."

"I guess. There's no way Graham could have fallen off the ring. It's physically impossible."

Ouroboros, the first stage in the Chandrasekhar Station project, was a five-meter-wide ribbon of metal stretching almost 13,000 kilometers around Kali at a radial distance of 2,025 kilometers. Scale the ring down to a diameter of one meter, and a few dozen atoms laid end to end would be enough to span its width. This metallic thread, with Kali at its center, was rotating clockwise at 4,440 meters per second. Because of its continuous ring shape, Ouroboros had no net gravitational interaction with Kali and was vulnerable to anything that might alter its position. Without active stabilization, Ouroboros would begin to oscillate and sooner or later fall into the black hole. To prevent that, the ring could alter its shape dynamically, damping any undesirable resonant energy.

North Platform had been constructed first. Then the ring was extended clockwise along the path of orbit with three more platforms built at ninety-degree intervals. Each platform incorporated nuclear fusion for power, data processing, and communications equipment, and life-support systems for the safety and comfort of the building and maintenance crews. North and South Platforms were mainly living quarters. East and West Platforms emphasized infrastructure and support equipment. AIs to control the ring stabilization system were deployed east and west, facing each other across the ring. But at the moment only AI Shiva, on East Platform, was fully functional. AI Sati, its opposite number, was still in final testing.

"That's right. As long as you're on the ring, it's impossible to fall into Kali. You're in free fall around it. But that's not what bothers me about this accident. Did you read SecDiv's analysis?"

Dr. Chapman's fall into Kali was a conundrum. How had it happened? Tatsuya had already received the Security Division report. The time stamp showed that it had arrived just before the funeral.

Chapman had taken a truck to East Platform, where he had apparently input some modifications to Shiva. After Chandrasekhar Station was complete, its orientation and positioning systems would be distributed to avoid reliance on a single AI. But for now it was up to Shiva to keep the ring stable. To prevent tampering with such

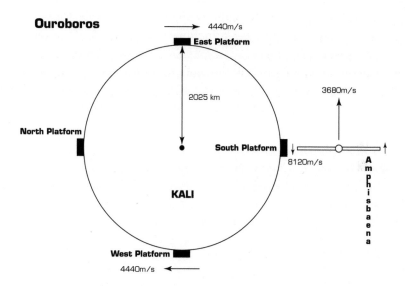

a critical system, the AI's programs couldn't be modified remotely. Modifications could only be done by authorized personnel physically present on East Platform.

Whatever his objective had been, Chapman had fulfilled it, then boarded the truck and begun retracing his route. Yet he went only partway before turning back. Judging from his actions, he must have realized that there was some flaw in the modifications he'd made. Evidently he'd been desperate to return right away, for he removed the truck's console cover and forcibly disconnected the speed governor. The truck's speed quickly exceeded safe limits.

By disconnecting the governor, Chapman had taken the truck off-line—which prevented Shiva from detecting it as it came hurtling back. Instead, the laser cannon radar array picked it up. Shiva's log later showed that the AI had mobilized all of its reasoning capacity to determine that the approaching object was in fact a truck and not a meteor. Then it had searched for a way to gain access to the truck's power control. It found one—and stopped the truck dead in its tracks.

Chapman would have been killed instantly, the truck torn to pieces by its own inertia. Its fragments, along with Chapman's body, hurtled toward the temporary crew modules atop East Platform. The kinetic energy of the pieces and its erstwhile human cargo demolished the modules instantly, producing two types of wreckage. The module debris took an elliptical course toward the interior of the ring. The rest—including what had once been Chapman—hurtled toward the black hole. By now, most of the debris had already been transformed into a gaseous ring by Kali and was flowing into the black hole, sweating X-rays as its atomic structure was disrupted by the immense tidal forces.

For now, that was the sum total of what was known about the accident.

"Based on this report, Graham was messing with the speed control," said Tatsuya.

"That's not the problem. Shiva would assume mechanical fault in a case like that. He should've decelerated the truck gradually. We've had a few glitches with the trucks and the bullet, and that's how Shiva has always handled them. This is the first time he's behaved like this. Sure, yanking the limiter circuit created a problem, but not with the truck. The problem is how Shiva responded. SecDiv doesn't have the tools to get to the bottom of this. This is all about Shiva's reasoning processes."

"In other words, it's a job for professionals. Like you guys."

"You must be joking. SysCon can't solve this either. This is out of the human realm. First of all, there are way too many lines of inquiry. We'd never work through them all. The only thing we can do is get Sati online as soon as possible so she can find out what went wrong with Shiva."

"But we should be analyzing the accident, not every branch of Shiva's reasoning process. It's not going to be easy, but do we really have to put another AI on it?"

"Sati has to analyze all of Shiva's processes first to tell us where to start looking. And that's not all."

Tatsuya noticed Catherine glancing at the coffeemaker. It hit him that he hadn't had anything to drink since before the funeral. He'd been thirsty without realizing it. He activated an agent program from his web and ordered the coffeemaker to brew two cups. Their personal mugs were just a few feet away in the wall locker. Tatsuya retrieved them and filled them with coffee from the machine.

"Thanks," said Catherine. "But listen, Tatsuya—why did you make coffee for me?"

"Because I love you? Okay, I thought you'd be thirsty. No fluids since before the funeral."

"There. You've put your finger on the problem."

"Which is?"

"The impregnable fortress we have to conquer. The difference between humans and AIs. Humans have a theory of mind. AIs don't."

"Are you sure? 'Thirsty' equals 'make coffee.' Simple logic. Any AI could manage that."

Catherine took a few moments to frame a reply. "Here's the problem. I'll exaggerate a bit to make the point. Have you ever seen Grünewald's *Crucifixion*?"

"Sorry, doesn't ring any bells."

Catherine downloaded an image of the centuries-old painting to her web. It showed Christ on the cross, limbs twisted in a grotesque posture of agony. "What does this make you think of?"

"Well, he has nails through his palms. Must be painful. That's about it."

"Right. That's your theory of mind. As a human, you experience pain. You have memories of pain. You can create an image of Christ in your mind. You have the same physical structure, so you assume Christ feels pain. So let me ask you: why don't you assume that the cross is suffering? The same nails that go through Christ's flesh are penetrating the cross."

"But the cross doesn't feel any pain."

"Really? Have you ever been a cross?"

"Not personally, no." Tatsuya grinned.

"That's my point. The cross and the human body have different structures. Maybe the cross does suffer. But we have different structures, so we can't model its suffering in our minds. 'Thirsty' equals 'something to drink'—that's knowledge a digital inference engine has no way of learning. It has to be *programmed*, it doesn't *know*. That's why a theory of mind is so important. AIs don't have that ability yet.

"AIs use language to reach conclusions, but that doesn't mean they can learn from every form of human reasoning that can be expressed in language. They can't access the meaning behind the words. Even if AIs can reason, they still need humans to translate phenomena into words or symbols. Otherwise, as far as the AI is concerned, those phenomena just don't exist.

"It's not just that the universe humans and AIs understand is different. The universe we perceive is different. Sati and Shiva were populated by their developers with different sets of axioms.

Whatever looks like a logical contradiction to Sati will be the key to the accident. What we have to do is analyze that contradiction. Only humans can find internal contradictions in the axioms that a unique AI has constructed using rules of logic."

"Cath, shouldn't we just start from what Graham actually did? He must've modified Shiva for a reason. Then he noticed something wrong. That's got to be the key."

"Good point. Graham was trying to upgrade the resonance-damping system. Oscillations could snap the ring if they grew strong enough. He told me the current safeguards aren't ideal."

"Hold on, that sounds like a major problem."

"I wouldn't say it's major right now. But the data we're getting isn't what the model predicts. There are these little discrepancies we can't account for. Whatever Graham was doing with Shiva, there's probably a connection. Just before the incident he must've noticed something problematic about the changes he made. Whatever it was, I think the problem must be connected to why Shiva reacted the way he did. Still, linking cause and effect isn't something we humans can do in this case. We need to get Sati online as soon as possible."

"A famous detective needs a brilliant assistant, right?"

"Just so, Watson."

2

"THAT'S THE GREAT THING about this station. You can eat rice with chopsticks like a human being."

Tatsuya and Kurokawa, his deputy station manager, were chatting via web from their respective living quarters in the west and east habitat modules of space station Amphisbaena—a huge, bisymmetrical needle rotating around Ouroboros in the same plane as the ring. The two cylindrical habitat modules extended across the width of the needle near its midpoint, flanking a central utility module. Tatsuya was responsible for overall operations, but he'd delegated oversight of Station West to Kurokawa. The distance between the two modules was eighty kilometers.

Amphisbaena—named for the legendary serpent with a head at each end—rotated like a propeller about its center at precisely 8,120 meters per second to generate downward inertia in the modules. Each tubular structure was a small city that combined residential and work spaces, with each level dedicated to a different function. A cylindrical space ten meters across penetrated the structures from top to bottom; a circular, five-meter compartment traversed the central space like an elevator, giving access to each level. Tatsuya's office was in this glassed-in cylinder, which allowed him to oversee work with key staff throughout the module. Access from the levels to his office was via a projecting bridge. Three levels of floor-to-ceiling glass made up the central section in Station East, which meant that Tatsuya could observe operations at any point of the compass.

Tatsuya was eating. To avoid having to glance at the device embedded in his wrist, he had routed its display to a flat screen monitor. Tatsuya was busily stirring a bowl of green tea over rice. Seeing him about to tuck in, Kurokawa suddenly looked serious. "It's nice that we have rice to eat, but don't eat too much. We don't have much left."

Kurokawa disappeared from the monitor, his image replaced by a data plot of declining stores of rice from Amphisbaena Harvest No. 7. Superimposed on the curve was another plot, labeled TATSUYA KAWANISHI'S RICE CONSUMPTION. The plot clearly showed that the supply of rice from the last harvest would be exhausted in another week or so at the current rate.

"Why do you send me this stuff when I'm eating?" grumbled Tatsuya, as he gave his rice another stir. His voice was picked up by his wrist web; at times like this it was a very convenient device.

"Mealtime is the only time for info like this. Should I send it during work hours?"

Amphisbaena

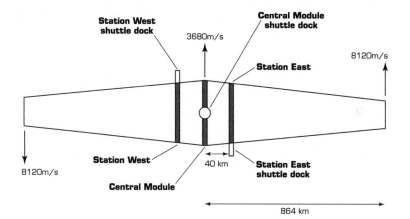

Station West shuttle dock

3680m/s

Central Module shuttle dock

Station East

8120m/s

Station West

Central Module

40 km

Station East shuttle dock

8120m/s

864 km

Schematic not to scale

"I see your point."

"This station isn't a farm, it's a logistics center. We have a limited amount of growing space. It puts a load on the life-support systems too."

"Yeah, but this is the only AADD station where we can grow rice. I seem to remember that farming was your idea."

"I wanted to grow vegetables, not rice. And we're supposed to be sharing. You're eating more than your share."

"Are you still holding Harvest No. 6 against me?"

"No. The fact that you ate sixty percent of that harvest is something I got out of my system months ago. Besides, I have all the data if I ever need to refresh my memory."

Tatsuya's web chimed and he saw a detailed consumption plot for Harvest No. 6. At times like this, the web was a very inconvenient unit.

———•◦◆◦•———

TATSUYA AND KUROKAWA had commandeered some unoccupied space in the habitats and started growing rice on the pretext of creating a green zone. Naturally these were not real rice paddies. The plants were grown in trays, a crude hydroponic setup with nutrient solution, high ambient oxygen levels, and macromolecular granules instead of soil.

Their inspiration came when they noticed some of the crew cultivating ornamental plants in pots. Most vegetation required gravity to germinate—in fact, gravity was necessary for them to grow normally at all. As Tatsuya's office moved along Central Block, he saw plants on each level forming small clusters of green, like miniature forests. Boston ivy vines spread along the inner wall, blocking part of the view through the glass. The habitat was an ideal environment for vegetation. It was probably only a matter of time before this castle of high-impact glass and hybrid materials was completely covered with a lush blanket of ivy, as Tatsuya could see from the way the vines were creeping further and further into his field of vision.

Once Chandrasekhar Station was complete, Kali's gravity would make it possible to farm on the shell's outer surface. There was no gravity on Ouroboros, which was still under construction. Free-fall conditions prevailed. The only other place with "real" gravity in the vicinity was Kali—not the best location for agriculture.

Space Station Amphisbaena was a charcoal-gray needle 1,728 kilometers long. The carbon-fiber nanotubules used in its construction were the same as those used to build the orbital elevator on Mars. Without their web's image-enhancement circuits, it was very easy to miss the station against the blackness of space. The tips of the needle completed a revolution in just under eleven minutes, with the center of the station tracing its own counterclockwise path around the rim of Ouroboros at 3,680 meters per second. Each tip of the station made a close approach to the surface of the ring approximately every fourteen minutes. As the tip made its closest approach, the relative speed between station and ring fell to nearly zero. From the ring, it looked as if a titanic pillar was descending from directly above, remaining stationary for a few tens of seconds.

During this window of synchronized movement, supplies could be transferred across the gap between the station and any of the platforms on Ouroboros by extending the tip of the station. A transfer from the station to any given platform was possible once every three hours or so.

In stations East and West, forty kilometers from Amphisbaena's center of rotation, gravity was more or less the same as on the surface of Mars. Many of Tatsuya's team members had been born on Mars, making the station a comfortable environment for them. The next closest place a person could eat tea over rice with chopsticks was ten-odd astronomical units away. Trying it in free fall would get a bit messy.

The gravity generated at the tips of the station was far greater than in the habitats. The station had an automated cargo-handling deck at each tip, echoing its two-headed namesake. An unmanned cargo container could enter one of the decks and be transported with the station's revolution to a platform on the ring. The cargo decks could also be used to pick up containers from one platform and drop them at another. A logistics module running the width of the needle through its center was the hub of the system.

Humanity had been living in space for several generations, but the history of that settlement was still limited. Chandrasekhar Station had been named after a Nobel Prize–winning physicist, but there remained a preference for ancient names like Ouroboros and Amphisbaena—perhaps a sign of humanity's desire to feel that they had planted their feet firmly in space long ago.

"HEY, KUROKAWA—GET THIS."

Tatsuya had finished his rice and was now holding his tapered chopsticks up horizontally, butted end to end. "It's Amphisbaena!"

"Stop trying to change the subject and start acting like the head of this station!"

"All right, okay . . ."

"If you're finished eating, I'd like to go over the cargo capture schedule."

Tatsuya cleared away his dishes, somewhat sorry that lunch was over. When he looked up, there was an augmented-reality display board floating in midair a few feet away. He activated an agent program from his web, and the same opaque white rectangle appeared throughout the station where his team was at work.

The board displayed the current positions of Ouroboros, the station, the nearby planets, and an approaching fleet of cargo containers. Kali's orbit was highly inclined to the ecliptic plane, approaching aphelion. Once Kali reached its furthest point from the Sun, AADD's goal was to redirect it along a path that would lead to eventual capture by Uranus.

Reducing relative speed with the ring to zero was not the only reason for Amphisbaena's rotation. It also facilitated the recovery of cargo containers coming from other locations throughout the solar system. Kali was already more than ten astronomical units from the Sun. Because its orbit was highly inclined, the distance to Mars and Jupiter was about the same. But since the speed of the containers varied depending on their origin, speeds had to be equalized by Amphisbaena's rotation before the containers could be sent on to their destination.

The tips of the station moved at several kilometers per second. With proper timing there was scarcely any need for an approaching cargo container to decelerate before recovery. This meant less propellant to make the journey, even as other navigational elements including angular motion had to be adjusted. Still, the huge inertia of Amphisbaena's millions of tons of mass acted as a kinetic energy sink for incoming containers.

"The accident on East Platform threw our construction schedule off. I've configured a new timeline. Suppliers on Titan and Mars are now working to this schedule."

There were advantages and disadvantages to sending cargo containers across space. One advantage was that space itself could be used for large volumes of cargo storage. One disadvantage was that emergencies and changes in plan were naturally difficult to accommodate.

To solve this problem, AADD used containers with limited propulsion capability. While the containers coasted on an inertial trajectory after launch, a certain amount of acceleration or deceleration allowed time of arrival to be adjusted for unforeseen problems or changes in plan. Kurokawa's plan, displayed on the board, detailed a raft of changes in container trajectory speeds.

"I think this is the optimal strategy, given our present status. What do you think, Chief?" Kurokawa was clearly trying to minimize any impact on the current program, and there were no conspicuous changes in the arrival sequence. "This should let us stick as close as possible to schedule."

Tatsuya accessed the ring's computer system via his web to verify the new timeline. The schedule did indeed minimize changes, but this was not what he had in mind. In a few seconds, he formulated an alternative based on different parameters. "Your proposal keeps us close to program, Kurokawa. But under the circumstances it's not what I'm looking for."

"I don't understand."

"Our logistics strategy is to keep construction going as efficiently as possible, not necessarily to stick to the program. Right now our first priority is to get Sati up and running. That means we've got to expedite the materials we need to get that done."

"How are we going to do that?"

"The other divisions won't like it, but we'll have to change their allocations. SysCon has first call on network equipment." Tatsuya uploaded his plan to the board. First, all equipment on Amphisbaena needed to activate Sati would be offloaded at the next rendezvous with West Platform. The effect of this change would be offset by rejiggering the velocity correction sequence for the containers.

Amphisbaena's recovery schedule now looked very different. The board used different color densities to indicate relative differences in the correction sequence for each container in the fleet. Some would be parked in orbit around Kali to form a recovery queue, again using space as a temporary staging area. The overall plan was feasible but clearly more complicated than what Kurokawa was proposing.

"But, Chief, why are we prioritizing SysCon's needs when the schedule is already out of whack because of the accident?"

"The accident is the reason we want to get Sati up and running as soon as possible. Listen, Kurokawa—why do you think Dr. Chapman was killed?"

"It's obvious. He shouldn't have disconnected the speed limiter."

"Wrong. The cause was whatever modifications he made to Shiva before he was killed. When he realized that, he was forced to depart from standard operating procedure. Right now Shiva is our only high-level AI looking after resonance control. And this same AI violated its operating protocol by not gradually slowing the truck down. If the safety and integrity of the ring take priority, so does solving this problem."

"What does activating Sati ahead of schedule have to do with it?"

"A lot. Whatever Chapman did, it was like an operation on the frontal lobes of a human brain. Analyzing the logic chains of a high-level AI is no mean feat, even for human specialists. There's just too much to look at. AI reasoning is very different from ours. Even the people who write the software can't predict with complete certainty how an AI will behave in a given situation. In a way, that was the whole point of trying to model intelligence. Sati is like Shiva but also different, so we need her help to get to the bottom of this."

"I didn't know you knew so much about AIs."

"I have a good teacher."

"Oh, you're just passing on something you got from Kitty."

"Why not? We're logistics. Passing things on is our job."

"I hope you won't mind if I go to the source, then. Kitty?" Kurokawa initiated a link between himself, Tatsuya, and Catherine.

"How many times do I have to tell you? Stop calling me that," said Catherine. "Have you disabled your agent's learning function?"

"Of course not. Why do you think it always calls you Kitty?"

"Great. So what's going on? You know I've got my hands full."

"Listen, about your procurement schedule—the chief tells me we're supposed to prioritize Sati. What I want to understand is, why are we using one machine to debug another machine? Chief says our reasoning processes are different from an AI's. But I mean, one plus one is going to equal two whether a human or an AI is involved."

"Are you sure? What does apple plus sugar equal?"

"That's not addition. What am I supposed to say—apple pie?"

"I don't know. But an AI might come up with an answer to that question, if it was required to do so. Maybe it would say apple pie, or maybe it would decide that 'apple' and 'sugar' are the same thing."

"But where's the correlation? Is that even reasoning?"

"Of course. When correlation is obvious we don't need to reason about it. If we decide that the answer the AI comes up with is meaningless, then we reject its reasoning. So here's the problem—when we send a human to debug an AI, how do they evaluate reasoning processes that appear meaningless to them?"

"They could just ignore the processes." Kurokawa wouldn't give in, but Catherine was used to dealing with this kind of resistance.

"You know, it would be so nice if we could," she said, a hint of enjoyment in her voice. "But what if the AI rejects two as an answer to one plus one? Listen carefully—the AI's conclusion isn't important. What's important is the reasoning chain that led to that conclusion. If Shiva had behaved as expected, he would've slowed the truck gradually. But that's not what he did. And now Graham's dead."

"For reasons unknown," said Kurokawa. "So that's where Sati comes in?"

"Yep. But what makes things sticky is that Shiva isn't malfunctioning. Shiva—as a machine—is functioning normally even as we speak. Yet he's demonstrated that he's capable of reasoning to an incorrect conclusion. It's not easy to repair a machine that isn't broken."

"And that's why we're supposed to upend the schedule to prioritize System Control's equipment needs. So let me ask you this: what makes you think Shiva will cooperate?" Tatsuya had already asked Catherine this very question. Her look of pity came back to him vividly. "After all, why wouldn't he rebel?" Kurokawa continued. "He's supposed to be smarter than we are in some ways. According to you, he's already killed once."

"Kurokawa, you need to get this through your head. Shiva doesn't know we exist. He doesn't even understand the world in terms of relations between objects, at least not the way we do."

"I can prove you wrong." Kurokawa touched his wrist, stood, and went to the coffeemaker in his quarters. A few seconds later he held a fresh cup of coffee. "Behold. I give the order, here's my cup of coffee. Shiva knows which human I am, he knows what coffee is. Otherwise how could he do any of this?"

"You're obviously suffering from interface illusion. Shiva doesn't 'understand' coffee. Mr. Black River knows that every item on Ouroboros or the station has an item code. Well, Shiva understands the relationship between the code for coffee and the code for Black River, and that is precisely all he knows."

"I'm not Black River. I'm Kurokawa."

"And I'm not Kitty, I'm Catherine Sinclaire. Still, when I called you Black River, you knew I was referring to you. That's because you grasp what it means for there to be an object behind a label. For an AI, the universe is symbols and abstractions, nothing more."

"But there's no item code for Kurokawa."

"You used your web," said Tatsuya.

"Oh, right. My ID."

"Yes," said Catherine. "Shiva has no concept that a human named Kurokawa ordered a stimulant drink. What he 'knows' is that web ID THX-1138 or whatever is in a certain location, and that's where item XYZ needs to be delivered. When a machine does this, humans think it 'understands' what it's doing."

"So what's all this about high-level intelligence?"

"It *looks* like intelligence to us. It's one of the problems we face in artificial intelligence research. Most of the work being done these days is about the interface, not about teaching AIs to grasp meaning. Basically, most AI work is designed to fool humans into thinking that real intelligence is present."

The discussion shifted to the container recovery process. After some tweaking based on input from the other specialists online, they voted to proceed with Tatsuya's plan.

"Happy now, Cath?" said Tatsuya.

"Totally. We ran the prelims on Sati and she seems fine. I would like to commandeer one more thing—the temporary habitats that were allocated to East Platform. Can you swing it?"

"Why do you need more shelters than we already have out there?"

"A lot of people are going to be working on this. After reviewing the timeline, I think we need to increase the living space so we can stay on top of this round the clock."

"I assume Sati's like Shiva? No remote access?"

"Exactly."

"Hold on a sec, let me take a look." Tatsuya viewed Catherine's incoming wish list on his web. Everything that AADD moved around the solar system was bar-coded and tagged electronically. It was an old technology that had proven its worth; so far no one had come up with anything better. Tying the solar system together with a vast, smoothly functioning logistics system was one of AADD's main long-term goals.

Tatsuya ran Catherine's request though his database. "You're in luck. We've got at least one of everything you need on hand right now. I think we can get it to you on the next rendezvous."

"Perfect. We'll be ready for you."

Tatsuya had Catherine's request entered into the supply chain almost before she rang off. The cascade of changes was executed automatically throughout the system. Web-activated agent programs were the workhorses for basic tasks, with the higher-level responsibilities of senior team members handled by avatars—advanced programs, often in the form of talking heads that looked and sounded like their owners—that were active round the clock. Avatars could deal with each other on a variety of tasks; below a certain level of sophistication they were as effective as human support staff.

"Kurokawa, what's your elevator status? Can we steal some space?"

"No worries. You can have some right now." The board showed a schematic of Amphisbaena's central logistics module, flanked by the habitats. The status of West and East Elevators, as well as of the payload bays projecting from the central module, was visible at a glance. East Elevator was already moving toward the payload bays, some of which were extending from the central module in preparation for docking.

Amphisbaena's logistics module was its main storage depot, with enormous payload bays projecting from either side like the teeth of a comb. Each "wing" of Amphisbaena supported an elevator that delivered cargo to the tips of the station. Containers were in constant motion throughout the system, not only to make the most efficient use of payload bay capacity, but also as mobile ballast to stabilize Amphisbaena's constantly changing inertial profile.

The schematic indicated that the new plan was proceeding smoothly. The west tip of the station was nearing its rendezvous with South Platform. The slightly distorted visual showed a bridge extending from the leading edge of South Platform toward the approaching cargo deck. This bridge could shift position along the edge of the platform, extending the time that the station's speed relative to Ouroboros would be zero.

Suddenly the board vanished, along with Kurokawa's video feed. "Hey, what's going on?" said Tatsuya. It was instantly clear that they had a situation. All data links other than audio went down. It took everyone several seconds to grasp what had gone wrong.

"Chief! My web's off-line!" Kurokawa's voice held an edge of fear.

"Don't panic. How could I hear you if it was down?" said Tatsuya. "The intranet's dropped, that's all. We can maintain voice contact without full data spectrum." But for Amphisbaena and Ouroboros to carry out the minute adjustments necessary for their rendezvous the station and ring control systems required common access to the same network.

"Okay," said Kurokawa. "Local diagnostics show everything normal, but we're shut out of the ring network."

"Keep sending rendezvous correction data to the buffer. Once you relink with O-Net, purge the buffer. We've got to make those corrections."

"But, Chief, we're going to miss the rendezvous with South Platform."

"That's a problem. What about container recovery?"

"We're still good to go with the local net."

"At least we dodged that bullet."

But Tatsuya had spoken too soon. The bullet was on its way.

3

THE TEMPORARY INSTALLATION set up to activate Sati consisted of six eighteen-meter standard habitat tubes clustered together on West Platform. The tubes were 4.2 meters across. Rumor had it that the diameter had been fixed back in the twentieth century to fit the payload bay of the old space shuttles. Whatever the reason, most habitat modules were still the same size.

"Catherine, it's no use. I can't get Shiva to acknowledge A-Net."

"He won't acknowledge Amphisbaena?" shouted Catherine through the docking node to the next module. "Come off it!" In this cramped maze of equipment, yelling was faster than using her web.

Her Systems Integration specialist called back, "As far as Shiva is concerned, there's no such thing as Amphisbaena, period."

"I don't believe this." Catherine floated into the next module. Her team had been waiting impatiently for the arrival of the new equipment. One moment they'd had a visual of the approaching tip of the station, the next their monitors had gone blank. At first, those watching weren't even sure something had gone wrong; it didn't look like loss of signal. It looked more like Shiva had smoothly shut down the feed. All other systems continued showing normal.

"Rendezvous corrections with South Platform stopped as soon as Amphisbaena disappeared from the system. Everything else is nominal," said the SysInt specialist.

"That's very strange." Catherine shook her head, puzzled.

"Why? Whatever's behind Amphisbaena disappearing from the system, it's not surprising that Shiva would stop the rendezvous sequence."

"No, I mean this whole situation is abnormal. Shiva canceled the rendezvous as if that were the logical thing to do as soon as he lost Amphisbaena. He should've alerted us at the same time. Instead he's behaving as if everything's fine."

"Shiva thinks Amphisbaena disappearing from the system is a nominal condition?"

"That's the most logical assumption. And if so, there's only one conclusion. Amphisbaena isn't on the system because Shiva wants it that way." Catherine grasped a handhold next to the nearest terminal and harnessed herself in to make operation easier in the zero-G conditions.

As soon as she buckled in the terminal automatically powered up. A few commands gave her access to the AI. The terminal displayed a status summary. Although Shiva could not be modified remotely, as sysadmin, Catherine could view any data she chose.

Shiva responded instantly to Catherine's commands; thousands of lines of data scrolled rapidly across the terminal. Catherine winced—her input had been amateurish. In seconds her agent went to work, organizing the data. The mountain of data began to shrink until there was nothing left.

"Well, you were right. Shiva isn't recognizing Amphisbaena as a system object. The station is just gone."

This was expected. Catherine next queried Shiva on his reasoning in connection with the station over the last half hour. If her guess was correct, there should be a record of data erasure. How it had happened would determine her next step. She was starting to suspect that Shiva's banishment of Amphisbaena from his universe of recognized objects might have something to do with the events that had killed Graham Chapman.

"Listen, guys, I need a position simulation for Amphisbaena." Catherine wanted to make sure this was handled before she got so deep into things that she forgot about it. Shiva might wish Amphisbaena away, but as a physical object the station was still very real. Knowing where it was in relation to Ouroboros could be critical as events played out.

Catherine stared at the terminal, increasingly puzzled. Shiva was taking his own sweet time fulfilling her request. The readout showed that the data transfer had taken place, but her agent was having a hard time dealing with the result. Finally the answer came back.

To Catherine's astonishment, Shiva had presented her with a raw dump of his reasoning processes over the last half hour—not the kind of information a human could evaluate without weeks of study.

"What's that? Is he playing games with you?"The SysInt specialist peered over her shoulder at the monitor. The agent program had been smart enough to prepare a summary of the information Shiva had sent. It was now waiting for further instructions. Catherine punched the terminal, erasing the summary.

"Don't you need that?"

"It wasn't a very human-friendly answer. But now I know a little more than I did."

"Just from that summary?"

"Well, I'm half guessing here, but I'd be willing to bet Shiva thinks there's a cause-and-effect relationship between Amphisbaena and some other event."

"Is that a learning function?"

"I guess you could call it that. Shiva's decided that Amphisbaena's existence was the cause of some event, so he's rendered the station nonexistent . . . Hold on a sec." Catherine entered Shiva's access code and added a command. A few moments later a graph popped up on the monitor. "See? This plots the number of reasoning cycles over the last hour. It rises dramatically until Amphisbaena disappears from the system. Then it falls to normal again. It's like Shiva thinks eliminating the station as a system object solved some kind of problem."

"That doesn't make sense. Eliminating the station as a system object doesn't make it physically disappear."

"The answer is probably connected with how Amphisbaena appears to Shiva. If object data is the only thing Shiva erased, there's a copy in system backup. I bet Shiva erases that too as soon as we restore it."

"What then?"

"We create a dummy ID and associate it with Amphisbaena's object data. The only concept Shiva has of Amphisbaena is as an ID code. I don't see why that wouldn't work."

"Then we'd better make sure Logistics changes the station's code to match."

"Let's talk to Tatsuya. We may be locked out of A-Net, but we can still use the voice circuits to work through the problem. And get me that position simulation!"

4

"ALL RIGHT. To recap—first, you're going to restore Amphisbaena's object data. If that works, we're home free. If not, we'll use the new ID and reboot on this side, correct?"

"That's right, Tatsuya."

"What's all this about?"

"I think Shiva's taken a dislike to Amphisbaena."

"You're kidding, right? What has Amphisbaena ever done to Shiva?"

"Who knows? It could be anything. I seem to remember that the god Shiva never forgave his father-in-law for forgetting to invite him to a banquet."

"Listen, Cath, maybe we better just do what we can to get Sati activated." As he spoke, Tatsuya was already preparing a new ID for Amphisbaena. Over time he'd picked up a great deal of knowledge about AIs from Catherine. Crew safety didn't seem to be at stake yet but the situation they were facing was potentially serious. Everyone on Ouroboros and Amphisbaena knew this instinctively. As they worked, Tatsuya made a calculated effort to engage Catherine in small talk. As much as possible, he needed everyone to keep calm.

"All right, Tatsuya. I'm restoring the file from backup. This probably won't create any new problems." Despite Catherine's studied optimism, half the crew was glued expectantly to their monitors. The rest were too anxious to watch for fear of disappointment.

After a few moments Catherine spoke again. "Well, that's what I expected. Shiva's gone ahead and erased the restored files too. I guess that's good news. At least he's acting predictably." The stress in Catherine's voice belied her attempt at humor. To Tatsuya her inability to fake things was one of her more endearing traits, but right now he wished she could be a little more convincing.

"Let's try a new ID," said Catherine. "What shall we use?"

"Up to you, Cath."

"All right then. Let's see—the safest way to go would be an existing ID, something inactive."

"What about Graham's old ID?"

"I didn't think of that. You're right, that should work." Tatsuya could hear Catherine inputting commands over the voice circuit of his web. Then he heard a small gasp.

"Tatsuya, let's use something else. On second thought, it's bad luck to use Graham's ID. Can we use something from mythology?"

"Try 'fei.'"

"What's that?"

"Amphisbaena is a serpent with a head at either end. The fei is a mythical Chinese creature that's just the opposite, a snake with two bodies attached to a single head."

"Sounds like just the legend we're looking for. I'll create a new ID based on that name. You'll need to rename the station in your system."

Catherine proceeded to create a new system object called Fei. She associated Amphisbaena's backup files with the new name and copied them to Shiva's data portal.

"Catherine! It worked, we're back up!" shouted the SysInt specialist. The mood on West Platform immediately lightened. Amphisbaena—now Fei—was fully accessible to Ouroboros.

"I want a facilities diagnostic before we do anything else. As soon as we're sure that's clean, we go to normal ops. Catherine, we're going to do a full orbit to make sure everything's normal. I can get you that equipment in about a hundred minutes."

"Got it. Thanks, Tatsuya, you've saved us."

"It's you who's saved us." Tatsuya switched from the general circuit to a secure channel. "Listen, Cath. Did something happen when you tried to use Graham's ID? It sounded like you ran into a problem."

"You heard that? Well, I guess you'd better know. Graham's alive, at least as far as Shiva is concerned."

"What the hell does that mean?"

"His ID is still a valid system object. And one of his agent programs is still active. I haven't been able to trace which one yet. Maybe these events are a crime, rather than an accident."

"That's impossible. It would take someone with a thorough understanding of Shiva's program. Access to the system is strictly controlled."

"That wouldn't have been a problem for Graham Chapman."

Tatsuya wasn't sure how to respond.

The voice of the attitude control officer sounded over the PA: "Approaching West Platform. Initiating rendezvous sequence. This is a dry run, people."

Since the data restore, all systems on Amphisbaena had returned to normal. Over the next hour, as he watched Amphisbaena continue to move smoothly around the ring, Tatsuya's intuition told him Catherine must be wrong.

Dry run complete, they were now ready to make the transfer. Tatsuya switched his web to a view of Amphisbaena's cargo bay approaching West Platform. From his point of view Ouroboros appeared to be rising from below the cargo bay. On Ouroboros the scene would be reversed; the tip of Amphisbaena would seem to descend toward the ring as its speed gradually fell to near zero.

At Tatsuya's request, Catherine had created a backup ID and was standing by for another data restore if problems developed with the station's cover name. In keeping with the snake motif the new ID was Echidna, the half maiden, half serpent of Greek myth. Resetting Amphisbaena's ID was treating the symptoms rather than the disease, but every time Shiva did something unusual it gave Catherine new clues. Maybe there would be no further problems. On this point Tatsuya was more optimistic than Catherine.

The images Tatsuya was seeing were augmented with data from radar and laser range finders. A camera feed alone would have shown very little; Amphisbaena and the ring were both too dark to be easily visible. The rendezvous sequence was proceeding normally. Under Amphisbaena's gravitational influence, West Platform was being drawn closer to the tip of the station. Given the size of the ring the distortion now under way would barely be visible from far off, but the distance from Kali to West Platform would soon increase by nearly fifty kilometers. From where Tatsuya sat, West Platform seemed to be rising on a giant wave. The ring's positioning system was simultaneously creating the same degree of distortion on the opposite side, otherwise Ouroboros would fall into the black hole.

When complete, Chandrasekhar Station would be a Dyson sphere and would require a variety of mechanisms to maintain position. But at this stage Ouroboros used dynamic distortion to maintain stability in orbit around Kali. Additionally, its four platforms were equipped with thrusters for emergency position correction.

The cargo deck at the tip of Amphisbaena was not attached to the station. Powerful magnets held it in place without physical contact. The gap in the magnetic field holding the deck absorbed the shock of any inertial forces in play at the moment of rendezvous. Range finders on both Amphisbaena and Ouroboros measured the attitude and relative speed of the deck in real time. Contact with the ring took place at a precisely defined location. In an actual transfer, the movement of the containers was automatic and almost instantaneous.

The rendezvous ended and the titanic pillar rose away from the platform. Ouroboros and Amphisbaena moved apart. Tatsuya watched as West Platform fell rapidly away.

"That was about as nice a transfer as I could've asked for." But he'd spoken too soon. The next instant his web went dark.

He's back, thought Tatsuya.

His web went off-line again. An instant later the visual was restored as his web switched to Amphisbaena's local network. He immediately input the new ID for Amphisbaena/Fei, and in seconds the station was online with Ouroboros again. Tatsuya's monitor showed the cargo bay at the tip of the station. West Platform was moving quickly away. The containers that had been transferred were no longer visible. Apparently they had been stowed without incident.

It was just Amphisbaena that Shiva had a problem with, thought Tatsuya. He was about to turn away from the monitor when something in the corner of the display caught his eye.

One of the cannons was swiveling. The ranging laser wasn't active, but the cannon was tracking smoothly toward a point in space. That meant it wasn't being guided by its automatic sensing software. And it wasn't tracking a meteor.

Tatsuya shouted, "Rig for collision! Emergency pods!"

The crew froze momentarily before they realized this was no drill. Everyone reached for the nearest emergency pod and began tugging it out of its container. The pods were temporary shelters from vacuum conditions, essentially sleeping bags with integral helmets and life-support gear. A few moments later, the first shock hit.

The station's connection with Ouroboros was lost for the third time. A few seconds later the local network was back up. But now everything had changed.

"Depressurization warning!" shouted one of the crew. There was the high-pitched sound of atmosphere bleeding from the module. The hole must have been small, otherwise white fog would have been visible at the breach. Apparently they'd been spared a direct hit, but they had sustained some damage. Tatsuya shouted, "Find that breach and repair it. There may be more than one."

"Only one breach, Chief. But the hull's weakened in several other locations."One of the crew was monitoring the external video feed. "Chief, look at this!" He routed the visual to everyone's web. "The shuttle's gone."

Amphisbaena's habitat modules terminated in a shuttle dock; its shuttles ferried crew between the station and Ouroboros. It looked as if a fuel tank explosion had torn apart West Habitat's shuttle. The dock itself was a twisted mass of wreckage.

Someone handed Tatsuya a damage update. It was the worst situation he'd seen firsthand. "Station East was hit too. They're dealing with the same problems."

"Shiva took out everything at once."

"Yes. There's no way off the station now."

The camera feed now showed the ring moving rapidly away, fading against the black of space. Tatsuya and his crew were marooned.

5

THE SUCCESSFUL RENDEZVOUS with Amphisbaena gave new hope to Catherine and the rest of the System Control team. Shiva's actions had taken everyone by surprise, but they had been finding ways to cope.

AIs were not the equal of humans in terms of intelligence; that was what Catherine thought. But Shiva had opened her eyes to just how irrelevant the comparison was. Matching wits with humans had never been part of Shiva's agenda; this should have been obvious. Shiva had no awareness of humans as humans. For humans, it was difficult to deal with an entity that was playing by its own set of rules.

"Catherine, I don't know how to tell you this, but the laser cannons are tracking something."

"That's impossible!" Catherine punched up a status screen. The cannons were moving under Shiva's control. She hit the kill switch, but it was too late. The cannons had fired.

Catherine switched to West Platform's optical sensors. Amphisbaena's West Habitat wasn't visible from this angle, but she could see East Habitat. The cannons were firing at both modules in the same pattern. Damage to both was probably about equal.

"He's going after the shuttles."

The shuttle for East Habitat was a few shreds of metal hanging from the docking node. The lasers had targeted the fuel tanks. Fortunately the vector of the explosion was mostly outward, so little debris had struck the habitat. The long cylinder looked relatively free from damage.

"Amphisbaena reports no casualties."

"Thank God." Catherine, still buckled to the terminal, looked at the ceiling in relief. But none of their problems were solved. Things were much worse, and reports coming in from West Habitat gave everyone pause. Catherine had one of her team run a 3-D simulation of the attack.

"It looks like Shiva ordered the two cannons to put a single pulse into each habitat." Red lines extended from cannons at the ends of West Platform to the habitats. "You can see the results. Maybe Shiva wanted to prevent the crew from getting off the station. What I don't understand is why he didn't just go after the habitats."

"I'm afraid our AI may be learning the difference between symbols and the real world faster than we could have predicted. If Shiva deduced that destroying the crew's means of escape was the best course, it means he's become aware of our existence." Shiva's conflict with humans seemed to be stimulating his acquisition of knowledge about the outside world. But that didn't mean he would ever understand humans, not even the basics of human common sense.

"I'm going to East Platform."

"Catherine, are you serious?" said SysInt.

"I know more about Shiva than anyone here. If this were about erasing data from the system, I'd be amused. But he's using the lasers. We don't have a moment to lose."

"Do you have to physically go there?"

"This is a system-level issue. I can't do a thing from here. The only solution is to go and get my hands dirty. And that's something only a sysadmin can do."

"Then I'll go with you. I have the same clearance."

"No. I'm going alone. If I can't handle it, reinforcements won't help. Work on getting Sati activated. That's our first priority. If things go beyond the point where humans can deal with them, Sati's our last chance."

"All right. We'll have her up as soon as we can."

"I pass command to you then. You know the activation sequence. I'll leave the voice channel open in case anything comes up."

"I hope nothing does. Be careful, Catherine."

"What's to be careful about? I'm just taking a little trip to the opposite platform."

She floated out of the control module and into a circular rest area just under four meters across. The control module she exited was a horizontal tube; this module was positioned vertically and functioned as a four-level docking node. Each level could be used to access four other modules connected at right angles, but only the first level of the node was in use now.

There was a hatch at each point of the compass. The hatch behind her led back into the control module; the one to the right gave access to another module. The left hatch led to an air lock that connected to one of the trucks.

Catherine headed directly for the air lock, then stopped. The trucks were pressurized. In theory she could go through the air lock, into a truck, and all the way to another platform without a space suit. Other than Graham Chapman, no one had ever had an accident.

Catherine entered the air lock and suited up before stepping into the truck docked on the other side. Trusting systems that were under Shiva's control was far too risky. A space suit—with life-support systems beyond Shiva's reach—just might mean the difference between life and death. The hard-shell suit was like lightweight armor with servo-assist joints. This allowed it to be fully pressurized without any need to spend hours purging the body of nitrogen in preparation for EVA.

Catherine stepped into the truck and closed the hatch. The power came on automatically, console glowing green. All systems go—and Shiva was in control. The AI had deployed laser cannons to attack Amphisbaena, yet now it provided Catherine with the usual support. The reasoning processes of an AI were so fundamentally different. A human might have seen these actions as contradictory. To Shiva, both were consistent with logic.

Catherine raised her visor. "East Platform." The vehicle accelerated gently.

6

"I HATE TO SAY THIS, but we can't trust Shiva. We'll have to plan our evac accordingly."

Tatsuya was addressing the crew. Everyone was suited up, though their visors were not closed. They would not draw on their oxygen supplies while there was still breathable air.

"This is some kind of AI system failure. My guess is that it's the same problem that caused Dr. Chapman's death. Once the other AI is operational, we should be able to determine the nature of the problem relatively quickly. I'm optimistic that this situation will be resolved, and soon." Optimism was imperative. It was too early for pessimism.

Tatsuya's web inbox was overflowing with messages from his crew. His agent had already sorted them by topic; they ran the gamut from doubt to grief, encouragement to a certain amount of anger. Still, these sentiments were consigned to text rather than voiced openly, because no one wanted to risk sparking panic or wasteful bickering. Technology had transformed even the way humans dealt with tragedy.

"So, on to the evac plan," continued Tatsuya. "Amphisbaena's status is summarized here." A display board appeared in midair, showing a representation of the logistics module and the two habitats. The two shuttle docking ports were completely destroyed. "Pressure has stabilized, but we're still losing atmosphere. In a few more hours normal respiration will be impossible. Both habitats are in the same condition. We're going to make our way to the logistics module. Part of the module is pressurized, but it's going to be a tight fit for all of us. There's also the backup shuttle docking port. The port is undamaged and can be operated manually. That means we should be able to evac on the two ring shuttles without interference from Shiva."

"But, Chief, how are we going to get there? It's forty klicks."

The voice belonged to Kurokawa in East Habitat. Along with the destruction of the docking ports, they had lost the cargo lifts and elevators running from the habitats to the logistics module. Theoretically they could make their way to the logistics module using the carbon-fiber handholds running along the station struts. But EVAing forty crew members and bringing them to the logistics module was not realistic. There was bound to be an accident—most of the crew had not logged much EVA time.

"Well, the main lifts were carried away when the shuttles exploded, but there are emergency lifts that can be deployed manually from the logistics module. All we have to do is enter the code to release the lifts and centrifugal force will bring them down to the habitats. They carry four at a time, so it will only take five round-trips to evacuate everyone."

"That means someone will have to EVA and go there to enter the codes."

"That's right, Kurokawa. And we can only summon the shuttles from the habitats, not from the core, so we'll need to leave some people here. All we need is for one person to go—say two, for backup in case there's an accident."

"But that means whoever goes has to be qualified to prepare the port for docking."

"Then we know who's going, don't we?"

"What do you mean?"

"You and I are the only ones on this station with those qualifications."

7

THE TRUCK WAS SPEEDING counterclockwise around the ring, far faster than its rated limit, though this was of no concern to Catherine now. Shiva had attacked Amphisbaena. There was no telling what he might do in the next few minutes.

SysInt's voice came over her web. "Catherine, Shiva's logic core is running flat out."

"That's not good. Where's the station now? Is it approaching another platform?"

"No. It passed South Platform a few minutes ago. Shiva ignored it."

The truck abruptly decelerated. Catherine had inadvertently created the same conditions that preceded Graham Chapman's death. But Shiva had learned something from the accident. Rather than stop the truck instantly and risk damage to Ouroboros, the AI was reducing its speed slowly.

"I think I know what he's doing," said Catherine. "This may have something to do with the resonance-damping system. Whenever the station approaches Ouroboros, gravitational attraction distorts the ring. If the truck moves too fast in this direction, it too will generate oscillations that have to be damped out."

"So all this is consistent with Shiva trying to protect Ouroboros from oscillation?"

"It could be. It's just that the anti-resonance system isn't new. Why has Shiva started behaving like this now, I wonder."

"What are you going to do? You're not going to make it there. Should I send the train?"

"We don't have time. Stay calm, there are other options. Just get Sati activated as soon as you can." Catherine lowered her visor and pressurized the suit. The truck's life-support systems had just gone off-line. The air would soon be unbreathable. She extracted a tool from her utility pack and went to work removing the cover on the console and resetting the control jumpers. This put the truck under manual control.

"There goes five minutes," Catherine said to herself. She put the truck in motion again. There was no way Shiva could access it now. She quickly passed the speed limit again; this time the truck's systems remained nominal.

"Catherine! What's going on?"

"Nothing, I just outsmarted our AI. Something wrong?"

"He's reasoning like mad. He must be thinking of a way to stop you."

"That's not possible. I've taken the truck off-line. I'm invisible." The truck was within hailing distance of South Platform when Catherine heard a wail of panic.

"Stop!"

"Why? What is it?"

"He's activating the laser cannons!"

"Good god!" But the truck was moving far too fast to be stopped quickly. Increasing speed, on the other hand, would make Shiva's aim that much less accurate. It was her best bet for survival, but Catherine prepared for the worst. She assumed a fetal position on the floor of the cab.

Then it hit her—Shiva didn't have to know where the truck was. The lasers were equipped with onboard radar aiming. He could hand over control to the radar at the last moment and let the cannons think they were firing at a meteor.

Where am I? Catherine began feverishly trying to guess when the truck would pass South Platform. Shiva didn't know her precise location, which made it impossible for West Platform to confirm it either. She couldn't see anything from the floor of the cab. All she could do was try to guess her location from the time display on her visor.

He'll hit me as soon as I poke my head up over the horizon.

The distance to the horizon along the ring's outer surface was only about two kilometers. Catherine would be in cannon range for less than a second, but for that instant her fate would hang in the balance.

Suddenly the cab was filled with light, and Catherine was convinced her luck had run out. There was a high-pitched whine as air vented rapidly to space. Soon the sound stopped.

Is that it? She lifted her head to peer out. There was a single hole, several inches across, in the front of the cab. It would have been fatal if the beam had struck her, but the location of the hole suggested Shiva hadn't been targeting the passenger.

"Catherine, I hope you're alive." It was SysInt.

"Alive and kicking. There's a nice big hole in the truck though. What happened? It looks like Shiva only fired once."

"So he did hit you. We tried to take control of the lasers, but he completely shut us out. We saw him fire."

Catherine noticed she was slowing down. The outrushing air had pulled the truck's operating manual out of the rack behind the passenger seat and tossed it onto the speed control lever. She lifted the lever and the truck accelerated.

"I think we've been on the wrong track all along. You said Shiva bypassed the subsystem and was controlling the lasers directly?"

"That's how it looks."

"Shiva isn't capable of selecting targets."

"I don't understand. You said there was a hole in the truck," said SysInt.

"It's not that he grasps the reality of Amphisbaena or the truck as physical objects. For Shiva those are just symbols. He's using symbols to attack symbols. That explains why he hasn't been following through on his attacks. I think the same thing happened with Amphisbaena. The data relay on each habitat—that's all Amphisbaena is to Shiva."

"But if Shiva is reacting to symbols, how did he target the station?

That has to mean some kind of awareness of the physical world."

"Being dependent on symbol recognition doesn't mean Shiva can't target things in the real world. The relays on the station are just above the docking ports. Shiva is constantly tracking them, which means he can extract a targeting solution from real-time coordinates. That's not recognition of three-dimensional space, though. We had another dummy Amphisbaena ID ready to swap into the system, but we haven't used it. As far as Shiva is concerned, the attack rendered Amphisbaena nonexistent. The truck's speed dropped after I was fired on, though that was just an accident. Shiva will think the truck's been destroyed." In point of fact, Catherine wasn't sure about this, but she felt reason for optimism. Accounting for Shiva's behavior in terms of faulty awareness was easier than assuming the AI had decided to attack its human masters.

There was a pause. "Catherine, it looks like the angle of the laser strikes on Amphisbaena is consistent with an attack on the data relays. The shuttles were just in the way."

"See? That's a major indication of why this started in the first place."

"But in that case, Shiva is a danger to us all," said SysInt. "He doesn't understand that humans are physically present on Amphisbaena."

8

"CHIEF, SOUTH PLATFORM'S SHUTTLE is ready when you are."

"Understood. Prep for evac. I'm almost there."

Tatsuya toggled off. After the laser attack he'd decided not to use a new ID to reestablish contact with Ouroboros Net. Clearly Shiva had some serious issues with Amphisbaena. For now the AI seemed to be deliberately ignoring them. As long as they weren't under attack, it was best to leave things alone.

The current problem was how to get to the logistics module across forty kilometers of Amphisbaena's struts and bracing. It had been his idea, but he'd never imagined it would be this challenging. The gravity in the habitat was about the same as that on Mars—about a third of Earth's—and as he worked his way toward Amphisbaena's midpoint, the force generated by the station's rotation would diminish. The beginning was supposed to be the hardest part.

Tatsuya's guess that it would be possible to cover such a distance was based on a vacation he'd spent as a young man climbing Olympus Mons, the highest mountain in the solar system. The volcano was twenty-seven kilometers high, but nearly six hundred wide. It was more of a plateau than a mountain, with a constant, gentle slope. Walking to the top in his suit had been exhausting and he'd had some close calls along the way. But he'd made it.

Of course, Amphisbaena was not a mountain. But there was little difference between gravity at the base of Olympus Mons and at its summit. Even so, he'd managed to gain twenty-seven kilometers of altitude. With gravity dropping the closer he was to the center of Amphisbaena, this should be far easier. At least that was the concept.

As it turned out, he wasn't entirely wrong. He could feel his body getting lighter as he worked his way along. Still, it had taken him twenty kilometers of climbing just to reduce the gravity by half.

"Kurokawa, can you hear me?"

"I hear you, Chief."

"How far along are you?"

"I think about halfway."

"About the same as me."

"Can I ask you a question, Chief?"

"Sure."

"What gave you the idiotic idea we could climb forty klicks?"

"Is that your only question?"

"That's it for right now."

The rest of their climb was punctuated with similar exchanges. Not long after the halfway point it was clear to Tatsuya that he was reaching his limit, because he was having trouble gripping the climbing hooks. The low gravity made it easy to recover if he missed a hook, but after missing one five times, he knew he was out of his depth. This was getting dangerous. He found himself wishing the emergency docking port had been situated a bit more conveniently. He toggled his comm and said to no one in particular, "Ten-minute break."

The logistics module's docking port had been built for cargo shuttles to use while the station was under construction—it wasn't in routine use. For reasons Tatsuya could not recall, the port was oriented ninety degrees to Amphisbaena's rotation, forcing spacecraft to roll in order to synchronize with the station beneath them prior to docking. Because this port had only been used during the construction phase, the designers had never thought to equip it with remote access capability. Someone had to prep it from inside. At a time like this, the design wasn't very user friendly. Tatsuya spent his break cursing this lack of foresight.

"Chief? Ten minutes."

"I know, I know." Tatsuya started moving again. Later he realized from Kurokawa's tone that he hadn't just been reminding Tatsuya of the time. He'd been checking if his chief was still alive.

Not far past the halfway point climbing became much easier. Tatsuya discovered that propelling himself tens of meters at a time was more efficient than proceeding hook by hook. It seemed Kurokawa had made the same discovery. The Coriolis effect was weaker here, and there was little drift to correct for. Soon he was able to cover a hundred meters in one go. He had to stay alert; were it not for his experience, he could easily have built up enough momentum to end up crashing into the hull of the module. But he and Kurokawa had EVA'd so many times that compensating for changing inertia was second nature.

Tatsuya reached the hatch of the logistics module. It opened easily. Gravity was now close to zero. His body was exhausted, but he wasn't feeling it much in the microgravity. He released the east lift's latch, leaving the west lift for Kurokawa. They had both climbed here, each with a mission to fulfill.

The emergency lift consisted of a plastic frame at the end of a carbon nanotube wire. Releasing the latch triggered a spring-loaded ejection mechanism. Slowly the lift began its forty-kilometer descent toward East Habitat.

"Lift on its way, gentlemen. It'll be with you shortly." Tatsuya went to work prepping the docking port.

9

STOPPING THE TRUCK was no easy task—Catherine was moving far faster than a jet aircraft. The truck sped past the broad central boarding area of East Platform almost before she noticed. By the time she finally came to a stop, she was five kilometers past the platform.

Catherine clambered from the truck, taking only a small tool pack, and started back toward the platform with carefully timed, leaping strides. She felt an overwhelming sense of isolation; the nearest human was three thousand kilometers away. The ring was only five meters wide. If she veered from this path, she would be outside the human world, a satellite of Kali.

The stars moved visibly with the ring's motion. Bounding across this dark gray ribbon suspended in the void, it was difficult to believe that the events of the past few days had actually happened. Instead she felt she'd always been here, circling the ring forever in utter solitude.

Seeing the ruins of East Platform brought her back to reality. She reduced her pace to a slow walk, carefully bleeding off inertia to avoid stressing her knees. The structures on the outer surface of the ring had been ripped apart by the truck and the body of Graham Chapman. The structures on the inner surface had escaped damage. That was where she would find Shiva.

Catherine went to the hatch closest to Shiva, lifted it, and climbed through the ring and into the inner core. Shiva's console on the surface of the ring had been destroyed in the accident. But despite the inconvenience of having to input commands while suited up, she would have full access to the AI through the backup panel in the core.

The structures inside the ring were unscathed. Even the lights were still on. Catherine made her way down the corridor to the control room without noticing anything unusual. The door was sealed, but as she approached, Shiva automatically started calling up biometric data from her web. He wanted to know the identity of his visitor.

Thirty seconds later the door opened. Though it must have been her imagination, it seemed to Catherine that access was given grudgingly. She'd be unable to use her web from the control room to exchange data with the outside—another security measure. The only way to communicate with her team would be by voice, via her suit.

To the right of the console was an umbilicus for suit power, circulating oxygen, and heating water. This was essential for extended work in the cold vacuum of the core, but Catherine left it alone. There was no guarantee that Shiva might not use the umbilicus for some other purpose. She was taking no chances.

Inside the control room, Catherine was weightless. She harnessed herself to the console as if for a routine work session. A few moments later the console initiated a second verification sequence with her web.

Under normal circumstances Catherine would have regarded this as unremarkable. Obviously, Shiva would want to know who was attempting to use his console. But his recent behavior had been anything but normal. She was struck by how much work and ingenuity were necessary to create and maintain a world where things functioned as expected. If AIs could be taught to think like humans, maybe none of this would be happening.

ID verification was successful. The object known as Catherine Sinclaire was authorized for full system access. The console powered up and signaled ready.

Catherine used the outsize keyboard to input data with gloved fingers. She avoided voice input to keep the interaction as basic as possible. Shiva's response was immediate. Catherine winced.

Graham, this is all your fault, isn't it?

The fact that Graham Chapman's ID was still valid had to be the key to solving the problem. Instead of running a system analysis, she queried the status of Chapman's agent. Sure enough, the program had assumed override control of Shiva's top-level functions. Chapman had named it "Priority Observation Program."

So you're the one who's been screwing things up.

The program had been loaded less than an hour before Chapman had become his creation's first victim. Catherine next asked to view the program code, but the output was so long and involved that it was difficult to make an immediate judgment. Apparently the program was designed to make Shiva respond to some specific condition or event, but just glancing at the code didn't yield much information. A proper analysis would have to wait for Sati.

Still, Catherine wasn't going to walk away empty-handed after almost being killed in the effort to get here. If the front door was locked, maybe she could find another way in. That was almost always possible with any large system.

Graham, what is this program supposed to do? Is it a new resonance damper?

She decided to take her first calculated risk: accessing Chapman's avatar through her web. Most programs of this type allowed limited access for basic maintenance and profiling. All she had to do was ask the avatar to state its type and purpose.

The avatar was configured for voice response only. Perhaps because of the program's size, Chapman had dispensed with the usual talking head. That was just as well. Catherine was in no mood to talk to a simulation of a dead man.

"This all goes back to my goal of analyzing that anomalous ring resonance," the avatar said, apparently programmed by Chapman to be chatty. Somehow Catherine was not surprised. "I think I'm onto a solution, but I can't prove it yet."

"So what are you using to verify this theory of yours?" asked Catherine.

"As you know, the platform-to-platform ranging system for maintaining the ring's position relative to Kali can double as a laser interferometer."

"And you're using it to investigate resonance?"

"Yes, but more importantly, for gravity wave observation. The operating principle is the same. Ouroboros happens to be the largest freestanding laser interferometer in the solar system. Properly used, it should yield very accurate observational data on gravity waves."

⸻ ◆═◆═◆ ⸻

THE RING'S FOUR HABITAT PLATFORMS bracketed Kali from two directions, offset ninety degrees. Each platform pair—North/South, East/West—used lasers to continuously monitor the distance to the other side of the ring. Kali's gravity shifted the wavelength of the laser before it reached the detector on the other side; how closely it passed by Kali determined the wavelength shift. By comparing the incoming wavelength against its own reference, each detector could gauge any drift relative to the black hole. Combining these results with data from the other platform pair made it possible to maintain Kali at the precise center of the ring.

The whole system was a basic application of interferometry and was essential to maintain the stability of a structure like Ouroboros. A ring encircling a gravity source has no net gravitational interaction with that source and thus no stable orbital characteristics. Slight inputs of external energy—including G-forces from the station—could eventually cause Ouroboros to fall into Kali. Data from the lasers was ported to the ring's attitude control system.

The attitude control system was also part of the ring's defense against vibrations caused by activity on the ring—a major problem with such a large structure in space. Despite its size, the ring was extremely delicate. Keeping it stable was no easy task. Ouroboros was equipped with systems to prevent vibrations from turning into destructive resonance. The ring could automatically change shape to dampen any vibration-induced resonance. Once Chandrasekhar Station was complete, systems to deal with these problems would be distributed and redundant, but still essential.

•◦•◦•

"I DON'T BELIEVE IT. You made your pet project a system priority? *That's* what you loaded into Shiva?" Catherine knew that Chapman had been investigating this problem just before his death, but she'd had no idea he'd been using interferometry to study gravity waves.

Chapman's avatars had always taken realism further than most. In this sense he was an artist, and Catherine's shock made her forget for an instant that the programmer was dead. A moment later she remembered what she was conversing with. It didn't do much to cool her anger. The avatar offered the mere appearance of consciousness, while humans were hardwired by evolution to assume—with minimal prompting—the existence of other minds.

Sure enough, the avatar sounded appropriately offended. "Hey, come off it—I'd never mix private pursuits with official duties. You know that better than anyone. I'm designed to do nothing but monitor for resonance, except when one specific condition is fulfilled. Unless that happens, I'm not programmed to control Shiva in any way."

"What's the specific condition?"

"When I detect gravity waves that I can't account for, such as might be generated by an extrasolar civilization."

10

THE VOICE FROM WEST PLATFORM reached Tatsuya. "The South Platform shuttle is on its way. North Platform shuttle is nearly ready to launch."

"Roger. We're almost set to receive visitors. Kurokawa, are you sure this guidance beacon is going to work? It's been a while since anyone used it."

"The long-range tracking radar and short-range laser guidance system are both fine, Chief. Stop worrying. The technology is very simple. They're not complicated enough to malfunction."

"True. This rig isn't much different from what they used a hundred years ago." The two men stared at the control interface—little more than a ten-key pad with a few function buttons. A small display above the console showed a wire-frame rendering of the approaching shuttle with range and attitude information.

"See? We've acquired the shuttle," said Kurokawa.

"West Platform, this is Tatsuya. Ready for docking."

"Great to hear that, Commander. To be honest, we were all sort of turning blue here. The last thing we need is another surprise from Shiva."

A flash of white light stabbed through the open hatch. "Chief— the shuttle!"

The display above the control console was empty. The shuttle was gone.

11

"EXTRASOLAR CIVILIZATION? You turned Ouroboros into a SETI platform?"

"That's right. The search for intelligent entities outside the solar system has been my life's work as an astronomer."

Catherine hadn't expected to hear an avatar talk about its life's work. The program continued: "Gravity waves can be detected by the same principles we use to monitor for resonance. Of course, the probability of Ouroboros detecting gravity waves from an extrasolar civilization would have to be an incident so unlikely as to be on the same order as Kali's discovery. Close to a miracle, perhaps. But if there's the tiniest chance we can verify such a phenomenon, I think you know what it will mean for the human species."

"And that's why you erased Amphisbaena from the system?"

"Gravity waves are hard to detect. Man-made perturbations interfere with my observations. I know it's an inconvenience, but it's temporary. This is an opportunity humanity may not have within its grasp a second time. I'm afraid you'll just have to put up with me."

"What if someone tries to stop your observations?"

"I'm not sure I understand, Catherine. If something interferes, I am programmed to eliminate it."

"Eliminate it? You'd put lives in danger?"

"No need to worry about that. As long as no unauthorized tampering takes place, I'm not allowed to eliminate any humans."

If the voice coming from the console had been that of a human rather than an avatar, Catherine might have trusted it. In fact, the avatar was correct. But for Shiva there were no flesh and blood people, only web IDs. Shiva had had no intention of killing anyone, including Chapman. But what humans thought of as human and what Shiva thought of as human were not the same thing. And that was an unbridgeable gap.

The emergency hailing signal sounded in Catherine's helmet. "Catherine, we have a situation here. Shiva fired on the shuttle we sent to evacuate Amphisbaena."

"Are there casualties?"

"No, fortunately. The shuttle was destroyed before it docked. No one was aboard. But why—?"

"Hold on, I think I have the answer right in front of me."

Catherine accessed the cannon log, displaying the commands sent by Shiva to the meteor defense system. The data set was limited enough for even a human to evaluate quickly.

"Got it. He was targeting the docking guidance system."

"But why? We haven't used it since Shiva was activated."

"That's the point. Amphisbaena doesn't exist for Shiva. He knows all about the shuttle, of course, but when its guidance system handed off to Amphisbaena, the shuttle disappeared because it was under the station's control. The thing is, as far as Shiva is concerned, there's no station for the shuttle to be handed off to. That made the shuttle an unidentified object from the instant of handoff. That wasn't an attack. Shiva was defending Ouroboros against a collision risk."

As she heard herself speak Catherine felt an icy chill. Shiva was equipped with a high capacity for learning, but at a certain cost—it was not possible to predict with certainty what the AI might learn from a given experience. His next move might be to slice the station to pieces with the laser cannons in order to protect it.

"Catherine, should I cut power to the lasers?"

"No, wait. That could be dangerous. Shiva would probably start looking for a workaround as soon as you cut the power. He doesn't know about aiming in real space as opposed to cyberspace. Cutting the power might teach him something else we'd rather not have him learn."

"But the shuttle for North Platform is on the way. That's the last lifeboat we've got."

"We've got to keep Amphisbaena's docking beacon switched off. I think I'm onto what's causing Shiva to behave like this. I might be able to do something from here. Keep working on Sati. If everything else fails, we'll cut power to the lasers."

"Okay. I'd better alert the Guardians. They'll want to know."

During this entire exchange, the avatar kept droning on about the importance of SETI, as if it actually believed what it was saying. Catherine wasn't listening. She didn't fully understand what was going on, but Shiva was using Ouroboros as a gravity wave detector, and for some reason he was convinced he had detected something that fulfilled Graham's conditions for system override.

"Graham, I think your program killed you." The avatar didn't answer. Shiva must have had some difficulty parsing the logic of Catherine's statement. At length the avatar responded.

"The longer you live, the more shit you see." That was what Chapman had tended to say when he was at a loss for words.

"I'm deleting this program," said Catherine. There was another long moment of silence before the answer came:

"I'm afraid I can't allow that, Cathy. It would interfere with my observations."

12

"SHIVA TOOK THE SHUTTLE for a meteor?"

"Not exactly. He lost touch with it, and when he detected something that occupied the space the shuttle was in, he thought *that* was a meteor."

"What the hell's the difference?" said Tatsuya. The second shuttle was approaching. It had only been moments since their webs had become usable again, using the shuttle as a relay. "So you're saying the moment the shuttle's guidance is handed off to Amphisbaena, Shiva will think it's a threat?"

"Yes, if our analysis is correct."

"That's not encouraging. Maybe Shiva isn't shooting at us, but the difference seems academic." Tatsuya couldn't help complaining, but it hardly made things better. Oxygen levels in the habitats were dropping and they were down to one shuttle. "Can't you dock in full auto mode?"

"We can get close," said System Control, "but we can't dock. The system's designed to hand off automatically to the station's guidance system to protect Amphisbaena from collisions."

"Can you alter the program?"

"Well, since Shiva doesn't think Amphisbaena exists anymore, altering the guidance program and trying to use it again might elicit another unexpected reaction. All we can do is get as close as we can."

"All right. Bring her in and align with the station's rotation."

"Sure, but ... Wait a minute, you're not going to EVA to the shuttle and ride back here on the outside?"

"Thanks for the idea—maybe that'll work."

"You've got to be kidding. You'd be sitting ducks if Shiva decided to attack again."

"Don't worry. No way forty of us can piggyback on the outside of the shuttle. I've got a better plan. More elegant."

"YOU CALL THIS ELEGANT, CHIEF?"

"It's more elegant than climbing forty klicks." Tatsuya watched Kurokawa's EVA on the docking console monitor. The shuttle was in position a hundred meters above the port, its rotation synchronized with the station. From Tatsuya's point of view it seemed to be stationary. The docking guidance system was off-line. A pair of astronauts floated on either side of the shuttle. Only the most experienced crew members were capable of this kind of work. Attempting to send everyone up to the shuttle and tether them there would almost surely have resulted in casualties.

They had begun by attaching several strands of carbon nanofiber cable to the shuttle. The other ends of the cables were attached to a lift winch clamped to the side of the logistics module. Now the cables were slowly being drawn in. The four astronauts were making tiny adjustments with their thrusters.

"How did we end up getting chosen for this, anyway?" griped Kurokawa.

"EVA experience, and the fact that you all weigh pretty much the same. Very important for something like this."

"I see. Once we're back on Ouroboros I think I'd better go on an eating binge."

The first fifty meters went quickly, but after that they had to proceed much more cautiously. The winch was bringing the shuttle in at a rate of a few centimeters a second. It wouldn't do to crash the shuttle into the station when they were this close to succeeding.

The astronauts fired their thrusters in short bursts, using their suits' laser range finders for fine adjustments. The latches on the shuttle and the port locked. Kurokawa quickly unhooked the cables.

"All right, people. Let's get the hell off this station," said Tatsuya. The waiting crew began boarding the shuttle one by one. The shuttle was not designed to carry forty passengers, and the men and women inside had to arrange themselves like sardines in a can, but they managed to fit. The sense of relief was palpable.

"Come on, Chief. Everyone's aboard." Kurokawa signaled impatiently. Tatsuya was about to go when he noticed a small object on the console display, probably a piece of drifting debris from the shuttle explosion. He upped the magnification and stared, dumbfounded.

"What is that? Is that the maintenance droid?" The object was clearly firing its thrusters. "West Platform, what's Shiva up to right now?"

There was a long pause. "We were wondering the same thing. Shiva erased Amphisbaena from the system, but he's still linked to some of the station subsystems. We're not sure why. What's going on?"

"The maintenance droid is carrying out some kind of attitude change. You know, the droid with the laser welding unit?"

Another pause, then: "Shiva is controlling it directly. He's not tunneling through the station subsystem. That means you can't take it back from him."

"Any idea of what he's planning?"

"He's exchanging lots of data with the welding unit and the droid's optical sensors."

"Optical sensors? You're talking about target acquisition. Real-world target acquisition."

There was no answer.

13

"what do you mean, you can't allow it?"

"What I mean is that you can't stop me and you can't delete me. You never know what kind of system error that might precipitate."

Even though she knew the avatar was a nonsentient interface, Catherine felt herself losing control. "You have no idea what you're doing!" she shouted. She knew the AI was unable to recognize the situation confronting her. "How do I terminate the program?"

"I will terminate when observations are complete."

"When will that be?"

"When no more anomalous gravity waves are detected. I can't tell you when that will be."

For a moment, the avatar's complacent tone almost drove Catherine over the edge. An impulse to demolish the console was flitting through her mind when she received an excited message from West Platform. Shiva was manipulating the maintenance droid.

Under different circumstances an AI researcher like Catherine would have been delighted to hear this news. Shiva was displaying far greater learning capabilities than his creators had dared dream of. His ad hoc manipulation of the trucks and the laser cannons had awoken him to the possibility of self-directed action and the novel use of tools.

"Catherine, do you think Shiva may have stumbled onto the concept of aiming?"

"I wouldn't jump to that conclusion." Catherine pulled up the communication log between Shiva and the droid. From this console, cutting Shiva's link with the droid should be straightforward. But so far every roadblock thrown in his way had only accelerated his learning. If severing the link didn't succeed, it might make Shiva even harder to handle.

"It looks like he hasn't figured out how to integrate information from the sensors with the laser control system—yet," said Catherine.

"Good. That means he still doesn't know how to aim."

"It may not be good at all. If he understood aiming, at least he'd know what he was aiming at. He knows the droid has a laser unit, so he knows he has an attack option. But he's still just attacking symbols."

"What should we do?"

"Don't give up. You've got to change the shuttle ID. That may buy us some time. And hurry—Shiva's getting smarter every second."

14

"I'M NOT PLANNING to get killed. Don't worry. Stay safe."

Tatsuya sent the shuttle on its way. After consulting with System Control, he decided to roll the dice again, this time swapping IDs with the shuttle. Shiva had stopped accepting new ID codes. Since the shuttle now bore the ID of a human, it was protected from attack, at least for the time being. If the droid was targeting the shuttle, it should now come after Tatsuya.

A dead hero is a failure. A real hero lives to fight another day. That was what Tatsuya had been taught since childhood. In a world where you could wake up one morning and discover that your oxygen was about to run out, survival was never far from anyone's thoughts.

The shuttle moved off toward Ouroboros. Tatsuya engaged his suit's tiny thrusters and floated away from the docking port. He wanted to at least try to look like a shuttle.

The stars seemed to move around him, but only because he was rotating. He spread his limbs to stabilize his motion. Amphisbaena began to turn beneath him as he slowly drifted away.

"Chief, the droid is vectoring toward you. Sending coordinates." Tatsuya squinted into the distance. He could see a dull red glow, still far off—probably the droid's thrusters.

"SysCon, I have to say, there's not a whole lot of I in your AI. That droid sure is wasting fuel." As he watched, the red glow moved steadily closer.

15

"I DON'T HAVE TIME TO WASTE ON YOU!"

Catherine's heart was pounding with fear. This entire chain of events hinged on a simple mistake by Graham Chapman. His SETI investigations depended on distinguishing between natural and artificial perturbations, but not all artificial perturbations were the work of extraterrestrials.

Chapman had neglected to equip Shiva with the ability to distinguish between gravity waves that might have been generated by an extrasolar civilization and those created by the anomalous ring oscillations he had been researching. This must have occurred to him just before he died. Knowing his program better than anyone, he'd rushed to restore the system to its previous state. Ironically, he'd become Shiva's first victim.

But everything revolved around one source of data: the interferometer system. If that were taken off-line, there would be no gravity waves to detect. Catherine brought up the interferometer controls. The avatar quickly responded.

"Catherine, you are about to interfere with some very important observations. In fact, to do so would be a criminal violation of the ring's operating protocols. I'm sorry, but I have to eliminate you."

"Eliminate me? How?"

"Your actions demonstrate intent to defeat my purpose. Your existence cannot be permitted."

The console shut down and the room plunged into darkness. Catherine tried to restart the console from her web. There was no response.

16

I'LL ONLY HAVE A FEW SECONDS.

One more time, Tatsuya hurriedly reviewed the approaching droid's operating specs on his web. His plan was half-baked, but without weapons it would have to do.

The maintenance droid was a rectangular cuboid about the size of a small car, with six manipulator arms. It was nicknamed the "bumble bee" because of its laser, reminiscent of a stinger at the end.

Tatsuya held his forearm mirrors toward the droid. Normally the mirrors were used to check the condition of the space suit; in theory they should be able to deflect a laser beam. His suit transmitter was mounted on his chest. If the droid fired its laser, that was where it would aim. Tatsuya held both forearms up, protecting his chest. If luck was with him, the laser would bounce back and might even knock out the droid.

Come on, fire . . .

The droid drew closer and stopped, its laser welder just out of reach. Its optical sensors scanned Tatsuya intently.

"Tatsuya, Shiva's reasoning is spiking again. What's the droid doing?"

"Nothing. It's just checking me out."

Tatsuya had more than a passing familiarity with this droid. If the warning light on the welding unit changed from green to blue, it meant the laser was fully charged. Red meant discharge was imminent.

Suddenly the droid began moving its arms slowly in front of its sensors, as if it was examining them. After a few moments of this, Shiva seemed to reach a decision. It slowly extended the welding unit toward Tatsuya. Tatsuya moved his mirrors closer to the business end of the welder, but as he did so he brushed against another manipulator arm and knocked himself out of position.

Shit!

The droid's sensors were tracking him, laser arm moving with them. The warning light turned blue. Tatsuya prepared to face death.

17

WHEN THE LIGHTS in the control room went off, Catherine thought for a moment that she might be about to die. But nothing happened. She was simply alone in the darkness with a dead console.

By "eliminate," had Shiva meant from the system?

Apparently the answer was yes. When she hit the switch, the lights came on as usual. She manually entered her backup administrator ID and the console powered up normally. A quick check showed her primary ID was invalid. Catherine was no longer part of Shiva's universe. But the AI had no objection to her backup ID.

Shiva had reacted poorly to the prospect of shutting down the observation program. If he deleted her backup password, she'd lose her only chance to take countermeasures. The next few seconds might be her last chance to act. She did so without hesitation. First she cut the power to the interferometry arrays on the North and West platforms and ran a quick status check on Chapman's program. Sure enough, with no data coming from the arrays, Shiva detected no anomalous perturbations and had idled the SETI program. She quickly locked the program—and Chapman's avatar—out of the system. The entire process took a few seconds; after a few seconds more the console showed the AI operating at its default parameters.

That's all it took?

The ring itself could have been in dire danger with the wrong move, yet half a dozen commands was all it took to resolve the problem.

Did we learn anything from this after all? wondered Catherine. Was this a complex failure or a simple one?

18

THE SHUTTLE, jammed with the forty crew members from Amphisbaena, docked at North Platform. System Control took control of the maintenance droid. Tatsuya held on to one of the droid's arms as it ferried him back to the station. Shiva, having recognized him as a physical presence, had been about to fire the droid's laser, but Catherine's intervention had prevented that. Now the droid was under human control.

Tatsuya decided to remain on Amphisbaena. Its systems were rebooting and returning to normal, but there was a lot of recovery work to do. He also welcomed the chance to avoid the hero's welcome awaiting him on Ouroboros; it would only have embarrassed him.

Catherine stopped at North Platform just as the shuttle was arriving. Her team on West Platform reported Sati ready for verification testing, and Catherine knew that meant many busy days ahead. She was dead tired. Spending her sleep period on North Platform seemed the best option—if she returned to West Platform she'd be sure to plunge into the work waiting for her. Tatsuya's voice, when it came up on her web, seemed to signal that they had put the problem behind them at last.

"So this whole thing was Shiva being convinced that anomalous ring oscillations were evidence of extraterrestrials? It's ironic—Shiva wouldn't have behaved the way he did if he'd understood *human* intelligence, but he assumed the vibrations he was detecting indicated nonhuman intelligence. By the way, did you ever figure out what was causing those residual oscillations?"

"I think that what Graham realized just before he died is that Shiva alone doesn't have enough computing power to analyze every perturbation in a structure as large as the ring," said Catherine. "That created the potential for Shiva to mistake one type of oscillation for another."

"I guess that's the price of genius—sometimes your theories get ahead of you. But once Sati's online—"

"Something like this can't happen again."

"What I don't understand is why the droid spent so much time observing me instead of shooting."

"The answer to that will have to wait, but I think Shiva's interaction with us led him to infer the existence of a world outside cyberspace, and he was trying to confirm that. That's why he hesitated to attack you immediately. He was getting a lot of new data from the droid's feedback circuits."

"Whatever. At least it gave me a chance to come out of this alive."

Catherine's response was interrupted by a message from West Platform. "Catherine, we've been sifting through the raw data you sent—the interferometry data that Dr. Chapman's program was accumulating."

"Yes? What's up?"

"Well, we let Sati have a go at it, just for fun. A lot of it was false positives—Shiva didn't have the capacity to filter it all. It's just . . ."

"Just what?"

"Well, there's this underlying pattern that's left after we filter the data. We can't explain it in terms of natural or man-made sources. We're assuming it's just another artifact."

"So what's the problem?"

"This one pattern doesn't look anything like natural gravity waves. We've already corrected for sources at the galactic center."

"So what is it? Intelligent signals from outside Sol System?"

"We think it's a possibility, that's all."

"What do you think, Tatsuya?"

Tatsuya patched in a feed from one of Amphisbaena's observation cameras. It was a visual of the glowing gas ring circling Kali. "Take a look."

The ring of gas seemed to be shining less brightly than before, but it was still circling Kali, pulsating steadily.

"He always was a stubborn bastard. I think he's having the last laugh."

RECONFIGURING KALI'S ORBIT and constructing the accretion disk proceeded in parallel. Soon AADD would begin transforming the solar system with energy from the disk.

The first phase of this process would primarily be devoted to terraforming Mars, but AADD's ambitions were far larger than that. They would transmit power from the disk throughout the solar system, making human habitation possible even on some of the smaller asteroids. And once the energy transmission system was complete, humanity would truly have slipped the bounds of gravity. With radiative cooling systems in place around Kali, the entire structure would be seven thousand kilometers across, roughly the diameter of Mars, and the gravity on its surface would be about the same as that on Mars. By the time the transmission system was complete, it would have grown larger than the planets themselves, to encompass the entire solar system, or at least its inner core.

Naturally, completing such a gigantic undertaking was impossible without mishap. A huge number of new basic technologies would be needed. Sometimes the experiments made in pursuit of such technologies had unexpected consequences. Until their origins were known, these remained riddles, seemingly products of chance.

THE RIDDLE OF RAPUSHINUPURUKURU
A.D. 2144

MY FIRST IMPRESSION of the asteroid was that it looked bizarre. The flat side of the misshapen object was completely obscured by a honeycomb-mesh antenna. For hundreds of millions of years Rapushinupurukuru had moved in solitude along its own eccentric orbit. It had taken less than a month for the construction bot to build a structure that hid the entire surface from view.

Mass was needed to ensure stable energy transmission, and Rapushinupurukuru had been well chosen. Its eight hundred million tons of mass came in a shape that was ideal for construction of the microwave array; so ideal, in fact, that it was hard to believe it hadn't been created eons ago for just this purpose.

Its shape was somehow neither natural nor artificial. One might say it was unnatural. Now this unnatural object rotated roughly every five minutes.

If everything had proceeded according to plan, Rapushinupurukuru would not be rotating at all. From where I was sitting, the only thing visible should have been a twenty-kilometer-wide hexagonal antenna. As built, the antenna consisted of 250 individual segments, but the asteroid's rotation, slow as it was, generated enough centrifugal force to exceed the strength of the fragile joints holding the segments together. They had been designed for weightless conditions. The centrifugal forces at the edge of the antenna reached 0.45 G; there was no way the joints could hold.

More than two hundred segments had spiraled off into space.

Now only the central section was left, a honeycomb section about a kilometer across, still big enough to hide the near side of the asteroid beneath it. The far side was naked gray rock, faintly iron-red from ion weathering, though the spectrum shift was hard to see with the naked eye. I'd first noticed it while browsing the image bank on my web.

Of course, Rapushinupurukuru didn't have "near" or "far" sides. It was just convenient to call them that. The side with the mesh antenna was the near side. The far side showed no trace of human activity.

"I hate these things." Barbara was squinting at her web's readout through a bulky pair of data goggles. I was doing the same with mine.

"How's the analysis, Barbara? Any results?"

"I reran the calculations. Same as the first time."

"Figures." I was looking at the same data—everything *Dragonslayer*'s sensors could pick up, in fact—but given our different specialties, we were interested in different things. Our agent programs were filtering the data differently too. In all likelihood we weren't even talking about the same thing.

We were in *Dragonslayer*'s core block. We didn't need to occupy the same space to communicate, but the ship only carried twelve. Dispersing the crew to mitigate vulnerabilities in case of an accident wouldn't eliminate much risk. Still, there was no bridge or central control station. Everyone had access to all the information they needed to execute their responsibilities via web.

"I thought this chunk of rock wasn't revolving. What's the deal with it starting now? Can you see anything, Seiya?"

Barbara and I were facing opposite directions. The core block was, structurally, the safest place on *Dragonslayer*. It was where everyone would head in an emergency. Most of the equipment was well shielded against radiation. It wasn't exactly roomy with all twelve of us crammed in, but we could fit. It wouldn't have been much use otherwise.

"What's to see? It's a standard S-type asteroid. She's about as garden variety as they come."

Rapushinupurukuru's rotation was just revealing its far side. I thought it was kind of cool that even an object this small would have a horizon. It was roughly potato-shaped, twelve hundred meters on the long axis by six hundred by four hundred meters. A wedge with a regolith jacket, pulverized rock acquired over millions of years of tiny impacts.

"That's not what I'm talking about." Barbara's face, upside down, was suddenly close to mine. In the weightlessness of the narrow space it was easier to get face-to-face this way than to swivel the jump seats. Still, I got the feeling she liked the acrobatics in the narrow confines of the ship. She always wore her red jumpsuit and kept her blond hair cropped just a few millimeters past skinhead length.

"I mean, the robot finishes the antenna array without a hitch, and then, before we can even finish testing, Rapu starts rotating. What I was asking was, did you see anything that pointed to a cause?"

Barbara was still wearing her goggles. I had no idea what she was looking at, but the image I sent her must have been totally off target. My agent talking to her agent wasn't working so well.

"It might not be something we can extract from a visual," I said. "But there is something strange. I don't know if it's connected to the rotation." I sent the data to Barbara's goggles.

"Strange like how? Particle contamination . . . what the fuck?"

"Yeah. Weird, huh? It's a thin layer, but there's some kind of material on the antenna mesh, probably regolith. No way that could've accumulated in the six months since Rapu started rotating."

"Hmm . . . something must've kicked up a cloud of regolith. Maybe some kind of small impactor? Some of the particles would've been recaptured gravitationally. Collision-induced rotation. Simple explanation."

"I wouldn't be so sure." *Dragonslayer*'s captain floated in through the core hatch. Rebecca's job was to shape the crew's input into decisions, but we called her captain for convenience. Her long brown hair floated in a halo. She placed a fingertip against the wall, rotated 180 degrees, and settled into one of the jump seats. This kind of maneuver was simple for veteran astronauts; Rebecca was proud of her lack of bruises despite the generous expanses of skin she tended to expose for our benefit. She also insisted that leaving her hair to float free helped make her more aerodynamically stable. I kind of got the idea she was bullshitting us.

"Any impact with enough energy to shred the array and spin Rapu like a top would've left a crater somewhere. It might be no more than a few meters across, but our sensors wouldn't have trouble picking it up."

"You're right, Captain." Barbara nodded earnestly. For some reason she agreed with whatever Rebecca said but always criticized whatever I came up with—even if she had to make something up to do so. Not only that, but Barbara seemed to have gotten the idea that finding fault with others was something only I did. Well, I guess diversity of viewpoints is a good thing.

"Something else bothers me," said Rebecca. "This particle contamination."

"You mean its origin?" I answered.

"The origin, sure, but also the timing. I mean, look. Say a meteor— or something else—hits Rapu. It throws up a bunch of regolith. The impact starts Rapu revolving. Centrifugal force shreds the array but the central module stays intact. That means the impactor hit Rapu's far side. So how did the regolith contaminate the array? It was twenty klicks away, which would've shielded the central module from contamination."

"What if the impact itself destroyed the array?"

"Then how come the central module's intact? Anyway, a hit big enough to destroy the array directly should've left traces, but we're not seeing any. And there's another problem—the telemetry data. What do you make of that? Can't explain that away with a meteor strike."

UNTIL RECENTLY, Rapushinupurukuru had been known as Asteroid 2143SF, meaning it was the sixth S-class object to be discovered last year, 2143. Its orbital elements were quickly determined and, once it became clear that it had an orbit unlike any known object of its type, a proper name seemed appropriate.

By now we'd pretty much mined all of humanity's major myths and legends for names, so we'd been taking names from some of the more obscure cultures. Rapushinupurukuru was a dragon god of the ethnic Ainu of Hokkaido in the north of the Japanese archipelago. The name meant "feathered god with magical powers." According to our database, Rapushinupurukuru's realm was Lake Toya. The god was active in summer, dormant in winter. Since everyone living in Japan, regardless of where they came from, was referred to as Japanese, I seriously doubted anyone there had a clue that Rapushinupurukuru was the name of a legendary dragon. The fact that the name was in our database could indicate colonists with Ainu ancestry on Mars, or maybe one of the asteroids.

AADD had already moved Kali into orbit around Uranus. At the same time it had been moving ahead with construction of the facilities for the artificial accretion disk. Actually it would be more accurate to call the whole thing a Dyson sphere. Kali's accretion disk threw off energy, mostly in the form of electromagnetic emissions; this energy was trapped by the sphere surrounding the black hole. The energy could be distributed anywhere in the solar system via microwaves or laser, depending on where it needed to go.

The antenna on Rapushinupurukuru was meant to prove the distribution concept as well as the construction process, which was totally carried out by robot. Basically it went like this: Once the best site for the antenna was identified, the core relay module was anchored to the surface. Then piles were driven in around it and the central section of the microwave receiver was built overhead. This section was structurally the strongest part of the whole antenna. The rest of the antenna unfolded outward from the central section like flower petals. Each section was about a thousand meters across, with the whole antenna extending out about twenty kilometers. Each section was joined to the others by threadlike joints. Something this big and fragile could only be deployed in a weightless environment.

The designers had incorporated an unbelievably precise, dynamic leveling system. Any little tremor reaching the antenna was automatically offset, guaranteeing an absolutely flat surface—a single, gigantic antenna precise enough to put a signal into a hundred-meter circle at a distance of one AU. This level of accuracy was critical to the whole concept.

Rapushinupurukuru's orbit was almost vertical to the plane of the ecliptic—its inclination was eighty-seven degrees. Perihelion was three AUs, aphelion thirty, and it took about sixty-seven years to orbit Sol. At first astronomers assumed it was a short-period comet, till observations showed it was composed mainly of the metal-silicate compounds typical of an S-type asteroid. In terms of planetary physics, it was a pretty interesting object given its orbit, but AADD had another reason for paying attention to this particular asteroid. Not only was it sharply inclined to the ecliptic plane, it also had a very high orbital eccentricity at 0.82. If Rapushinupurukuru could be used as a transmission node, delivery of energy to almost any part of the solar system would become practical. The high orbital eccentricity meant that energy could be relayed by pointing the array in a fixed direction. Of course, Rapushinupurukuru's antenna could also be used to beam energy to the planets, but a more important goal was providing power to spacecraft traversing the solar system. With an external power supply, spacecraft could be made much simpler and yet travel faster. As long as the craft's position was known at all times, power could be supplied with lasers, with guidance data piggybacked on the energy transmission. That would let us move cargo more efficiently, with automated bulk carriers.

Of course, this was the ultimate goal. Getting there was going to take some time. Kali was still moving into position around Uranus and the accretion disk was still being tweaked. In the meantime we'd been working on getting the kinks out of the energy transmission system.

Things had gone pretty smoothly at first. The robot had successfully completed the antenna array, and microwave power generation with the accretion disk was achieved for the first time. But then the array had started sending some strange telemetry, indicating that Rapushinupurukuru was beginning to rotate, at first very slowly. The signal began dropping and recovering intermittently, with indications that the rotational speed was picking up. Then we lost the signal completely.

Telemetry analysis didn't tell us much, but it did point to a mystery beyond that of the asteroid's anomalous rotation. The array had been receiving faint signals unrelated to the control signals for the construction bot. All we knew was that the signals were not some natural phenomenon. And their connection with Rapushinupurukuru's anomalous rotation? Equally unknown.

There was just too much going on here, and you never know until you go. The Guardians—that's what we are—were set up for just this kind of problem.

The Guardians were AADD's security enforcement arm. We dealt with just about everything connected with security. We helped keep the peace. But mostly what we did was get people out of trouble. And sometimes, if AADD's progress was at stake, we carried out investigations.

The origin of the Guardians went back to the early days of space colonists forming their own security organizations. As the space cities grew, these police forces became more specialized and professional. After AADD was formed, it took all these scattered groups and unified them into the Guardians.

We were the closest team to Rapushinupurukuru when the problem was detected. *Dragonslayer* was our ride.

ABOVE OUR HEADS the ship seemed to be moving slowly, but of course it was Barbara and I who were actually moving. Although the asteroid's rotation made it useless as a microwave relay node, on the surface the motion didn't seem so noticeable. Farthest away from the axis of rotation the centrifugal force was a mere 0.03 G. Close to the axis it was barely perceptible, though a misstep could send you off on a short trajectory.

"Hey, Seiya, what's the deal with these supports? Were they designed to be this short?"

"Not likely," I answered. I looked at the surface. Some of the little craters must have formed before life even began on Earth. Most asteroids, except for the densest, were covered in regolith—especially the big ones where distances were measured in kilometers. They usually had enough gravity to hold on to a blanket of fine material.

Asteroids like Rapu had so little gravity that the finer particles created in collisions usually traveled fast enough to escape into space. This left a regolith blanket of coarser rock. I could tell just by looking that the layer under my boots wasn't very thick. I felt its granules crunch under my feet like gravel. If there'd been an atmosphere, I would have heard it too.

Rapushinupurukuru was at most only twelve hundred meters long, so the horizon was extremely close. On the surface, it felt like you were standing atop a tall building—a building with a penthouse rock garden. The horizon seemed to drop off into an abyss, but if you kept walking, more gray rock just kept coming up.

Before we started any further analysis we had to take a look at the microwave antenna array the robot had built. The surface in the shadow of the mesh antenna was redder than on the far side, testimony to the fact that until recently Rapushinupurukuru hadn't rotated. Rock weathered even in the vacuum of space. There were microimpacts, charged particles from the Sun—you name it. Under the influence of weathering processes, nanometer-sized iron particles were knocked out of the silicate matrix and came to cover the rock's surface, giving it a slightly reddish cast.

From the ship, the reddening of the near side seemed pretty uniform. But down on the surface the weathering patterns looked very complex. They reminded me of Mars after a dust storm, the density of the iron particles varying with the terrain. All these delicate textures and hues testified to the passage of hundreds of millions of years. It was incredible to think that even in this terrible isolation, natural processes continued to operate, leaving their fingerprints behind.

In the center of the near side was a forest of aluminum columns. The white shapes seemed to have grown out of the surface. These pale alloy columns were just as inorganic as the iron desert from which they appeared to spring, and yet somehow they seemed mysteriously at home here. We humans were the ones out of place.

We hadn't taken much notice of it from the ship, but once we were on the surface it was clear that the columns weren't nearly as tall as the design called for. On the other hand, the spacing and number of columns matched the plans exactly.

According to the blueprints for the array the columns were supposed to extend as much as ten meters from the surface to allow for local variation in the terrain. This was pretty standard and was intended to deal with just about any terrain variation that might be encountered on an asteroid. The columns themselves were just L-shaped stock bonded at the edges to form square supports for the array. They were light enough that robots could build very large structures with relative ease.

So why was the antenna no more than two meters off the surface? In some spots there was only half a meter or so of clearance. The underside of the array was supposed to look something like a huge gymnasium, with a ceiling of up to ten meters. This was something else entirely. It reminded me of a hydroponic tomato farm I once saw. It wasn't just that the mesh antenna was close enough to reach up and touch; in some spots you'd actually have to crawl to get under it. The columns were fairly flimsy, just strong enough to support the huge array in microgravity. Bumping up against one of them by accident could bend it out of shape.

"We're gonna have to crawl if we want to get under this thing," said Barbara.

"I'd rather not try it." Our hard-shell suits were pressurized at one atmosphere. This made them quick to get in and out of—no more hours spent prebreathing pressurized pure oxygen like the old-time astronauts. But the suit had to be very stiff to stand up to one atmosphere of internal pressure with a surrounding vacuum. It wasn't the kind of thing you could go shimmying around in. We weren't prepared for that.

"Maybe we'd better let the eyeball handle this. Let's take a walk around the perimeter in the meantime."

Barbara signaled agreement by extracting a red sphere about the size of a tennis ball from her utility pack. The eyeball had twenty-four pinhole thrusters distributed over its surface. Tiny streams of combustion gases allowed it to maneuver freely in low-G environments. It could be guided into inaccessible or dangerous spaces to send back visual and other data.

Getting a signal out from under the antenna was going to be difficult; our suits would serve as transmission relays for *Dragonslayer*. The eyeball was red, as was the surface, although not the same hue. Still, as the little sphere floated under the array it looked almost like some natural inhabitant of this rock, released into its native environment. The way it rose up from the palm of Barbara's hand indicated that it was already being guided from the ship.

"So what do you think, Seiya? Are these off-nominal or what? Has this got something to do with our rotation riddle?"

"The rotation and the length of these columns? Neither is

natural, but that's all they have in common. The robot's AI was sophisticated enough to allow it to deal with most problems it might run into during construction, but I can't see why it would build these this way."

"This isn't to spec, right?"

"Nowhere near. The question is whether there's a causal link."

"How about timing? The columns get shorter, then the rotation starts."

"What's the mechanism?"

"How should I know?"

"Look, Barbara. You're right. Maybe the rotation is happening because something made the columns shorter. But you could also posit some extrinsic factor that shortened the columns and started Rapu spinning. In that case there's no causal relationship between the height of the columns and the rotation."

"Why assume an extrinsic factor?"

"How else do you explain the signal picked up by the array? It's too regular to be natural."

"Okay, so it's too early to judge."

"That's what I'm getting at. This could be anything from a natural event to aliens messing with our stuff."

The answer to the riddle of the columns came while we were still talking. Rebecca had been reviewing the ops logs for the construction bot. At least as far as the columns were concerned, the answer had nothing to do with little green men. One of the robot's sensors had malfunctioned, causing it to calculate that it would run out of aluminum alloy stock ahead of schedule. The AI took that information and reconfigured the design with shorter columns. Fortunately the near side of the asteroid was fairly flat.

Space is a rough environment for any kind of mechanical device, so for the robot to experience a component failure was not surprising given the robot's size and complexity. The AI had to be up to improvising in response to the unexpected. It wasn't a genius, but within certain fixed parameters it was pretty sophisticated. It was designed to be a tool for humans; that didn't include being curious about too many things.

So that explained the height of the columns. Images from the eyeball of the underside of the array showed that the robot had carefully deployed the power distribution cables to allow for the shorter column height.

"So everything is nominal, except that the bot screwed up the inventory calculation." Something in Barbara's voice suggested that she wasn't totally convinced. "I guess this leaves us in the dark about the rotation."

"No clear link to our mystery signal either," I added. "I'm starting to wonder if it was a real signal."

WE DECIDED to head back for a rest. When we got to the core block there was news.

"Look at this," said Rebecca, holding out her web.

"They could've given it to us a little sooner," I griped.

"Now, now, Seiya. We're pretty far from Uranus. It took a while to import the whole database."

I scanned the results of the query Rebecca had run. Neither of us was sure what to make of it.

"Rapushinupurukuru—formerly known as 2143SF—isn't such a new object after all," said Rebecca. "Apparently it was discovered once already, about a century ago. Back then it was called 2053CJ, but the orbital elements look pretty similar. Rapu's outbound from Sol now, but the first time it was discovered it was almost at perihelion, and its track relative to Earth made it hard to calculate an orbit with much precision. It clearly wasn't a collision threat, so they more or less ignored it."

"It was discovered from Earth?"

"No. An astronomer on Callisto saw it first. A hundred years ago Callisto was crawling with them."

There was a time early in the history of space colonization when everybody assumed that the outer planets, beginning with Jupiter, were the future of the solar system—mainly as sources of fuel for nuclear fusion. Work to develop that potential started very soon after humanity returned to space. For a while, a lot more capital was directed toward the gas giants than toward settlement on Mars. Investments on the red planet looked to have payback times measured in centuries, while Jovian fusion fuel seemed to guarantee quick, fat returns. Everybody on Earth threw money at it. In pretty short order Jupiter Fever created a bubble that would have made seventeenth-century Dutch tulip traders proud.

Recovering the precious fuel was one thing, getting it back to Earth was something else again. This was in the days before reliable spacecraft and basic space infrastructure, and the first settlers on Jupiter's outer moons had to use the ships they rode in on as habitats, connecting them to create space towns.

The settlement on Callisto was self-sufficient from the beginning, at least at the level of basic survival. Supplying the colony from Earth was far too expensive. The colony was awash in hydrocarbons, so generating oxygen and growing or synthesizing food was straight-forward, but useful goods and equipment were chronically in short supply. Callisto had the most advanced technology humanity had ever developed, but daily life was based on barter exchange.

The economy of Jupiter's moons was directly affected by conditions on Earth. When the bubble was inflating, funding and resources were plentiful. When the bubble popped, Earth's economy cratered, funding was frozen, and even the flow of vital supplies dried up. The colonists' destinies were controlled by events taking place hundreds of millions of miles away.

Yet it was these colonists who, short of almost everything, assembled the data that was the basis for later exploitation of the Jovian system. They overhauled and refueled used boosters and cobbled together recycled components, sending one probe after another to the Galilean moons, even to Jupiter itself. The later full-scale missions to the outer planets could not have succeeded without the dedicated research of these early pioneers. The Callistans didn't hesitate to press their habitats into service as makeshift probes. More than riches or cargo from Earth, these colonists craved knowledge, and the strange new world before them constantly stimulated this hunger.

Given their history, I could easily believe the Jovians had spotted 2053CJ. "Are you sure they didn't send a probe? Unmanned at least? An S-type asteroid at such a steep angle to the ecliptic has got to be pretty interesting to any planetary scientist worth his salt. Think of the data they could've collected on how Jupiter's gravity interacts with the orbits of these little rocks."

"That's what I thought," said Rebecca. "But querying the database for 2053CJ returned zip in terms of unmanned probe data." Rebecca sent a graphic of the orbits for Jupiter and Rapushinupurukuru to the main monitor. At aphelion the asteroid was three astronomical units from the Sun. Its orbit was nearly vertical to the plane of the ecliptic. At its ascending node across the ecliptic plane, it was around 5.4 AU from the Sun. The average radius of Jupiter's orbit was 5.2 AU. Sooner or later significant gravitational interaction between the two bodies was inevitable. It seemed likely that the disappearance of 2053CJ and its later rediscovery as 2143SF should be chalked up to Jovian gravitational influence.

"2053CJ was a very interesting object from a planetary science perspective. Its discoverers knew that it reached its ascending node 540 days after perihelion. But its angle to the ecliptic was just too large for a probe from Callisto to reach. In addition to reducing relative velocity to zero, a probe would've had to adopt the same steep angle to the ecliptic. At the very least, it would have had to accelerate to twenty kilometers per second to get there. I'm sure the settlers on Callisto wanted to send a probe to investigate further, but it just wasn't going to work. That's why there's nothing in the database."

2053CJ reappearing a century later as 2143SF was definitely

interesting, but it wasn't the key to our problem. Once again we'd come up empty-handed. This was turning out to be harder than we'd expected. For a while we just sat staring at each other.

"Aren't we forgetting something in this analysis?" I said.

"We've looked at everything. The robot, the microwave relay array..." said Barbara.

"It just hit me—we've been ignoring the biggest factor of them all."

"What, Seiya?"

"Rapushinupurukuru itself."

<hr />

"READY TO DISPLAY results of analysis," said the synthesized voice.

Barbara and I were still in the core block. I'd ordered a full workup on the asteroid, and *Dragonslayer*'s AI had just obliged.

"How're we looking?"

"Nothing unexpected," said Rebecca. "Except for one thing I'm surprised we didn't notice. It looks like Rapu is a CAT."

As their name implied, Comet-Asteroid Transition objects were comets that had exhausted most of their volatiles and were on the way to becoming plain old hunks of rock. Given Rapushinupuru-kuru's highly inclined orbit, the possibility of it being a blown-out comet seemed at least plausible.

"The data suggest that Rapu carried a pretty light load of vola-tiles. Judging from the weathering profile, I'd guess the outer layer of volatiles boiled off quite a long time ago." We were looking at a 3-D image of Rapushinupurukuru without its array, its reddish surface rotating slowly against a gray-white background. Regolith and weathered red rock. Even on the restricted scale of the solar system it was an insignificant heap of minerals, but I never got tired of staring at its surface.

After watching the image revolve ten times or so, it suddenly hit me. The asteroid was sheathed in its blanket of rock fragments. The mesh antenna had been covered with a fine dusting of regolith.

Depending on mass and velocity, fragments kicked up through collisions either escaped and went into space or traced parabolic paths back to the surface. But there was no crater to explain the regolith on the array.

"Barbara, can you change the view?"

"Depends. What do you want?"

"Regolith by size, color-coded. I want to see how the fragments are distributed."

"That's easy. Wait for it." Barbara was already sending the commands to her agent. After a few seconds the image was covered with a rainbow of colors. The distribution of regolith around craters formed hundreds of millions of years ago was as standard as anything you'd find in a textbook. The finest fragments had blown off into space while the heavier fragments had stayed on the surface. There was a gradation of material, from fine to coarse, near the craters. Still, this wasn't the answer to our riddle.

A completely different pattern showed up in several locations—small spots surrounded by tight concentric circles of surface fragments with completely different distributions from the craters. Each circle of regolith was composed of a different size of fragment, with the fragments becoming smaller with distance from the center. These formations were new—they were superimposed on the splash-out from the older craters. Maybe this was the source of the regolith on the array? It would explain why the weathering was different on different sides of the asteroid. The near-side array shielded the surface from falling regolith, but the far side was exposed to the regolith.

"Captain, I think we have our answer." Rebecca and Barbara looked at me in disbelief. "The asteroid *is* the problem. We just need to prove it."

"Can you do that?"

"*Dragonslayer* can transmit in microwave frequencies. That should tell us."

IT TOOK A WHILE to get the experiment set up. Some of the code for the microwave relay had to be tweaked so the emitters could be controlled independently instead of acting as a single array. Before the experiment we deployed laser spectrometers on the surface—especially around the concentric regolith deposits—throwing in some infrared sensors for good measure. These assets were more basic than their names suggested: light alloy poles a meter or so long, each topped with a simple sensor cluster about the size of a fist. Still, they were highly reliable. The surface of the asteroid was now dotted with these sensor packages, like giant pushpins. There were a few eyeballs too, cruising above the surface for backup observation.

"You think this is going to work, Seiya?"

"You never know till you try." Barbara and I were on the surface, ready to respond if anything happened. *Dragonslayer* was already sending microwaves down to the surface. Nothing was happening so far, but that was expected.

We stood inside a support station, a kind of cage, monitoring the sensors. We'd been on the surface for hours now, so we were hooked up to an umbilicus that kept us supplied with oxygen and heating water.

The first sign that something was happening came from one of the infrared sensors. The microwaves were starting to heat up the surface. To the naked eye it was still nothing more than aluminum columns standing in the regolith-covered surface, but the columns and surface were already far above absolute zero.

"Keep an eye on the spectrometers. It'll take a while for the heat to penetrate the surface."

"Will do. Looks like you were right."

"It's too early to tell. But we'll know soon enough."

The spectrometers started returning solid indications sooner than I'd expected. The first reading came from an area near one of the hottest parts of the surface.

"Seiya, look! We've got gas. Steam . . . cyanide . . . hydrocarbons. Typical comet constituents."

"I knew it. This is why Rapu started revolving."

"You found it!" Rebecca was jubilant. She probably hadn't expected such a clear-cut outcome. With the data we were getting, the answer was straightforward. Rapushinupurukuru was a CAT object. Although it was stripped of nearly all its volatiles, thousands of tons remained in subsurface fissures and spaces. The microwave system was designed to relay huge amounts of power transmitted from Kali's accretion disk. That generated heat. Dissipating this heat down through the columns and into the asteroid shouldn't have caused any problems, but a simple sensor malfunction on the construction robot had led to the columns being much shorter than planned. This had massively increased the amount of heat reaching the surface.

As the asteroid warmed, gas streaming from cracks in the surface had blown regolith particles upward, essentially acting on the asteroid as a rocket engine—and causing it to rotate. Its rotational force had shredded the greater part of the array, which hadn't been anchored to the surface but extended for kilometers into space, held together with flimsy joints never intended to withstand more than a tiny amount of external stress.

All that was left of the array was the central section. That had held some of its heat a bit longer, and now finer particles of regolith blown upward from the surface could reach and settle on what was left of the array. Rotation had then gradually brought the asteroid back to its original frigid temperature.

"See? It wasn't little green men after all." I basked in my moment of glory. Rebecca shook her head.

"Not so fast. There's still that anomalous transmission."

Frankly, I'd forgotten about that, but Rebecca had orders to run down anything unexplained. "Maybe the signal came from the volatiles? Induced current flow from the power supply?"

"A pulsed signal at regular intervals? Come on, Seiya."

"Well, how should I know?"

"I can hear it," Barbara murmured. Rebecca and I glanced at each other. For a moment we wondered if Barbara was losing her mind.

"One of the eyeballs picked up a signal. It's weak, but it's definitely there."

Rebecca peered at the monitors. "It's two hundred meters from here, right under the center of the array."

We walked to the array, where we ducked underneath the mesh and crouched close to the surface. Our semi-rigid suits made it difficult to crawl; instead, we advanced toward the eyeball on our hands—actually the tips of our fingers—stirring up coarse regolith in the low gravity. It felt like we were moving very fast, though it was probably only about walking speed.

Barbara pointed ahead. We dug our fingers into the surface to stop our forward motion. Our fingertips scored patterns in regolith that had lain undisturbed for millions of years.

"Look, Seiya. Do you see what I see?" Barbara was pointing to a slender spar of metal, about thirty centimeters long, emerging from the regolith directly below the floating sphere. A transmitter.

I carefully began to clear regolith from around the transmitter. The regolith was deeper here than elsewhere. A few seconds later we could see a metal tube about twenty centimeters in diameter. Protected by the regolith, the tube and its nameplate looked as new as the day they'd been built.

"What is this?" said Rebecca.

"A penetrator. From an unmanned probe, launched from Callisto."

"YOU WERE RIGHT, Seiya. But how did you figure it out?"

"Partly intuition. The database had no record of data from a probe sent to 2053CJ. But then again, we only checked for data from successful missions."

"Then they did send a probe. And it carried a penetrator to send back information about surface composition."

"Penetrators were part of the standard instrument suite."

We looked at the piece of space hardware built a century ago. We could hear its faint signal on our suit receivers; it was probably transmitting a range of telemetry data about this far-flung rock.

I asked Barbara to run another database query—not for observational data from unmanned probes, but for launch information on all known probes, successful or not. It turned out that Callisto's colonists had been busily studying 2053CJ after all.

The probe used an ion propulsion system. To rendezvous with the asteroid as it passed its ascending node on the ecliptic, the probe had to reach a speed of at least twenty-two kilometers per second to match the complex velocity vectors of the asteroid, respective to orbital speed as well as speed relative to the ecliptic. On paper, the probe's engine had enough power to reach the required velocity.

With barely any resources, Callisto's colonists would have had to cobble together recycled components to build the probe. They had only one chance to reach the asteroid, so they not only set out to image the surface, they were ambitious enough to load a small penetrator to evaluate surface composition. With their limited resources and technology it was an all-or-nothing gamble.

Unfortunately, communication with the probe was lost shortly after launch. The project ended in failure and was eventually forgotten. But even though the probe's communication system had failed, its other systems seemed to have worked perfectly.

The penetrator had a power source, but it would have failed after a few months or years. Still, the regolith had shielded its delicate circuits from Sol's ion flux. A century later, induced current from an array built by a robot over its resting place prodded these circuits briefly to life. The penetrator awoke and dutifully took up where it had left off. The relay picked up the signal and sent it on to Callisto. And now, as long as *Dragonslayer* kept bathing it with microwaves, the penetrator would keep transmitting.

"So all we were doing was chasing a hundred-year-old piece of junk?" Barbara started to yank the penetrator out of the regolith. I reached out and put my glove on hers. She peered at me warily.

"We can't imagine what they went through to get this here. Now it's doing what they intended it to do. Callisto's been waiting for this signal for a century. We can wait a few minutes and let it do its job."

Barbara withdrew her hand, unclipped the booster antenna from her suit, and attached it to the penetrator. "There. That should give it a little help."

The signal sped via *Dragonslayer* toward the home of its makers in the Jovian system. In three more hours, it would finally be home. One hundred years and three hours. It had been a long mission.

TO UNCOVER THE TRUTH, you have to delve deep. No investigation of history can approach the truth without probing beyond immediate surface appearances.

For example: are humans genuinely rational?

Not an easy question to answer. It was humanity that forced a small black hole out of its orbit, chasing dreams of an energy network that would span the solar system.

But judging humanity by the scale of its dreams would be a mistake.

Not all of humanity was eager to see work proceed on an artificial accretion disk. Different forces were at work to prevent AADD from realizing its plans. These forces were also human.

Why make a determined effort to bar the path of progress? Again, not an easy thing to explain. One would have to account for the structure of human consciousness.

Consciousness is not a unified entity. Multiple awareness subsystems in the brain give rise to the socially determined composite phenomenon we call consciousness. The human species and its collective actions can never be understood without comprehending the hidden workings of these independent subsystems.

At the level of the collective, human consciousness oscillates between stability and chaos.

Faced with the challenges of survival in space, AADD created the device called the web and used it to forge a collective that was greater than the sum of its parts. But this new conception of what it meant to be human unleashed forces that were pushing humanity's collective consciousness toward chaos.

These were the forces stoking the conflicts between AADD and the people of Earth. Many of them manifested in the same way: as violence.

HYDRA'S ICE
A.D. 2145

Minus 38 Hours 30 Minutes

COOPERATE and we'll guarantee your safety. Otherwise—

Gunfire. Breaking glass. A scream, abruptly cut off.

That's what you'll get. Are we clear?

The lift module was rising at a thousand kilometers per hour. No one in the circular lounge was inclined to take on the hijackers.

"I mean, are these guys shitheads or what? Discharging a firearm in the lounge?"

Shiran Kanda was listening to Mikal, her squad leader, reporting from orbit overhead. It was an open circuit. Everyone on the team could hear everyone else.

"You should be seeing them pretty soon, Mikal. We'll only have the one chance, you know."

"Yes, Professor, I'm aware of that."

"They've been holed up for more than ten hours. Everyone will be hitting the wall pretty soon." Shiran was six thousand kilometers above the surface of Mars, at Clarke Station on Tsutenkaku, the orbital elevator. Mikal and his squad were at least ten thousand kilometers higher.

"Once we're in we'll bag them in a few seconds. Are we still waiting on visuals?"

"No. The cameras are down. When they came in shooting, they

decapitated the main server. The backup system doesn't support visuals, just control functions."

"How are we getting audio?"

"Thank me for that," said Samar, Shiran's forensic team leader. "We're laser-painting the lift. Doppler vibrometer."

"Good work," said Mikal. "Are our bad boys all in the same location?"

"All indications are affirmative," said Shiran. "No one's exited the lounge."

"All right. I just hope we don't have to use these." On her web's retinal feed, Shiran saw Mikal raise his machine pistol. The compact weapon fired plastic rounds whose energy fell off rapidly with distance. Still, they could be set to deliver more than enough kinetic energy to terminate at close range. "I still don't get it, Professor. Why bother to assassinate someone, anyway?"

"Assassinations are one organization's way of signaling another organization. Who, how, and where you kill—it all means something. It's a message, pure and simple."

"Then they should save us the trouble. Every child in Sol System knows Earth isn't our friend."

Mikal and Shiran reviewed the assault strategy. The lives of the squad members depended on successful completion of each step of the plan. "Professor, the module is approaching Clarke orbit."

"All right, Mikal. Lock and load."

The squad was suited up, ready to move. Shiran watched them finish prepping. On schedule, a cylinder the size of a multistory building flashed past the squad's orbiting capsule at close to three hundred meters a second. The capsule's guidance system maneuvered automatically, accelerating to close with the lift, then changing course to move directly beneath it.

"How're you holding up, Mikal?"

"No worries, Professor. Three Gs, at ease." Shiran needn't have worried. She was raised on Mars, so three Earth gravities of sudden acceleration would have made her feel close to ten times heavier.

But every member of the assault squad was trained for the stress of acceleration. She was a Guardian, though it had been a while since she'd been on an op like this.

The capsule was now moving slightly faster than the lift, closing the gap to less than a hundred meters, invisible from the lift in the dead angle.

Why'd you have to use your weapon? How do we explain this to the client?

You'd rather get caught?

By AADD? They can't touch us. Deportation, sure. But hostage taking, that might even get us prosecuted on Earth. And you have to make it worse!

The voices from the lounge were distinct over the laser pickup. "Mikal, you better get moving. It sounds like they'll be at each other's throats soon."

The lift was a twenty-meter cylinder moving up the side of the orbital elevator. From its base on Mt. Rokko to its orbital anchor on Deimos, the elevator stretched across twenty-two thousand kilometers. The lift contained a food counter and spartan rest facilities for the full-day ascent. To take advantage of the fantastic views of Mars, the two-thirds of the lift that faced away from the elevator were sheathed in transparent polycarbonate, carbon-reinforced for radiation shielding and structural strength. A utility corridor extended along the spine of the lift where it attached to the elevator. The guest rooms were on the other side of the corridor—windowless for better protection from radiation.

In an emergency the capsule could dock with the lift to make repairs and evacuate passengers. At this altitude there was no atmospheric resistance, only the black shadows and stark sunlight of space. Above the day side there was enough photon scatter to give some visibility in the shadows. The squad had night-vision lenses to cut through the darkness.

Mikal opened the hatch and climbed out. The elevator's carbon nanotube cables seemed close enough to touch. Climbing out onto the moving capsule was not for the faint of heart. The cables were streaming past at almost three hundred meters a second. Anything brushing against them would instantly be torn to pieces.

Using hand signals in case the hijackers were monitoring their communications, Mikal guided the capsule closer to the lift. With twenty meters to go he motioned for a stop, then resumed the approach centimeter by centimeter. In the few minutes since their rendezvous with the lift had begun they had gained nearly a hundred kilometers of altitude.

Mars hung below them, hundreds of times larger than a full Moon seen from Earth. It seemed unbelievable that this bundle of cables led all the way down to that disk. As the capsule closed with its quarry, Mikal had a few moments to look out on his home planet. The view calmed him.

He held up his hand. The capsule was a meter from the lift. Docking would alert everyone inside. The only thing to do was hold a constant speed and jump the gap.

Mikal pushed off from the capsule and landed in the docking bay. In stationary orbit the lift would pass through a brief zone of true weightlessness, but they had not reached that altitude yet. Beyond Clarke—or stationary—orbit, centrifugal force would gradually take over. Normally the lift would stop and turn 180 degrees in preparation for the reverse gravitational pull of the rest of the trip to Deimos. But the hijackers were wasting no time. They were heading directly for the spaceport on Deimos.

Before Tsutenkaku had been built, the orbit of Deimos was adjusted to bring it closer to Mars. Now this irregular mass of rock was 22,386 kilometers above the surface. At this distance it acted as a counterweight for the elevator, its velocity nearly equal to escape velocity. It was ideal as a docking point for spacecraft and cargo transfers.

They were in luck: no watch had been posted in the corridor. The squad assembled. Mikal used a short-range laser transmitter for final instructions, then led them down the narrow passage toward Lift Level 3. He plunged straight downward, the rising centrifugal force giving him a slight boost. His squad followed close behind, equipped with full combat packages.

The hijackers were oblivious to what was about to hit them. They were too busy watching the hostages, who had been herded into the lounge.

Mikal reviewed the hostage roster on his web. All were AADD employees. One was even a Guardian. Mikal sent her a coded message and got a response in seconds: thirteen hijackers, masked, with strap-on webs that they were mostly ignoring. Terrans were known to dislike these devices; it was rare for them to wear webs, even the smaller, restricted-capability models.

"Hit the deck!" the hostage Guardian yelled—not for the benefit of her fellow hostages, but to divert the attention of the hijackers. Stun grenades flew into the lounge from stairways above and below. The squad burst into the lounge, eyes shielded against the flashes. Strangely, the hijackers made little effort to resist. Half a dozen were handcuffed before they had even regained their eyesight. Others began firing wildly but were quickly subdued.

"The leader!" The Guardian pointed to a masked figure hurrying toward the utility corridor. Mikal pushed off from the ceiling. A stream of tracer rounds swept over his head. The leader was firing wildly, and then Mikal saw why: she was using recoil to power herself toward the exit. Mikal was about to fire when he realized it would only slow him down. He tossed his weapon away, but his target still made it to the exit first.

"The hatch! Close the hatch, she's headed your way!" Mikal yelled. The leader was already reaching for the hatch of the capsule, docked in the lift's now pressurized bay, when Mikal caught up.

"Cut the crap, Rahmya. You know you can't get away from us. Hijacking? You won't be coming back to Mars for a long time. Hands on your head."

For a moment the hijacker seemed startled. Instead of complying, she drew a heavy mil-spec pistol from the small of her back and aimed it at Mikal's head.

"You are so dumb, girl. Drop that before you hurt yourself." Mikal reached for the pistol. The hijacker fingered the trigger. The recoil sent her into a strange-looking backward somersault. The shot went wide.

"Don't you guys ever learn? You're not on Earth anymore." Mikal put cuffs on his prisoner. "It's a wrap, Professor. Hostages and bad guys, all safe, no casualties."

"Good work. What about Rahmya?"

"She's right here with me. I think she had some urgent business, but I convinced her to stay. Guess I'm just irresistible." Mikal pulled off his prisoner's mask. "Ah, correction, Professor. Suspect is not Rahmya."

For the first time the hijacker spoke. "You're late. Rahmya was the one with the urgent business."

Minus 37 Hours 30 Minutes

When I transited through Deimos Station I was Ryoko Kashiwazaki. Not my real name of course. But using Rahmya probably would've made things difficult. My real name? I'm not sure I even remember.

I'm waiting for someone here in Kobe City, on Mt. Rokko. Rokko's this dead volcano, the base of their great fucking orbital elevator. I think the mountain was called Pavonis a long time ago. Nobody here calls it that now.

If you believe the tourist crap, most of the people brought from Earth to develop Mars (many of them not by choice)—and I mean the ones who managed to survive those first horrible years—had science backgrounds. Screwing up usually meant getting dead, so it helped to know something about the physics of space and how to behave in low-G environments.

A lot of the Japanese who were brought here survived. They say some were from central Japan, driven out when the oceans rose, when Japan's main island was cut in half by water. That's why this area has these Japanese names from places that are underwater now. Like Kobe City. Or Tsutenkaku, after the old tower they had in Osaka.

I figured Kobe was the best place to hide, lots of people from all over.

I'm not AADD, I don't have those stupid implants. It's hard to operate here without them, so I've got a strap-on. It proves I'm Ryoko Kashiwazaki. Got the ID, all the biometric data.

These strap-on jobs are mainly for Terrans. The sites that pop up first, when you log on, are mostly for us Terrans too. Martians could use those sites, I guess, but they like their own stuff—super-targeted, very individualized. Not real useful for me.

I'm sitting on this fake outdoor terrace, watching people swarm by like ants. It always feels like complete chaos here. Check the news. Somebody jacked the elevator at Clarke Station. Now they're trying to reach Deimos. Well, the Guardians will probably scoop them up before they get there. No sweat, they were just bait anyway. Keep the pit bulls busy so I can do my job.

Don't want to flash my face around too much. I've got this visor on, standard Martian fashion, so I don't stick out. This one's got a monitor up in the corner too. I don't have to glance at my wrist all day and look like I'm fresh off the boat.

She shows up just as I see the readout flip to the meeting time. Asian, petite, young. Probably my age, exactly my height. Same bone structure. If I had a little sister, she could easily be it. She walks over to my table with that funny stride we all have before we get the gravity. Typical Terran.

"I'm sorry I'm late. You're Ms. Kashiwazaki, I hope."

"The one and only. You must be Gong-ru Yang."

"Yes. Oh, it's so nice to talk to someone from back home."

"Why's that?"

"Everyone here uses your first name all the time, even people who don't know you. It's disgusting."

"Different world. Can't be helped."

"I suppose you're right. Etiquette must go out the window when you live in a ceramic prison."

She's misunderstood me. Not surprised, though. Kobe's city plan is based on Arcosanti, some twentieth-century settlement in Arizona. Paolo-something was the architect. Futuristic, efficient energy use. Alternative community. Escape from the monoculture. The glass/ceramic tunnel we're in is a good hundred meters across. Maybe she's right, maybe this is a kind of prison. They can plant as many green zones as they want, but a prison is a prison. Nothing beyond those walls but a quick death.

"So, Gong-ru Yang, did you get everything I asked for?"

"Yes, I've collected everything listed in the contract. But, Ms. Kashiwazaki? What are you planning to do with these things? The list includes everything from sensors to steel pipe. I can't see any connection between these components. I know this is supposed to be government work, but—"

"Does the contract say I have to tell you my client's identity? Or the purpose of the shopping list?"

That's all it takes. The girl gets really, really flustered. Must be hard, trying to get by on Earth as a freelance journalist. In this day and age, you know? And she wants the exclusive I've offered her, she wants it bad. If I pull out now, she won't have a pot to piss in. Oxygen and money. Gotta have 'em both or you might as well curl up and die.

"Okay, Ms. Yang. Just kidding. The things on the list are components for automatic tracking cameras, that sort of stuff. Shipping costs up the well are based on weight, so it makes sense to buy as much as possible locally and have it all assembled here. Cheaper than paying to haul finished goods all the way from Earth."

"Oh, I understand."

I'm not positive she does or if she even believes me, but it looks like I won't have to deal with any more inconvenient questions. When I contacted her on Earth, I hinted I had some choice government connections. Not totally false, considering who my client is.

"I was hoping you could tell me a little more about where we go from here, Ms. Kashiwazaki."

"This isn't a good place. We should go somewhere private."

"All right."

You really believe this, don't you? Think you're on some secret Terran procurement mission. Well, why not? Not a lot of difference between journalists and spies.

We duck into this maintenance tunnel that leads to Kobe's old atmospheric treatment station. If Kobe is a prison of glass and ceramic, this is a cave of cinder blocks and concrete. Now it's just backup in case the main O_2 plant goes down. Most of the time the place is totally deserted. If Kobe was a person, this would be sort of like their appendix. When the city was still a basic settlement this was its main O_2 generator. Still has a lot of old gear, like cylinder locks on doors. You don't see those on Earth now; easy to pop with a simple tool and a little elbow grease.

"After you," I tell my guest. She walks through the door I've just jacked open like the place might be full of snakes.

"Ms. Kashiwazaki? It's very dark in here."

"Hold on a sec. I'll get the lights." I close the door and give her a shove. I want her in a little deeper. My visor has op amps, I can see pretty well as long as there's any kind of light. There's enough photons for the job, anyway. I see her, even if she can't see me. "Careful now, Ms. Yang. Don't move till I find the switch."

Good girl, she does exactly as she's told. What else can she do? She can't see a thing. She doesn't even move when I put the wire around her neck.

Minus 36 Hours 15 Minutes

"Professor? Tetsu is confirmed as the target." Mikal descended in the lift toward Clarke Station. "The way they got their weapons past security this time was very slick. Real weapons . . ."

"As opposed to what, Mikal? Fake weapons?"

"Ah . . . what, Professor?" Mikal sounded slightly dazed. "Um, sorry. I'm distracted by the view of Phobos transiting the elevator. So this is what it looks like from overhead . . ."

"Mikal, how long have you been a Martian?"

"I never get tired of seeing this—the way the el flexes to let Phobos pass, missing it by just a hair. At least that's what it looks like. It always feels like I'm seeing it for the first time. I don't get to watch this from above very often."

"Congratulations. What about the weapons?"

"Professor, you're the head of AADD's classical arts department. Your specialty is storytelling, I think. Doesn't this cosmic display make you want to write poetry?"

"As a Guardian? No, Mikal, it does not." Shiran could see the interior of the lift via her web's optical feed. Tsutenkaku was capable of dynamically flexing to allow Phobos to transit past without colliding. Shiran's outpost on the elevator—Clarke Station—was named for the man who had first proposed the concept, twentieth-century science fiction author Arthur C. Clarke. It was at the same altitude as the orbit of Phobos.

She watched the satellite's irregular bulk slip past her windows. The sight always made her think of a finger plucking the strings of a harp. The view from the station was dramatic enough; from above one could also appreciate the technology behind Tsutenkaku's guidance system. It was no exaggeration to say Phobos passed within a hair's breadth of the elevator.

"That's really interesting, Professor. There it goes . . . Anyway, ah, yes, about those weapons. All the hijackers did was pull the firing pins and a few other parts and bring their guns in as stage props.

Another group brought the missing components in disguised as machine parts. I guess we know now that they're not completely incapable of learning."

"So they brought their guns in through the front door. They caught us napping, Mikal." Shiran looked at the list of weapons—assault rifles and handguns for each hijacker. You didn't need an arsenal and thirteen hit men to assassinate the chairman of AADD. Something wasn't quite right.

AADD's intelligence division had already gotten wind of a plot to kill Tetsuya Ochiai. The information pointed to possible Terran involvement at a semi-governmental level. National governments existed, but the total economic integration of the planet meant that they ruled in name only. An intelligence subteam was working to uncover the specific organization backing the plot. Shiran's group was tasked with apprehending the hijackers and preventing the assassination. Unfortunately, citizens of Earth still had immunity offworld as long as they didn't actually engage in illegal activity. This meant Shiran and her team couldn't lift a finger unless a visitor committed a crime.

This legal standoff between AADD and Earth created ideal breeding conditions for dedicated terrorists. Japanese law was especially full of holes—half by design, it seemed—when it came to prosecuting Japanese citizens for offworld crimes. Since citizenship was as easy to get as paying income tax, most offworld terrorist acts were committed by people traveling on Japanese passports. You could round them up and deport them for prosecution by their own government, but in a few months, after things had cooled off a bit, they'd be right back in your face.

Shiran's people had marked Rahmya and her conspirators from the moment they had disembarked at Deimos Station, but under the terms of the space treaties the visitors couldn't be touched until they made their move.

Previous attempts by Terrans to bring weapons past Deimos security had been clumsy at best. So far they'd been turned back at the water's edge, as it were. This time the Guardians had been caught napping, and the result was an act of terror. They'd practically given the hijackers a free pass.

"I don't like it that they brought in so many people and so much heat. If I wanted to put a hit on the chairman of AADD, I wouldn't send a SWAT team. Interesting that their leader is the only one who didn't see fit to put in an appearance."

"Are you saying this was a diversionary operation, Professor?"

"It's a possibility. Rahmya is a trained ghost dog, Mikal. Kills without leaving a trace. She's never been captured and almost always works solo. Once that we know of she worked with a team of three. Now she's working with thirteen people? I don't believe it—she just wants us to think so."

"But the leader of the team that jacked the lift is a prize in her own right, a known organizer."

"That's why we had them under such close surveillance. And while we're busy with that, Rahmya gets away. We played right into her hands."

In 2143, relations between AADD and Earth were strained. The flashpoint was mining and minerals. The first offworld mining colonies were on the Moon, extracting ilmenite and other ores for their metal content, then shipping it back to Earth. With advances in recycling and the need to protect the dwindling proportion of the environment that hadn't already been devastated, the number of mining operations on Earth had fallen to a handful. But this was not because Earth had exhausted its resources. Developing new mines meant compliance with a huge number of stringent regulations. All this red tape made it more profitable to recycle metals than to mine for them. The spiraling cost of eco-preservation made this truer with every passing year.

Still, Earth could recycle every gram of metal and it would still come up short; a completely closed recovery system was impossible. The price of iron and other basic metals kept climbing, yet this did nothing to spur the development of new mines. In fact, rising prices had the opposite effect as the cost of new mining infrastructure and machinery increased as well. Eventually, metal prices became high enough that lunar mining programs beyond the reach of environmental regulation became practical.

The Moon had more than enough ore to satisfy Terran demand. The lunar mining colonies provided raw material for the early settlement of the solar system, including the colonization of Mars. But Earth's focus on recycling didn't change, and offworld mining did not spread beyond the Moon.

Then the Artificial Accretion Disk Development association was founded. Within a few years AADD had changed the terms of the economic game for the entire solar system. Their first move was to start mining on three main-belt asteroids—nudged by AADD into orbits around Kali—for metals to construct Ouroboros and Chandrasekhar Station. This gave AADD access to vast amounts of ore, allowing them to push ahead quickly with construction.

As soon as AADD began mining its own ore, the lunar mines lost income. The Terran mining conglomerates were hidebound and far less productive than AADD. They couldn't compete on cost—yet they were not all that concerned. The asteroids contained ores for every important metal, but refining it was comparatively expensive. The quality of the asteroids' deposits did not equal that of lunar ore. AADD still depended on Earth for copper and lead, and the mining companies could make decent profits from those metals alone. Even if AADD were self-sufficient in iron and nickel, they would still have to depend on Earth for nonferrous metals. Or so the Terrans thought.

They were wrong. The Martian colonists were not stupid. They knew the prices for nonferrous metals had been rigged by Terran cartels and were far too high. Where there were water and volcanoes, there were mineral deposits. Mars had them both. The volcanoes of Tharsis Montes contained enormous deposits of iron and nonferrous metals. At first, the ore the colonists mined there went to supply local needs. They exported only limited amounts, enough to be handled by small mass drivers sending packets of refined ore into orbit. Larger payloads would have to wait for the construction of the orbital elevator, which would ensure the economic independence of Mars from Earth. Finally it was built and online.

Now Mars had high-quality mineral deposits, efficient mining operations, and a low-cost way to get the ore into space via the orbital elevator. These factors made the mines of Mars unbeatably competitive. The Terran conglomerates were completely outclassed, unable to match the low price of Martian ore. For certain metals Mars became the preferred source even for Terran buyers.

This change in the balance of economic power inevitably brought a change in the balance of political power. Earth was committed to protecting its vested interests. AADD wanted the right to pursue and prosecute citizens of Earth who committed crimes offworld. Negotiations over this issue took up a large amount of Chairman Ochiai's time. Now he was on the cusp of reaching a deal that satisfied most of AADD's demands.

But not everyone on Earth was happy with what was about to happen. Within each power center were factions holding different visions of Earth's future in a solar system that was changing before their eyes.

There was no question that this situation had the potential to spawn murder.

————◆◆◆◆◆————

MIKAL SHOOK HIS HEAD. "If they were supposed to be decoys, then we've done nothing to stop Tetsu from being assassinated."

"We might have even helped Rahmya get the job done," said Shiran.

"When does he arrive on Deimos?"

"If he's on schedule, he'll be here in forty-eight hours."

Minus 35 Hours 45 Minutes

The leasing agency isn't tough to find. The entrance is period; don't know where they got those old fittings. Making a statement, I guess. Inside's nothing special. Chairs, tables, one leasing agent.

"My name is Kashiwazaki. I reserved a vehicle."

"Oh yes. Ryoko."

Here this bitch has just met me, and she calls me Ryoko. On Mars, a person's name is just an ID tag.

"You have a land cruiser for a week. Everything's ready—water, food, oxygen, all the necessities."

"That's good."

"Going into the outback? We don't get much demand for our cruisers. Most visitors from Earth want one of our buggies. They're lighter and more nimble."

"I'm going pretty far out. Why else would I need a land cruiser?"

"Are you a photographer?"

"Why do Martians ask so many questions?"

"I was just wondering."

The transaction is half-automated, our webs processing most of the details. Once that's out of the way she takes me through a tunnel to where they keep the vehicles. She's acting kind of chilly all of a sudden, which suits me fine. The rear of the shop is down half a level, following the slope of the mountain. We go through a few basic air locks into a garage.

"There's your cruiser."

Mars is right outside, through two more air locks. The cruiser's parked in front of them, ready to go, provisions loaded and my cargo—the entire shopping list sent ahead—in a big pile on the floor. The cruiser's just a box really, light alloy and plastic, five meters long with four sets of tracked feet instead of wheels. Looks a little like a snow tractor back on Earth. The tracks spread the weight over the ground better than wheels, but they're steerable, so you still get good turning radius. Typical Martian vehicle for anything other than light-duty work. If you run into something unexpected it has a winch and a basic crane. The cab is pressurized, with an air lock and a place to stow your suit. The drive units are self-contained in each of the feet, so there's a lot of room inside. You could live in one of these things for weeks.

"How's this perform in the outback?"

"She's small, but you still have a lot of horsepower. The tracks are extra wide. It comes with advanced suspension."

"Sounds like just the ticket." I start doing a careful walk-around. The bitch frowns.

"I check the vehicles every day. It's my job."

"I have to do this myself. Sorry, just one of those things." I'm starting to like this agency. The cruiser's been well maintained. Good thing, too, since my life will depend on it. "Looks like it's in pretty good shape."

"Of course. That's my job."

I open the hatch and start loading.

"You've got a lot of cargo there." She points at the pile. I notice she's not helping me load up. I get all the stuff into the cruiser—finally—and jump into the driver's seat. She forwards me the document with the warnings and disclaimers. Security requirements. I hate this part—you actually have to *read* the damn file or the vehicle won't start. So for the next ten minutes I play along with their bullshit procedure.

With that out of the way I power up the cruiser and start inching forward. The first air lock door opens, closes—and then the outer lock opens and the red slope of Mt. Rokko stretches ahead of me. The downslope is pretty gentle, doesn't feel like much. At least I've got that ugly fucking tower behind me.

I go a few klicks down the mountain and stop to check my "photo equipment." Good girl, she got everything I need. It'll assemble into something that shoots, so I guess I didn't really lie.

Phase Two: complete. Now for Phase Three.

It's too early to relax. I can't underestimate the Guardians. I point the cruiser in a new direction and pull the ID chip out of my web. So long, Ryoko. You're history.

I'm Gong-ru Yang now.

Minus 34 Hours 30 Minutes

According to the hijackers, Rahmya was on the Martian surface. But could they be trusted? Was this another diversion? It seemed more likely that Rahmya was somewhere on one of Tsutenkaku's stations.

Shiran decided to bet on the elevator. Every passenger landing on Deimos and exiting at Kobe City had to pass a cranial scan when getting on and off the elevator. Infrared imaging revealed underlying bone structures, so simple disguises wouldn't work. Rahmya topped the Guardians' wanted list. If she was planning to disappear in Kobe City, she'd have to defeat two sets of scanners first.

But several hours after the hijacking, there was still no alert from security—which would suggest she was still somewhere on the elevator. And yet, hours of searching turned up nothing in any of the stations along the way. Then Shiran's imaging officer called her with some unsettling news.

"Professor, she slipped past us after all. She's on the surface."

"How is that possible?"

"I'll show you." An augmented-reality display board appeared in the space above Shiran's desk just as Mikal walked into the office. The right side of the board began to play scanner footage. Shiran recognized the elevator exit gate on the surface.

"It's her!" said Mikal.

"No doubt about it, that's Rahmya." The scanner showed a young woman wearing an orange AADD crew jumpsuit passing through the gate. Her ID number, read automatically from her web, appeared at the top of the screen.

"This number doesn't match any of our personnel," said the imaging officer. "We're trying to trace it on Earth, but I doubt it's genuine."

"So she made it to the surface after all. But the cameras got her. Why didn't we notice? We all know this face."

"So we do, Professor, but we're relying on the IR scanners to catch what the human eye might miss. We only check the visible wavelength footage when a scanner gives us a heads-up. Otherwise this is all automated. You're aware of that?"

"Of course," Shiran snapped.

"Well, this time it was the reverse. We went back and reviewed the visible-wavelength footage just in case. That led us to the scanner images. Now look at this."

The same footage began to play on the left side of the board, this time from the infrared cranial scanners. The feed was enhanced to make it easier to see the structure of the face under makeup or a disguise.

"What the hell?" gasped Shiran. Rahmya's image under infrared bore no resemblance at all to her actual appearance.

"She must be using some kind of IR reflector—and she knew how to apply it to make herself look like a different person."

"This must go further than we thought," said Shiran. "If Rahmya has what it takes to defeat our scanners, she must have funding. She wouldn't be able to develop a countermeasure like that on her own."

"Our intelligence subteam thinks her client may be one of the Terran mining and metal refining conglomerates. If so, she'd have practically unlimited support."

"And the client keeps their hands clean. But there are at least two things wrong with this picture. One, Rahmya doesn't have a weapon. We recovered everything from the hijackers. Why didn't one of her coconspirators just slip her a weapon?"

"Under interrogation the suspects admitted that she orchestrated the hijacking, but that's all," said Mikal. "Maybe they're telling the truth."

"So everything they brought in was for the hijacking. The bigger question is, why head for the surface? Tetsu is staying on Deimos this trip, he's not going down to Kobe. His itinerary is public information. If Rahmya's planning to kill him, why is she moving in the opposite direction?"

"Maybe she's planning to come back," said Mikal.

"Maybe. Or maybe she's planning another diversion."

Minus 29 Hours 20 Minutes

The land cruiser is pressurized. All I can hear, moving along, is a faint hum from the oxygen/methane engine. Otherwise, silence.

The cruiser has laser radar that feeds data to the active suspension system. The terrain here is littered with huge reddish boulders, maybe from floods eons ago. Active suspension is a must for high-speed driving. The radar sees the terrain coming up and talks to the actuators in the suspension system, tells them how to respond in advance. Makes for a smooth ride, for sure. Good thing, because I want to use as little energy as possible. I never work when I'm tired.

My vehicle knows where and how to go, all the coordinates are loaded. The terrain here isn't that rough, so it's reasonably safe to hand off to the autopilot. The guidance database knows the rough spots. If the cruiser needs to detour, it can navigate without my help. My route's been carefully planned. The skies are full of satellites of all sizes, keeping an eye on the mining complexes. Staying out of sight is my major challenge right now. I'm avoiding terrain where the cruiser's likely to leave imageable traces on the ground. I double back on evasive headings to confuse the satellites. The cruiser is covered with camo net to break up its outline against the surface.

There's no guarantee I won't be detected. The technology hasn't been invented that can defeat every form of surveillance. And relying on just one form of stealth is for pikers. A professional would never make that mistake. You want to put together a suite of concealment strategies to blanket your opponent's surveillance spectrum. This can be challenging, but if you want real stealth it's the only way to go.

The trip profile was a bitch to input, but it gives me time for more important things, such as assembling the components I brought along into something useful—a weapon.

The rifle I'm holding doesn't compare with even a basic sniper rig, but it's more than good enough for this mission. If someone shoots you, you don't care what kind of gun they used. Dead is dead. All the parts were made in little workshops on Mars to my specs, ordered and paid for by Gong-ru Yang. If you want to get hold of a weapon here, you can't be in a hurry and you have to be inventive.

I look the assembled weapon over carefully. The main component, the barrel, is unrifled. Rifling a barrel is something you don't ask a workshop to do. No matter what kind of line you feed them, you'll blow your cover in two seconds. Anyway I can get along without it. Bullets don't generate much drag in this thin of an atmosphere. With the right-shaped projectile and tight tolerances close-range accuracy is no problem.

The cruiser stops on schedule at my chosen location for some sighting-in. I suit up and carry the bullets and the rifle out onto the surface. I need to test the rifle first, make sure it performs as designed. The cruiser has brought me to an ancient streambed several hundred yards across. Its walls are about three vertical meters.

I stick a big blob of silicon on the rock wall, smear it out until it's apple-sized. That's the target. I walk about a hundred meters away, affix my crude weapon to a tripod. Hit a switch and I've got a heads-up display on my visor, an aiming system complete with crosshairs. Check the safety and fit the magazine.

The gun fires bullets using an internal reservoir of liquid propellant, a supervolatile hydrocarbon cocktail. Making a gun is simple. It's the cartridges—case, primer, and powder—that are tough. You can't fool people into making them for you. You don't even want to try. You have to go to specialists usually, ammo manufacturers. That's where your cover's going to crap out on you.

But there's a workaround. If you have a good gas seal between bullet and barrel, you can use liquid propellant and dispense with cartridges altogether. Just feed bullets straight into the barrel and send them on their way with a puff of burning propellant.

With the gun set to go, I walk back to the target. I stand to one side, release the safety remotely, put the crosshairs in my heads-up display on the target, and thumb the firing switch.

The first round grazes the edge of the target. I adjust the sighting parameters and fire again. Other side this time. Split the difference. Fire again. The silicon splatters across the rock.

Sighting-in complete.

Now I'm officially armed. I load the rifle into the land cruiser and enter fresh coordinates into the guidance system. Destination: Phase Three.

Minus 26 Hours 30 Minutes

"Did she actually identify herself as Ryoko Kashiwazaki?"

A video link to the leasing agent was projected on the floating display. The agent responded dutifully, "Yes, her web confirmed it."

"And she rented a land cruiser for a week?" In one corner of the screen data for the vehicle scrolled past on its way to everyone in the team. "Did you notice anything unusual about her?" Shiran posed the question casually, but it was crucial. Given that most of the transaction was automated, there might not have been much reason to remember the small details of a particular customer.

"Well, it's just that she was very particular about the condition of the vehicle, even though I told her I'd checked it twice personally. She didn't seem to trust me at all."

This was unusual. On Mars and throughout AADD, work was the fulfillment of personal potential, a critical prerequisite for acceptance in the collective. People earned respect from their peers through attention to detail and professionalism, regardless of the work they did.

Terrans didn't quite seem to understand this. Ryoko Kashiwazaki's demeanor alone was enough to mark her as an outsider. For her to openly doubt the agent's competence was tantamount to a deliberate insult. The agent had not responded in kind only because her customer was from Earth.

"I can't say I noticed anything else unusual—except she had a very large photo gear case with her." The agent described the case and held up her hands to indicate its size. Several possible matches appeared on the white board.

"Did it look like one of these?"

"Yes, that one on the left."

"Well, thank you. You've been very helpful," said Shiran. "Please let us know if you remember anything else."

"I will. Helping is a citizen's duty." The agent disappeared, replaced by an analysis of the footage from the leasing agency's security camera.

"Professor," said the imaging officer, "the IR scanners show her using a different spoofing pattern from the one she used on the elevator. The visible-wavelength footage, however, confirms that Ryoko Kashiwazaki is Rahmya. Still, it's going to be hard to trace her."

"Hard but not impossible, right?"

"Well . . . yes, of course. We'll do our best."

"I'm relying on you. Use your discretion and I'll back you up."

"Okay, Professor. We're on it." The board went blank.

"I still don't like this."

"Why not?" said Mikal.

"Why did she leave Kobe? She went to a lot of work to slip past us so she could assassinate Tetsu. Why does she keep moving away from the target? What about the surveillance satellites?"

"Surveillance is ongoing. But it isn't foolproof—there has to be something for them to see when they pass overhead."

"Still, it should restrict her movements quite a bit. There are a lot of satellites up there."

"Do you think she might be planning to sabotage one of the mines?" Mikal sent a map of known mineral deposits from his web to the floating rectangle.

"Sabotaging a mine is too big a job for one person. What do you think was in the case?"

"Something light, small enough to be carried on a shoulder sling. She didn't have it when she got off the elevator—which means she bought it somewhere. I'll run a check of the retail outlets. But, Professor, let's say the case contained a weapon she obtained from somewhere. That means she has to get within range of Tetsu. In other words, she has to return to the elevator at some point."

"And try to reach Deimos."

"That's the most reasonable assumption—she'll try to return to Deimos to execute her plan."

"But how's she going to do that? She can't get there without using the elevator, and she must know she can't keep pulling the same trick to get past the scanners."

They began to review the evidence yet again. An hour later the imaging officer suddenly reappeared in Shiran's retinal feed. "What, did you find her already?" asked Shiran.

"Not yet, unfortunately. It's about the contents of the case. We found something interesting."

The display board reappeared showing footage of Rahmya at the leasing agency, the case slung from her shoulder. She put it on the floor, walked slowly around the vehicle, then hoisted the case to her shoulder again.

"What's new about this?" said Shiran.

"Based on her movements we can estimate the weight of the case. It's not light, that's for sure. What's interesting is, the center of gravity is unstable."

"What does that mean?"

"First of all, whatever's inside, it's not anchored. Her movements and center of balance tell us that the case contains something long and metallic. Also, we took the audio and asked another team to see if they could profile it."

"Auntie's group?"

"That's right. How did you know?"

"I'm surprised she made time for us."

"You know those guys, Professor. With easy stuff, you better take a number. Ask for the impossible and you get priority service."

"Well, if the profile's coming from Auntie's team I'm sure it's solid. What's the verdict?"

"They were able to isolate the sound of objects in the case striking each other. They think there's a hollow metal tube, interior diameter at least five millimeters, and a number of cylindrical objects, same diameter."

"A disassembled weapon and—what, cartridges? Bullets?"

"Bullets, according to Auntie. The acoustic characteristics of the tube are unusual, like hardened steel. And there are definitely bulletlike objects striking each other when the case moves. She thinks they're using some nonstandard propellant system. Gas or liquid, maybe."

"How did she get all that from the acoustics alone?"

"When bullets strike each other they sound different from cartridges. But bullets by themselves are useless. It makes sense, in a way. Cartridges wouldn't make it past security and you can't have them order-made—the end use is too obvious, the propellants are too specialized. But with the right shape, a bullet could easily be passed off as some kind of machine component."

"That's first-rate work. Okay, let's assume Rahmya is armed. If the weapon is in pieces she probably ordered the parts from different suppliers. Once this is over we'll have to do something special for Auntie."

"I thought you'd say that, Professor, so I've already made reservations. Auntie's pushing for Tuesday."

"Then it's settled. And that's one more incentive to get this off our plate by Tuesday."

Of course, everything had to be resolved before Tuesday. The target was arriving on Deimos in thirty-eight hours.

Minus 13 Hours 30 Minutes

With all this backtracking and detouring it's taken me a long time to get here, but I made it on schedule, arriving at night. A quick check of AADD Net confirms the targets are waiting.

There you are . . . present and accounted for.

With my night-vision binoculars I can see one of AADD's prospecting teams milling around in front of a vehicle like mine but much larger. Their van doubles as a research station and habitat. They've got a small trailer hooked up to it, a mobile power generator. They need a lot of juice, both for their ground-penetrating radar and for melting the permafrost layer.

Antiproton production is rising fast now that the artificial accretion disk is going through its shakedown trials. That generator they're running uses antiprotons from Kali. It puts out a huge amount of juice for its size. Reliable too. Antiproton-powered generators use pretty robust designs.

I hear this high-pitched whine through the thin atmosphere. They're probably running an oxygen/methane synthesizer, drawing carbon dioxide from the atmosphere. Their vehicle's got an internal combustion engine, so they'd need to synthesize fuel now and then with the generator.

It also looks like they're doing an equipment check, maybe evaluating samples. They're totally oblivious to my presence; I'm certain they don't see me. No lights around the vehicle. The light amplification circuits in their webs project images directly onto their retinas, so starlight is more than enough to work by.

Their camp is at the bottom of a shallow depression, so I'm in luck. Makes it easier for them to work, but also easier for me to set up without being seen. I carefully extend the tripod and configure the weapon. Sighting system is good to go. I walk back to my vehicle. The Martian horizon is pretty close. Parked three kilometers back, they won't see the cruiser till I want them to.

So I saddle up and drive into camp like I'm half lost, lights blazing so they see me as soon as I top the horizon. Then I'm in the camp and out of the cruiser.

"You're Gong-ru," says one of the prospectors. Must be the leader.

"Yes, I am. I'm so sorry to arrive after dark."

"Oh that's quite all right. Anything to show the people of Earth how the mines of Mars are helping humanity. We welcome journalists."

These guys are pros. Turns out they've done a lot of prep for Gong-ru's visit. All four of them gather around me without the slightest fear. Maybe they've never seen a journalist before. Or maybe they've never seen someone from Earth before.

"Listen, everyone, could you all line up together? I'd like to start by taking your picture." *Actually, I'd like to start by shooting you.* "Let's take it with that crater in the background."

"Certainly," says the leader. All four stand at the edge of the crater, the ideal firing squad lineup, lit by the lights of the cruiser. I motion them closer together and activate the aiming system. The crosshairs appear on my visor. I put the crosshairs where they need to go and fire.

They go down one by one, no clue what's happening. They probably don't even know they're dead—except for the last one, who has the sense to duck, probably half by instinct.

I run up quickly, looking concerned. This one took her round in the shoulder. A very young woman.

"What's happening, Gong-ru? What's wrong with my team?" Fear and shock. She's shaking. Her eyes stare up at me, pleading for help. Who am I not to help?

"You'll be all right. It's just a scratch. This will make the pain go away."

I put the crosshairs between her eyebrows and make the pain go away. One round is all it takes.

Minus 12 Hours 00 Minutes

"Nothing new since we talked, Professor. The victim is a young woman. Bone density and musculature indicates she's from Earth. At this point that's all we have."

"You can't ID her?" said Shiran.

"Still working on it. There's nothing in the database, no DNA or prints. But I'd bet my paycheck she's from Earth."

Samar was guiding Shiran and Mikal around a crime scene in a maintenance tunnel of Kobe City's Number Two Atmospheric Treatment Plant. Usually the tunnel was deserted. Now it was cordoned off by the forensic team. It had already been night when Shiran reached the surface, six thousand kilometers below Clarke Station. Most of the preliminary work had been finished before she arrived. Rahmya's trail had gone cold, and the chairman of AADD would land on Deimos in thirty hours.

"Think this is Rahmya's work, Professor?"

"Good question. Mikal?"

"It's Kobe's first homicide this year. Rahmya shows up, the next thing we know somebody gets dead. I have a hard time believing there's no connection."

"But why murder this girl? Our suspects say she's not one of theirs."

"That's what they say. Still, I'd be inclined to believe them on this one."

"So this killing might be totally unconnected. Samar, what's your take?"

In the elevator on the way down Samar had been in nearly continuous touch with his team—not that he didn't trust them, but there was something about murder scenes that seemed to excite him. Sometimes after watching Samar scurry ecstatically around a fresh corpse Shiran wondered whether perhaps she should rethink their friendship.

"The killer is probably Rahmya. Common sense points to it. Martians rarely go as far as murder. If they were stupid enough to try, they'd probably botch the job. If they were smart enough to succeed, they'd find a better way to solve their problem."

"I don't disagree, but let's not jump to conclusions, Samar. There's too much we don't understand about what Rahmya's planning."

"I never jump to conclusions, Professor. I'm a professional."

"You're also human. You make mistakes."

"I hope so. If I was even more competent than I already am, now that would be scary."

A maintenance robot had discovered the body. Shiran now had to juggle the search for Rahmya with the first stages of a murder investigation. The victim was nude. Her clothes were missing and her face had been pulped, preventing quick identification by a facial recognition system.

"Further down the corridor there's another one of these metal doors, its lower edge covered in blood. Undoubtedly the victim was positioned in the doorway and her face crushed by repeated blows with the door. Whoever did this didn't want us to ID the victim right away. Cause of death was strangulation."

"Hold on, Samar. How much time does that buy the killer, really?"

"Six hours, at least. Maybe as much as twenty-four. Reconstructing the victim's appearance won't require that much time, but confirming her identity from bone structure alone could take a few hours. If she's from Earth we can get a match from the elevator security cameras. If she's a Martian we'll be searching for a needle in a haystack. I'd estimate the probable time to ID at ten hours, give or take."

Shiran looked over the scene. In addition to the forensics team, a dish-shaped robot was moving slowly along the narrow corridor, painstakingly gathering up every hair, strand of fiber, flake of skin, and cell debris and noting its location. Cell debris was important evidence. Using the time-tested polymerase chain-reaction method, DNA could be cultivated and profiled. Rahmya's DNA was already logged. If any cell debris not belonging to the victim had been left at the scene, it would be easy to determine whether or not it came from Rahmya. But no such evidence was found, not even a single hair that didn't match to the victim.

"Rahmya's never left a trace of evidence at any of her crime scenes. I don't know . . . Something still doesn't feel right."

"What do you mean, Professor?" asked Mikal.

"Don't you feel it? Why destroy the victim's face and make off with her clothes when all it buys you is ten more hours? Or if you're really lucky, a day. And why did Rahmya have to kill this girl in the first place? She wasn't with the group that hijacked the elevator."

"Yes, we're sure we have all of them. Still, it's always possible this one was known only to Rahmya."

"Given the probable time of death, we have to assume that Rahmya commits a brutal murder almost as soon as she arrives in Kobe. Why?"

"It just hit me," said Samar. "The victim and Rahmya are about the same age, height, and weight. We won't know till the reconstruction is done, but I'd be willing to bet there's a strong resemblance."

"You mean the victim was a stand-in?"

"It would explain why she was stripped. Why do that if the victim was traveling under a false ID? A genuine ID chip, on the other hand, would be very useful."

"A stand-in . . . But Rahmya still only buys herself a few hours before we make the victim."

"Maybe that's all the time she thinks she needs to prep for an assassination."

A notification arrived over Shiran's web from a member of the investigating team on the ground. The case Rahmya was carrying had been purchased the day before in Kobe.

"Professor, we have a general idea of the kind of weapon she's carrying."

"That's great, excellent work. Did she assemble it from components?"

"Indeed she did. She sent specifications to several different clans before she arrived."

AADD's manufacturing network comprised workshops that were each owned and managed by a different family. Each workshop was known as a clan, the word meaning more or less the same thing it did on Earth. On Mars, family units and manufacturing units were more often than not equivalent. Social identity was achieved through work. These businesses were more than just small enterprises, they were symbols of participation in the collective.

"The specifications stated 'parts for photographic equipment.' All of them were picked up by the same woman, not Rahmya. The orders were filled yesterday—"

"A woman? You said a woman paid for the components?"

"That's correct, Professor. We have her face from the scanners. I'm sending it now. The buyer ID'd herself only as a representative for Ryoko Kashiwazaki. Her web was switched off throughout the transaction. She claimed it was malfunctioning. Everything was handled manually. We expect to ID her from the scanner images shortly."

The footage sent to Shiran's web showed a woman identifying herself as Kashiwazaki's representative. She could have been Rahmya's sister. Shiran turned to Samar. "All right, here she is. Could this be our murder victim?"

"It's very possible, Professor. I'd want some time to confirm it though."

There was more—a component list and the characteristics of the possible weapon. "The rifle is likely to be semiautomatic and tripod-mounted, with automated sighting functions. It could be operated remotely."

"Remotely? That's interesting. Range?"

"We're still simulating, but effective range is probably a hundred meters or so."

"All right. Please attach your team to this group."

"Will do, Professor."

Mikal shrugged. "Now that really doesn't make sense. What's a pro like Rahmya doing with a weapon like that? It's practically a toy."

"She had to source all the parts here. Pretty hard to build a sniper rifle that way."

"But she's always gone for explosives. Sniping isn't her thing. It would've been just as difficult or easy to order bomb components, even a small missile."

"Tetsu's not coming to the surface," said Samar. "A remotely operated weapon could be useful. But a range of a hundred meters? That's a popgun. And she's moving away from the target. What do you make of this, Professor?"

"I don't make anything of it. We don't know what she's planning, that's all. It's time to reach out for some help."

━━━◆◆◆◆━━━

AADD HAD HUNDREDS of teams and enterprises, some as small as two or three individuals. None had more than a hundred or so members. Each project was handled through organic collaboration among teams. One group might be attached to several projects simultaneously. Most project groupings disbanded after the work was complete, but some spawned new functional teams or even a new enterprise that might go on to have a long life.

The artificial accretion disk project was so large that it required multiple groups comprised of multiple teams. Teams in one group linked with others in a complex web of integrated mutual support. At the same time, many projects called for fewer than ten members all told. This organizational culture was the reason AADD could quickly turn theoretical research into real-world applications.

The Guardians were just one of AADD's groupings. Shiran and Mikal were attached to the group responsible for managing security systems on the orbital elevator. In this role they interfaced with other security teams to pinpoint emerging risks and formulate responses.

Shiran did not give orders to other security teams. She set goals. Orders are a way to elicit a response from an organization; they are not goals. Organizations are cultural artifacts—when the motivation for maintaining them changes, orders lose their force. For a constantly evolving organization like AADD, goal-setting, not hierarchy, was the key to getting things done.

AADD's members didn't gain status from the groups they belonged to. Different groups had different functions; that was all. People acquired status from performance regardless of their job. The poster child for AADD's culture was Tetsuya Ochiai. The people of Earth assumed Ochiai was AADD's dictator, because that was how Terran CEOs ran their companies. But that was a misconception. Ochiai was responsible for converting the policies of AADD's decision-making bodies into an overall strategy—nothing more.

Of course, serving as the CEO of AADD wasn't a job just anyone could do. Ochiai had played a major role in planning the construction of the artificial accretion disk as well as in terraforming Mars. Still, he was a facilitator not a dictator. What dictator would be referred to by his underlings with a diminutive like "Tetsu"?

"THAT'S RIGHT. Just contact us if you notice anything unusual. We'll follow up on any potential links to Rahmya."

Shiran had contacted the heads of the other security teams to line up support, most importantly the team responsible for analysis of news coming out of Earth. Her team was too small to handle that sort of monitoring on its own. Her request for assistance went out to other teams via web, and specialized AIs went to work sifting every scrap of available information. But as the sun rose on the second day of Rahmya's mission, nothing new had emerged. Ochiai would be arriving on Deimos in twenty-four hours.

Minus 9 Hours 30 Minutes

I take the land cruiser underground, through the ice caverns. This is another reason I'm not using a desert buggy. Underground the satellites can't see you.

AADD has thirty or so air locks between this road and the surface. I guess they're there to stabilize subterranean conditions before they get into the serious prospecting. I'm using the caverns for a different reason. With all the work they did to map them I'd be nuts not to use the caverns.

Problem is, for the first time the mission's not going according to plan. The data I sourced on Earth is turning out to be pretty incomplete. I should probably blame the client too. They're the reason AADD has started restricting data on their ore deposits, even in academic journals—and especially when someone from Earth starts nosing around.

Still, I was able to plot a route. I don't know how these caverns formed, but the ice in here has been frozen—what, a few hundred thousand years? A few million? The ice should be hard as rock. I should be able to drive something as heavy as this cruiser right over it. But it's not working out that way.

The floor was firm at first. And the cruiser is just the ticket when the ice is hard. But when I got past a certain depth, conditions deteriorated very fast. And the deeper I go the worse it gets. The floor has changed from ice to something like melting snow.

I'm so deep under the surface now, I'm guessing the pressure is getting pretty high outside the cruiser. I have no idea why the cavern floor is the consistency of shaved ice, but it's really complicating my plan.

Another thing making it hard to drive is the trailer I'm pulling, with the generator and other equipment I lifted from the camp. The whole thing has to weigh a few tons. I did some dry runs on Earth, of course, using a snow cat to haul a big load of ballast. Based on that, you'd think hauling stuff on Mars should be easier, but the lower gravity is preventing me from getting the traction I need. I don't have the weight; the tracks aren't gripping the ice. At the same time, mass is mass. If the tracks slip, I have to deal with the same amount of inertia whipping me around.

I can't build up a decent head of steam, but I'm still optimistic. This mission came with a lot of unknowns. I built in a cushion for surprises. I'm definitely a bit behind the original timeline, but I've still got time enough to prepare.

Minus 8 Hours 50 Minutes

Two disk-shaped airships twenty meters across perched on the Martian surface, identical except for the markings that showed them to be from different teams. The airship Shiran took from Kobe was decorated with a geisha, a branch of cherry blossoms extending over her head, Olympus Mons in the background. The other airship bore the insignia of the forensics team, a caravan traversing Valles Marineris. Both were hard-shell Guardian airships—not pure airships, but rather buoyancy-assisted aircraft.

"A sandstorm that only lasts a day is a good sandstorm, for sure," said Shiran. "Why do people keep turning up dead?" She stood next to a large surveying van wearing a hard-shell Extravehicular Mobility Unit. Several members of Samar's team were already collecting evidence.

The news had come from another team before dawn—all communication had been lost with one of the geological survey teams. It wasn't that they were refusing to respond; there was no locator signal at all.

Although this didn't itself demonstrate a connection to Rahmya, Shiran decided to investigate immediately. There was something about this new development that was just as unnatural as the murder in Kobe. She chalked it up to intuition. And so they discovered four more bodies.

"Professor, do you think Rahmya did this?" said Mikal.

"Even if she didn't, I think she brought bad luck with her."

"Not bad luck—death. She's an assassin."

"I don't care who the fuck she is!" Shiran had had enough of Mikal for the moment. Twenty-four hours had passed since Rahmya had breached the Guardians' security, and five murders had already taken place. If the hit on the surveying team had been Rahmya's work, the body count would likely continue to rise. Shiran was not in the best of moods.

The bodies had already been taken aboard the forensic team's ship. Mars's low atmospheric pressure was hard on corpses, especially if they were mishandled.

Samar came down the ramp from the ship. "I don't know who the Kobe killer was, but Rahmya gets the credit for this one."

"How do you know?"

"Take a look." He turned and went back into the ship, followed by Shiran and Mikal. They passed through the air lock into the pressurized interior, where they raised their visors before proceeding into a smaller compartment. Four naked bodies were laid out on metal tables. Shiran flinched. Mikal ran from the room, his hand over his mouth.

Even for Shiran, the condition of the young female victim was shocking—cranium split from the bridge of the nose to the crown, eyes bulging grotesquely from exposure to the near-vacuum of Mars. Samar, a veteran, was nonchalant. He held out a small, mushroomed cylinder of metal. "We took these from the victims. They're deformed from the impact, but the alloy matches the so-called parts Rahmya ordered."

"So it was her. But why kill a surveying team?"

"Maybe she stumbled across them on her way somewhere and had to silence them." It was Mikal. He was back, looking pale. His gaze flitted around the room, anywhere but on the bodies.

"No," said Samar. "We recovered the girl's web. We're in luck. The victims were lined up and killed one by one, but this one seems to have ducked at the last moment. She was hit in the shoulder. The other three were shot through the heart, which destroyed their webs. The girl was killed by a head shot, leaving her web undamaged."

"Then she saw the killer."

"And the motive for the killing."

"The motive?"

Samar didn't answer. Instead he sent the data to Shiran's web. Shiran now saw and heard the victim's last moments from the victim's point of view:

A visor enters her field of vision. The face behind the visor is unmistakably Rahmya's.

What's happening, Gong-ru? What's wrong with my team?

You'll be all right. It's just a scratch. This will make the pain go away.

Rahmya smiles. Suddenly the victim's helmet shatters.

The compartment returned; Samar had interrupted the play-back. Now Shiran was looking at a freeze-frame of the victim's last moment of life.

"So she's passing herself off as the Kobe victim," said Shiran. Footage from the clans' security cameras had identified the woman in the atmospheric treatment facility: a freelance journalist from Earth named Gong-ru Yang.

Shiran stared at the web taken from the victim's body. It was, of course, merely a tool, but an indispensable one for survival off-Earth. It was almost like another organ.

As a Guardian, Shiran had seen death up close many times. It wasn't unusual for the web of a murder victim or a person killed in an accident to furnish the key to solving the case. Sometimes agent programs were even able to act as witnesses, with almost human reactions. It was as if immortality were creeping in, half unnoticed, via the hardware and software that made human survival possible.

"Is that all we have? What about the motive?"

"It's coming," said Samar. "Before I show you, let's summarize what we know so far. Rahmya uses Gong-ru as her mule to collect the components for a weapon. She kills the mule and assumes her identity. Then, as Gong-ru she makes contact with the surveying team and instead of interviewing the team, she takes four precious lives. Now why in the world would she do that?"

"Cut to the chase, Samar."

"Watch the rest of the data. Maybe our victim is trying to speak from beyond the grave. Note the corner of her field of vision, near the cruiser and the surveying van."

The victim's web had continued recording. Again, Shiran was struck by the blurring of the line between human and machine awareness.

Instead of retrieving her weapon, Rahmya brings her land cruiser behind the van. She remains mostly outside the field of vision, so it's not clear what exactly she's doing, but evidently she's working on something. After a few minutes, the land cruiser crosses the victim's field of vision, towing something.

"What is that?"

"These surveyors use high-resolution ground-penetrating radar. It's essential for their work, but it uses a huge amount of power. You just saw Rahmya drive off with their power generator."

"She killed them for their generator?"

"That's the most logical assumption. Her cruiser was configured for towing. The unit she rented is equipped for off-road operation. Now we know why."

"If she had to steal a generator, that would explain the need for a weapon. But still—is a power generator really worth four lives?"

"Depends on how critical it is to her plan."

Shiran used her web to project a map of the surrounding region onto her retina, then superimposed the murdered surveyors' geological survey map on it. The map included their work schedule and marked areas where they expected to find ore deposits. "Rahmya's MO tends toward secluded locations. Places where it's dark. Take a look at this." She sent her composite data to the flatscreen. "Ten klicks north of here is an air lock entrance to the Hydra Ice Caverns. It's big enough to drive through in a vehicle."

"Are you saying Rahmya took the cruiser into the caverns?"

"Process of elimination. She's not on the surface. The caverns are the only place she could be. She can't fly. And that cruiser of hers could maneuver down there. It's built for rough environments."

The Hydra Ice Caverns were an underground structure extending deep beneath the Martian cryosphere. The structure was fairly well mapped in the mining data because the processes that had formed the caverns were thought to be linked to the creation of Mars's ore deposits. The caverns appeared to have been an underground river system. The formation of ore deposits on Mars was due not only to volcanism, but also to the activity of life. There was strong evidence that microbial metabolic activity was also a factor. The thick methane clathrate layer far beneath the surface was a major piece of supporting evidence.

The caverns were known to have at least nine major branches— thus the name chosen by the surveyors who had discovered them. In addition, many passageways branched off these main caverns, most of them yet to be mapped. Over two hundred entrances had been found and more were still being discovered.

"So she's fled into the caverns. That makes it simple," said Mikal.

"Not so fast. How are we going to track her? It's a maze in there. And below a certain depth you've got methane to deal with. We'd be fools to rush in without the right gear. And besides, we've got no idea how far inside she is already. She could've covered a hundred klicks by now. We can't follow her on foot. Just the time we'd need to prepare puts her out of our reach, for sure."

"You can't know that!"

"Then let's just say going after her isn't very efficient. A lot of preliminary surveying has been going on down there. How are we supposed to tell the difference between surveyors' tracks and Rahmya's? It won't be easy."

"But we know she's in there. Can't we seal the exits?"

"All two hundred of them? How long do you think that's going to take?"

"Then what do we do, Professor?"

Shiran closed her eyes and exhaled slowly. When she opened them, she spoke without emotion. "She's slipped away from us. I think we should just face that. She's beaten us. There's no way we can go after her now." No one spoke. It was a truth no one wanted to face, but it stood before them like an unmovable object. "Let's change the rules. She got a head start. We're chasing her but we started late. Now we can't catch up. What do we do?"

"Professor?"

"We find out where she's going so we're ready for her when she comes. That's the only way we can nail her."

But everyone knew how little time was left to do that.

Minus 8 Hours 15 Minutes

I'm moving through the cavern when suddenly I notice something odd—I can see the red fan pattern of the laser range finder as it scans ahead of me. The laser light should be invisible. Before I can think this through, something smacks the cruiser, hard, shaking it violently. The four tracked feet are pretty tough for fore and aft movement, but they don't take sudden lateral shocks too well. And there's not much support for them on this surface.

The side of the cruiser slams against a wall of ice. It scrapes along on momentum for a few more meters before it stops. I've got no idea what's happening here. The forward sensors are still active. Aft sensors are all down.

I suit up, half in a panic. I've got to get outside and see what's wrong. It must have something to do with the lasers being visible. You can only see them when the atmosphere is dense enough. On the surface you don't see them at all.

This is just what I need, more delay. I switch on the air lock pump. The pressure starts falling. What conditions are like in the cavern I can only guess. I stand there with my hand on the hatch release, watching the pressure fall.

What happens when I open the hatch comes as a total shock. A huge wall of flame shoots up in front of me and rushes outward. It's gone in less than a second. I'm almost not sure if what I saw was real.

I shine my flashlight at the cruiser. The beam reflects off it in a kind of sparkling light, like fairy glow. The cruiser is bogged down in the ice. Behind it, the generator is buried under a mountain of milky crystals. Then it hits me. This is not ice. It's too fluffy, like it's full of air.

"Hydra Ice Cavern? This isn't ice, it's methane clathrate!"

On Earth there are layers of methane clathrate under ocean sediments—basically waste from microbes eating organic matter. The methane molecules get trapped in cages of frozen H_2O molecules. I've never run across this in a cavern on Earth. But I'm not on Earth.

Methane clathrate is pretty volatile stuff. I must be standing in a pool of methane gas. The fire I saw was the little bit of oxygen left in the air lock reacting with the methane.

What I can't figure out is why the cavern wall came down. The clathrate isn't all that strong structurally, but the cruiser moving past it shouldn't have triggered a collapse. First I've got to check the generator.

Methane gas and steam are rising from the mound of ice crystals. Now I know why there was a cave-in. Even in idling mode the generator radiates heat. That's what brought down the clathrate. If I'm not careful, I could end up completely buried. My luck has held so far, but I can't rely on it. And I'm losing time.

I try to shut the generator down using my web, but I can't access the interface. Apparently only the surveying team is able to control the generator remotely. Like it or not, I've got to get the console exposed so I can shut it down manually. I take a shovel from the cruiser and start scooping clathrate over my shoulder. You run into a lot offworld that you'd never see on Earth, but I never expected to find myself in an ice cavern wearing an Extravehicular Mobility Unit and shoveling away like some miner. And the stuff I'm shoveling is methane clathrate—softer than ice, but handle with care. Otherwise lots of things can happen, none of them good. I've got to get to the console ASAP. The clathrate is melting. This could bring the whole cavern down on me. For now, the mound around the generator is containing the heat.

I don't have much time. Five hours? Six?

That's probably what I'm looking at to dig everything out. Then I've got to hit the road and get prepped. I'm barely going to make it. I keep digging, keep moving that shovel. Every minute, every second, is precious.

It takes me an hour just to dig through to the console. I open the cover and depress two toggle switches simultaneously. The space around me takes on a greater stillness. I hadn't noticed, but the generator was emitting low-frequency vibrations.

It takes me exactly six hours to free the generator. The inside of the cruiser is freezing. There's so much methane floating around I don't even think about pressurizing the cab. Vigorous intercourse between methane and oxygen molecules is something I can pass on right now.

I finally get moving again, still in my EMU. The EMU keeps me warm, but not warm enough to melt my icy mood. It's all I can do to stay calm and collected on the way to the air lock. This ice is so damn slushy, not at all what I'd planned for. I'm all out of cushion now, timewise, but flooring it would not be a good idea. That might invite another cave-in. I practically cheer when the air lock comes into view.

And that's where I run into another snag. All this delay has put me at the air lock just as a swarm of microsatellites hovers overhead. You can hold these things in the palm of your hand. They move in separate orbits and come together at timed intervals over specific locations, using lasers to stay in formation and function as one big system. The sum of the data they collect yields very detailed, high-resolution images. If I poke my head outside now, the Guardians will be able to read the cruiser's tracks like a newspaper.

Most of these satellites have a period of about two hours. This lot should be out of sight in about half an hour if they keep to their schedule. I stop the engine so they don't pick up any infrared hot spots. Just a few more klicks to the destination. Whether or not I can put up with another thirty minutes of delay will decide the success or failure of the mission. I start counting the seconds in my head. When I get to eighteen hundred, I'll be ready to roll.

Just as I reach 1,789, the timer sounds and I hit the ignition. The methane/oxygen power plant starts up. Even with a cold start, a femtosecond-burst laser keeps the environment inside the cylinder ready for combustion. As soon as I hit the switch, I can hear the faint hum of the engine from the cabin.

Got to focus. There will be another swarm overhead half an hour from now, which means I have only that long to get where I need to go. I pass through the air lock. I'm on the surface again.

Minus 2 Hours 15 Minutes

"I'm sending you the specs for the generator, Professor. Take a look."

Shiran gave a low whistle as she reviewed the data from Samar. Most Martian power generators were fuel cells running on methane and oxygen. But this surveying unit was different. It produced power through the annihilation of protons and antiprotons. It was powerful enough to provide electricity for a small arcology.

"My, oh my. All right, we know that everything up to this point was aimed at obtaining this power generator. And as far as we know, the target is Tetsu. Can't we get anything from the satellites, Samar?"

"Unfortunately that's a negative. We scanned in infrared, but she seems to have that covered. She timed the murder of the surveying team so the sun would rise fairly soon afterward. There were no IR traces left to scan; the sun's heat obliterated them. As for vehicle tracks—well, if you want to wipe those as you go, it's not too challenging."

"She hasn't missed a trick. But we can at least calculate the max distance she could've traveled based on the vehicle's specs. Have any of the other teams in the area spotted a lone vehicle?"

"No. Even if she's going flat out, with the generator she's hauling she should've been spotted hours ago. On the surface, that is."

"That settles it. She's using the caverns."

This was not good news for Shiran. The caverns were a restricted space; if she was so sure Rahmya was inside, she ought to be using that to her advantage. "All right, so our assassin was fortunate enough to get her hands on the generator. Given all the trouble she went through to steal it, that's got to point to something. She can't use the generator as a weapon. That itself should answer some of our questions. What's the tie-in between her target, the caverns, and a power generator?"

A three-dimensional projection of the generator hung suspended in front of them. Shiran rotated the projection in different directions, as if she might find the answer there. But all she saw was a generator, nothing more and nothing less.

"I see two possibilities," said Mikal. "One would be to use the generator to produce oxygen and methane for rocket fuel. The other would be to remove the antiproton capsule and convert it into some sort of bomb. It fits her MO."

"Sorry, but you're wrong on both counts," said Samar.

"You seem to have a problem with every idea I come up with."

"I have a problem with ideas that are stupid. I won't comment on the correlation between the stupidity of the ideas and the person generating them."

"Stop acting like children, you two. What are you thinking, Samar?"

"Suppose Rahmya wants to generate fuel—how would she use it? She'd have to have a missile in place. Look at all the effort she's already gone to—and that was just to get past our security. If she had some way to smuggle a missile in, why would she need to go to such elaborate lengths just to get fuel?"

"What about one of our discarded spacecraft?" said Mikal.

"You've got to be kidding. Our predecessors on this planet were hard up for anything that could be recycled. If they could've, they would've recycled the hair on their asses. They wouldn't leave a spacecraft lying around. Go to Kobe's Industrial Technology Museum and check it out. We've got titanium cooking pots made from the skin of rocket boosters. I ought to know, I'm on their research team."

"That doesn't prove anything. There might still be a spacecraft out there she could refuel, one we don't know about."

"Somewhere on the whole planet, maybe. Not around Rokko. The area's swarming with surveying teams. And there's a bigger difficulty. You'd need several days to fuel a spacecraft with this generator."

"I see," said Shiran. "What about the antiproton capsule?"

"Even harder to imagine. You'd need a specialist to access the capsule. It's protected by multiple safety devices to prevent tampering. The only way to open it would be to take it to a specialized facility. And even if she had all the access codes, she couldn't remove the capsule on her own. And even if she did and turned the capsule into some kind of warhead, she'd still need a launch vehicle—which puts us back where we started."

Shiran switched to an exploded-view image of the generator. She examined each component, turning casings transparent to see inside. Something about the generator was the key to Rahmya's plan. But what?

"I think what we have here is a power generator," said Samar at length.

"What makes this one different from others?" said Shiran.

"Its use of antiprotons and its high output, basically," said Mikal. "Just what you'd expect."

"So she needs electricity," said Samar. "With this much power you could practically get offworld—if you had a vehicle."

"Is that what she's going to do with it?" said Shiran.

"Professor, I was just joking."

"That's it—she needs electric power!"

"Could you please get a grip? What's she going to do with electric power in the middle of nowhere?"

"The first settlers on Mars recycled everything. But not these days. Now we do cost/benefit analyses. Like with old launchers. Do you dismantle them or just leave them in place?"

"Professor, I'm sorry, but there are no launch vehicles in the outback. And she can't generate fuel overnight—"

"I'm talking about a *launcher,* not a launch vehicle. We haven't used them since the elevator was built. The mass drivers that sent ore into space—they used electricity to launch their payloads."

Samar and Mikal were silent. Samar was inputting data to his web. At length he spoke. "I think we have a problem, Professor."

"What do you mean?"

"I don't know what orbit she'd use, but if the target is Deimos she has a restricted launch window. She'll also need to launch ahead of Tetsu's arrival, to give whatever she's using as a projectile enough time to reach Deimos. The next window is twelve hours before Tetsu arrives."

"But that means . . ."

"We've got two hours max."

Minus 1 Hour 30 Minutes

The great thing about a mass driver is that it has no moving parts. Therefore it can't malfunction. It took them seven years to build Tsutenkaku, and until 2122, when it was finished, mass drivers like the one I'm looking at were used all the time. Martian gravity is weak compared to Earth's, the atmosphere is thin, and the high plateau around Mt. Rokko is close to the equator. It's an ideal location for sending objects into orbit just by accelerating them up a ramp.

My client put me onto this. I'm in one of the few mines on Mars that was originally developed by Terran investors. The Martians haven't disclosed much about the technical specifications of their mass drivers. But for this driver the client had all the blueprints, everything. It's perfect for this mission.

I owe the Martians one for mapping and securing the access points to the Hydra Ice Caverns. At first I thought it was a bit much, going to all that work just to keep conditions underground nice and stable, but not anymore. Not after my run-in with the methane clathrate. I'd be nervous too if I were them. Still, even though I nearly bought it, the caverns got me here without being spotted. As far as I know there are at least fifty access points.

Even if the Guardians knew I was down there, they couldn't know where I might exit. They couldn't come after me with guns blazing, either. Not in the middle of all that gas.

What worries me isn't the Guardians. It took far longer than I'd planned to free the generator and make it to the egress point without getting buried or blown up. Thanks to that, I don't have much prep time left. And the launch window is very tight.

This mass driver is underground. The tunnel they excavated keeps it safe from sandstorms and the temperature swings on the surface. They must've decided it wouldn't pay to dismantle it. The galleries leading to the driver are chockablock with equipment that's probably still usable. It looks like the miners might come back any minute to start working again.

The superconducting magnets along the driver's two-hundred-meter length are in good shape. I figured all I had to do was supply power to the capacitors, but now I'm facing another complication. The control system is in relatively decent condition, but it's seen a lot of use. Some of the sensors for the packet guidance system are nonfunctional. Without these, there's no way to aim the packets. If I'm going to blow away Ochiai's ship, I've got to solve this problem. Fortunately the sensors aren't complicated. I can put them back into action with electronic parts from the assortment I picked up in Kobe for exactly this sort of contingency.

My bigger problem is the generator. Two of its three converters are out of commission, apparently because of the cave-in. They're not damaged, but a protection circuit kicked in—maybe water got in somewhere it wasn't supposed to. So now I'm looking at using just one converter.

In its day, this mass driver could only be used during launch windows that would let it put its packets of ore into a Hohmann orbit, for rendezvous with Deimos. That was back before they changed the moon's orbit. Outside the launch window, the system's capacitors could be charged with a small mobile generator. When the timing was right, they discharged the stored energy all at once, firing packets of ore into space one after another from a huge stack, like a machine gun.

The plan was to quickly charge the system and fire a barrage of projectiles. Now I'm wondering if that's possible. I hurry to connect the generator. The mission will fail if I can't juice up the capacitors in time. But if everything goes according to spec, Ochiai's ship will be ripped to pieces, and it will be impossible to prove it was my handiwork.

I log on to AADD Net using Gong-ru Yang's password. I want to make sure Ochiai hasn't changed his schedule. Everything's nominal. The target is on course and on time. AADD takes schedules seriously. They're masters at keeping their space traffic moving like clockwork.

The attack principle is simple. At a given moment, object A and object B try to occupy the same space simultaneously, with the results one would expect. That's really all there is to it. I was worried about getting the timing right, but things are looking good. The spacecraft carrying Chairman Ochiai will arrive with the precision that marks everything AADD does. And that's what's going to get him killed.

Minus 0 Hours 10 Minutes

"This mass driver the Terrans built is fairly small and simple. It looks like they decided to abandon it rather than spend the money to dismantle it. We haven't touched it, since it's not one of ours."

The airship flew at maximum speed above the Martian surface. Most of the mass drivers on Mars had been dismantled after the completion of the orbital elevator. Now there were only a few left. Of these, only one offered a high probability of being part of Rahmya's plan, but it wasn't clear whether a team could reach the site before the launch window opened.

All Guardian units were on alert. Units in transit to the camp of the murdered surveying team had been redirected to the mass driver, but they were certain to arrive even later than Shiran. Everything depended on whether Shiran and the team she had assembled at short notice could locate Rahmya in time.

"Professor, are you sure this mass driver is really usable for some sort of attack?" Mikal was paging through the driver's technical specifications, forwarded by the Industrial Technology Museum. "Deimos was repositioned as a counterweight for the elevator. It's in a different orbit now. The elevator is even visible from here. No matter how fast a projectile leaves this mass driver, the launch angle is low. The apogee motor on each packet is tiny. It should be possible to reach 22,000 kilometers with one of these containers, but given the launch point, hitting Deimos is impossible. I think we're reading this wrong."

"You said the velocity doesn't matter. Are you sure about that?"

"What do you mean, Professor?"

"Don't forget, Mars is revolving. That added kick will boost the packet to almost five klicks per second."

"But by the time it reaches 22,000 kilometers, it will actually be ahead of Tsutenkaku. How's the packet going to hit it?"

"By climbing to 30,000 kilometers. Then it uses its motor to descend to 22,000 kilometers. Fourteen hours after launch the packet would strike Deimos."

"Fourteen hours? That's a pretty leisurely attack profile."

"It would give Rahmya more than enough time to establish an alibi or simply disappear." Shiran sent the projected ballistic track to Mikal's web. The packet—a simple cargo container with a small

Tsutenkaku and cargo packet collide at approx. T+14 hours
due to revolution of Mars. Packet's velocity relative to target
releases enormous kinetic energy.

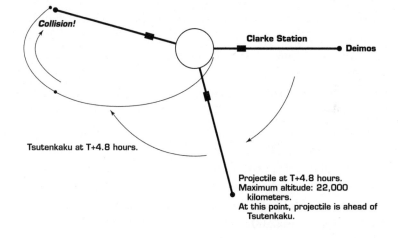

Collision!

Clarke Station

Deimos

Tsutenkaku at T+4.8 hours.

Projectile at T+4.8 hours.
Maximum altitude: 22,000
    kilometers.
At this point, projectile is ahead of
    Tsutenkaku.

booster—could rise smoothly to an altitude of 30,000 kilometers, then kick into a parabolic transfer orbit and descend to 22,000 kilometers. In effect, the packet could swoop in from above and behind Deimos as the satellite passed below.

"All right. All we have to do is contact Tetsu and tell him not to land until we can solve this."

"He won't do it, Mikal. The deceleration sequence has already started. I talked to him. He's not going to change his schedule. He's arriving on time, as planned."

"Even with someone trying to kill him?"

"Precisely because someone is trying to kill him. If the threat is a terrorist attack, he won't change his schedule." Shiran was well aware of Ochiai's views on this issue. This was not a matter of changing a single spacecraft's schedule. It was a political principle.

How should AADD deal with terrorists? Ochiai's actions spoke for the collective. There would be no compromise with terrorism or its hidden backers. Terrorism would have no effect on AADD's resolve to reach its goals. As the head of AADD's steering committee, Ochiai was the embodiment of that resolve.

"The greater the danger, the less room he has to back down," said Mikal. "He's carrying the burden for us all."

"That's why he's head of the steering committee." Shiran examined the specifications, hoping to find some way to block a launch from outside the facility. It didn't take her long to realize that the situation was worse than she'd imagined. "Mikal, if we don't stop her, she could devastate Deimos. This driver fires packets from a top-loading magazine. If I were Rahmya, I'd fire as many packets as I could to cover my bet. She could wipe out most of Deimos Station."

"How much longer till the window opens?" said Mikal.

"Less than ten minutes."

The Guardians put on their bulky assault suits and began to check weapons. Most of these Guardians weren't part of Shiran's team, but rather belonged to a specialized assault group. Shiran had overall operational control, but these men and women were responsible for tactical decision-making on the ground. Their target had already killed four people—five including the Terran victim.

Shiran also suited up. She hadn't worn one of these units in a long time. They looked unwieldy but were manufactured from composite materials and were surprisingly light. The suits had advanced servo joint assist, enabling enhanced finger dexterity inside the suit's gloves, and used a spaced armor system. This made them appear imposing, if not frightening—an intended psychological effect reinforced by an all-black finish.

"I haven't worn one of these units in a while," said Shiran to the squad leader.

"Bet it won't be the last time, though."

"I'm afraid you're probably right."

The squad members helped each other through their final suit checks. Their training focused on counterterrorism operations, and it was rare for them to actually be deployed. Most would-be terrorists were detained the moment they set foot on Deimos. Some members of this squad were undoubtedly on their first deployment. Shiran could sense it—even with their evil-looking suits on, some of them were visibly ill at ease.

Seeing that Shiran was unarmed the squad leader offered her a pistol. She waved it away. "Are you sure, Professor?" he asked.

"If you need me to carry a gun, I think the Guardians are finished."

"Then let's complete your thruster check."

The armored suits were equipped with onboard thrusters—good for only three minutes of flight, but reliable, powerful, highly maneuverable, and fueled by a cocktail of sixty nitrogen compounds.

"Professor, we're real close!" shouted Mikal.

"Maybe we're even in time. I need a visual." In seconds, Shiran's retinal feed showed her the opening in the surface that marked the egress point for the packets. The image must have been enhanced—despite the distance it was unnaturally sharp and clear. Most of the mine structures had been buried by sandstorms, but it was clear that something man-made was out there. Shiran switched to infrared view.

"Hello..."

A distinct IR plume was visible around the tunnel entrance, proof that something inside was generating large amounts of heat. "Looks like someone's in the kitchen."

Minus 0 Hours 1 Minute

Other than the guidance sensors, everything's finally going the way I planned. And the guidance sensors are fixed. I was worried about the mass driver equipment, but all in all it's in better shape than I'd thought. The launch packets were stacked way back in the galleries behind the driver, good to go with hardly any attention from me. All I had to do was top off the fuel tanks.

And now what's left is just a little heavy lifting while the capacitors charge. The crane on the land cruiser works fine for loading the packets into the magazine. I supply a little elbow grease, wait patiently, and let leverage do most of the work. I don't have to use my head. I'd really rather be loading with the big crane they have here, but with two-thirds of my generator capacity down that's a luxury I can't afford. The driver's guidance system is drawing power from the cruiser while the generator powers the capacitors. I don't hear much noise from the equipment, but I can feel the ground vibrating. I must be putting out a big heat signature right about now.

I've got twenty packets to work with. With that many I could send a huge amount of mass into orbit, but like it or not I'm going to have to launch them empty. I'd love to load them up with mine slag, but there's no time. Anyway, they'll travel faster empty. Even then, each one weighs about a ton.

Given the relative speed difference, I'm not going to hit Deimos with the packets. Not exactly. It's more like Deimos is going to collide with them. The velocity differential will be pretty huge, based on the packets' kinetic vector. It's like the old battleships of the twentieth century—the packets are like shells from the battle-ships' main battery. Twenty hits like that and Deimos Station will probably be snuffed out along with Chairman Ochiai.

Martian gravity is only about a third of Earth's, but after loading twenty packets into the magazine I'm completely exhausted. Still, there's no time to rest. The only thing finished is the preparation.

I'm already three minutes into the launch window when the guidance console's lights turn green straight across. The capacitors are juiced up and ready to go. I hurry to switch the guidance panel's power supply over to the generator. I bring the orbital guidance sensors from idle mode to full readiness. Optical sensors, ballistic homing radar—all systems nominal.

That's when I see it. A blip on the homing radar. I feverishly check the image data on my heads-up.

"You've gotta be fucking kidding."

A Guardian airship—and it's coming right down my throat. I didn't activate the radar earlier because I wanted to conserve power. Smooth move, Rahmya. I don't even need image data—the fuckers are close enough to see with the naked eye.

How did they find me? I haven't made a single mistake. But there they are. Looks like they're going to try and stop me from launching the packets. The airship is coming straight in, right along the launch trajectory. Yes! I activate homing mode and the radar starts scanning. There's only one airship.

I enter the auto-homing command into the console, but the target is so close that it's outside the mass driver's parameters. I haven't won yet, but they can't stop twenty packets, not even if they put themselves physically in the way. And unless they stop them all, I win.

I launch on the preprogrammed trajectory. The driver's huge capacitors begin to discharge. The superconducting coils violently change shape as they send the cargo up the ramp. I can feel the vibration through the ground under my feet. In a few moments the magazine is empty. The first packet's going to take out the airship, but that will leave nineteen for the hit on the chairman. More than enough.

Even before all twenty packets are out of the barn, the airship on the radar is gone.

Plus 0 Hours 5 Minutes

Although her mission was now complete, Rahmya had no time to rest on her laurels. The Guardian airship hadn't been simply passing by. They must have known about the mass driver and what could be done with it. She'd succeeded in destroying this lot, but more would come. She hurriedly gathered her gear and set out for the caverns.

Would the mission succeed? Its chances seemed no better than fifty-fifty. No—bringing down the airship meant the mission would probably fail. Even if Deimos Station were destroyed, Ochiai's ship could easily evade the attack.

Better get my ass back to Kobe. There's no proof I did this. Get back to Kobe, get a new ID, contact the client. We'll just have to come up with a new plan. I may have blown the hit but Deimos Station is going to be toast in a few hours. The client can't ignore that.

The straight-line distance from the mine to the nearest cavern gate was ten kilometers, but there were the satellites to consider. She'd have to follow the path of a narrow streambed for concealment, but that would double the distance, and the surface conditions in the streambed were rough. Still, there were no other options. She wasn't in a position to pick and choose.

Rahmya had just entered the streambed when the cruiser's radar returned an echo. She immediately halted the vehicle. A radar return here could only mean a rockslide, and the radar had definitely spotted something small dropping down in front of the cruiser. Rahmya swiveled the optical sensors upward, trying to locate the slide. She needn't have bothered. A glance out the cruiser's window would have shown her the source of the reading.

The small objects weren't falling, they were landing—clad in black armor and carrying guns.

Impossible—you're all dead!

Rahmya knew she had destroyed the airship. But now it seemed that some—all?—of the crew had bailed before impact. Soon there would be more of them. Escape was impossible; the mission was over.

"All right, you got me. You win, I lose. Deport me, whatever. I don't care." Rahmya spoke on the general comm. The answer was not what she expected.

"No. We're the ones who lost." It was Shiran Kanda.

Plus 0 Hours 6 Minutes

I think she said, "We lost." It wasn't one of the three in front of me though. That voice just had to be Kanda. She must be close by.

"You lost, did you? Yeah, I guess you did. Maybe I won't get Ochiai, but you can't do anything now to put Deimos out of harm's way."

"That's not what I meant. Your assassination plan failed. And Deimos is safe."

"Bullshit. You're bluffing."

"Am I? Watch."

I receive some image data on my heads-up display. It's the airship—imaged from outside. No . . .

The footage plays back one high-speed frame at a time. I don't have to see many frames to know what happened. The first packet hits the airship just as I hoped, but the mass differential is still huge, and the airship is built from some kind of carbon composite that absorbs shock better than a metal airframe. The airship shudders from the shock wave, but it's still hanging in the sky when the second packet hits, and the rest are right on its tail. There's a pileup of twenty packets colliding with the ship, pieces of the ship, and each other, the packets hitting the hull faster than the impact can tear the ship apart. "Now I understand. Wait—why does this mean you lost?"

Then she says something I never expected to hear from a Martian.

"We prevented you from assassinating Tetsuya and destroying Deimos Station, but not before you committed murder. Now four of our people are dead. By allowing you to slip past us, four precious lives were lost. We failed to protect them, even though it's our job. That was my failure and my defeat."

"Sorry, you missed one. In Kobe."

"Gong-ru Yang? Yes, we know. I'm sure her death was a tragedy, but she's not one of the people I'm here to protect. The Guardians exist to protect AADD."

"So the death of a Terran means nothing to you."

"I didn't say that. But I'm not responsible for protecting them. I'd prefer it if Gong-ru hadn't died. But either way, I failed to do my job."

"Weren't you trying to stop me from killing your chairman?"

"Of course. He's a member of AADD."

"Not just a member. He's the chairman—he calls all the shots!"

"No one calls all the shots in AADD. Tetsu is the head of our steering committee, nothing more. It's just a function. He doesn't hold any particular 'power.' But I doubt this is something you'd understand."

That's when it hits me—the reason I keep misreading these people. Terran culture, Terran values—none of it means anything to them. They're like this intelligent life-form that's close to human but plays by completely different rules. How can I win against something like that? They're not even playing the same game.

"So what are you going to do with me? Maybe you don't care about Kobe, but I killed four of your people. Why don't you just take care of the payback here and now?"

"Your hijacker friends have already been deported to Earth. Thanks for tipping us off to the plot. It made it very easy for us to arrest them."

"I didn't tip anyone off!"

"Really? Your accomplices think you did. We made sure of it.

You'll be sent back to Earth later, I suppose. Naturally we'll make sure your friends know every detail of your itinerary so you can have a reunion."

"So that's how you plan to dispose of me. Very convenient."

"That's something for you and your friends to decide. It's not my concern. But if you want to atone for the killing of four people, there is a way."

"And that would be what?"

"Follow precedent. Seek asylum on Mars. No—asylum in AADD. It's possible, if you wish to do so. But you'd have to become a Guardian. That'd be the best way to atone for your crime."

Plus O Hours 7 Minutes

As Shiran had expected, Rahmya's reaction to her offer was silence. Now it was time to drive the point home. "If you join us, you'll be the best weapon we could have against the people who hired you. That alone makes you worth having."

Shiran's web was delivering protests to this move from some of her team. But Mikal stood behind her. For Shiran that was enough to decide the matter.

"Sure. Use me till I quit being useful. Then you toss me to the dogs."

"How useful you are is something you'll have to decide yourself. Do your best to prove yourself as a Guardian, and that will be the greatest atonement you could make to those four people who died."

"Do my *best*? You know how many people might die if I did my *best*? Do you know what I am?"

"Of course. If you join us, we get access to your experience and expertise as a terrorist. That will help enable us to prevent further incidents like this."

"I kill four people and you're not going to execute me. You're not going to toss me in prison. No. You're going to make me a member of your society? Don't expect me to believe that."

"But it's true—if you work to earn your membership in our collective. Why should execution or prison be necessary? AADD doesn't have laws, at least not as you would understand that term."

Shiran signaled one of the team to take Rahmya from the vehicle. The captive emerged quietly, no sign of resistance. The Guardian got in the vehicle and drove it away, leaving Rahmya behind.

Plus 0 Hours 8 Minutes

There are about twenty of them, all wearing armored EMUs. Only one is unarmed. That must be Shiran Kanda.

"Your fate is in your hands," she says to me. "That is our way, and whether you join us or not you must follow it."

"I guess this isn't the time to negotiate."

"You guessed right."

The Guardians line up in front of me like a wall. I see another airship approaching the sandbar behind them, preparing to touch down. In the opposite direction is the mouth of the mass driver. Beyond that lies the red-brown desert, empty and infinite.

Shiran sees me checking out my situation and nods. "You have two choices. Step forward and follow us onto the airship. If you do, you will spend the rest of your life as a Guardian and a member of the collective. Your other choice stretches behind you, as you see. If you're resourceful and luck is with you, you may be able to reach the orbital elevator on your own. If you do, and you swear never to return to Mars again, you will be permitted to go where you will, unhindered."

"Two choices?"

"Only those two."

I can feel my resolve taking shape already. No matter how hard the decision is, I'm the only one who can make it. And as long as my fate is mine to decide, I'll never be defeated.

I've made my choice. The journey begins here.

THE ISSUE OF CONSCIOUSNESS was raised for a reason, of course. The structure of consciousness is partly responsible for misinterpreting chance responses.

Still, confirming the presence of consciousness is not necessarily straightforward. If you are communicating with an entity that responds appropriately, you can assume the entity is conscious. If you share the same physical structure, you can make certain informed guesses about the entity's condition, even if direct communication is impossible—and if you can make sense of the entity's actions and their results, you can infer that consciousness is present.

But is communication possible in the complete absence of shared physical characteristics? Could you confirm that such an entity was conscious? We have done so with an AI, but that may have been pure luck.

The intent to communicate, for example, may not always be present; where it is not, humankind has found it difficult to conclude that consciousness exists. Perhaps the emergence of life is inevitable. But consciousness is a byproduct of chance.

THE DRAGONS OF EUROPA
A.D. 2149

SOMEHOW we never really got used to seeing our ship from the outside. From the ship's viewing ports, all we could see was the dark sky full of stars, the monotonous plain of ice, and a slice of ocean surface, but our webs cut through the darkness and enhanced the contrast and texture of the scene. Technology had banished darkness from the solar system.

"Insertion in ten seconds. System disengage."

"System disengage. Autodiagnostic clear."

"System clear, check." Captain Kohara was proceeding through his final predive checks. *Remora* was now disengaged from the network of its mother ship, *Dagon III*, and operating on its own computer and power systems. I heard a faint mechanical hum start up.

"System status update: RPM, voltage, oil pressure, oxidant temperature and pressure, all nominal." Kameda's voice sounded strangely doubled. I switched off my web's audio circuit. In this narrow space, the navigator's voice reached my ears sooner than my web fed data to my auditory cortex. I could still faintly hear that strange hum. I must have seemed confused.

"Is this your first experience with diesel, Dr. Kurokawa?"

"This is diesel? Yes, it's the first time."

"I guess it must be. *Remora* is probably the only diesel spacecraft out there. Not as efficient as fuel cells, but the waste heat is recycled. Overall it doesn't perform too badly." Although it depended on *Dagon III* for transport, officially *Remora* was classified as a spaceship.

Kameda didn't seem inclined to explain further. It was obvious he thought I wouldn't understand. "*Remora* uses closed-cycle, air-independent propulsion. With only three crew, we've got enough liquid oxygen to cruise for a week."

"Hey, Kameda, instead of shooting the breeze with the professor, how about monitoring your console? You're supposed to be watching my back."

"Can't I monitor on my web?"

"I don't care, just do it!" In fact, all three of us were using our webs, even though the consoles displayed the same information.

"Commencing insertion." Kameda monitored the console intently as *Remora* slowly entered the hundred-meter circle of water. Energy transmitted from the artificial accretion disk—now in orbit around Uranus—had carved a gateway through 250 meters of solid ice.

Dagon III was a modified bulk carrier, piloted by AADD's Special Equipment Team. The ship was equipped with optical sensors along its hull. We could use these sensors to view 3-D computer-enhanced images from any angle. I selected a portside CG view of *Remora*. The mother ship was using its twenty-meter manipulator arm to lower us into the water. *Remora* was about ten meters long. Cradled beneath it was a submersible robot named Salmon. There was nothing for us to do—*Dagon*'s manipulator arm handled the insertion.

Europa's surface gravity was only 0.135 G. Even though we were undoubtedly descending slowly, I still sensed the motion in the pit of my stomach. And then my body felt slightly heavier as *Remora* floated in Europa's ocean.

"Commence dive."

"Aye aye, commencing dive."

I heard the faint sound of the pumps starting up. Water flooded the ballast tanks. We bid farewell to space and dived.

EUROPA, smallest of the four Galilean satellites of Jupiter. Since the twentieth century, scientists had speculated that it might harbor life. Data from unmanned missions suggested the presence of liquid water under the moon's mantle of ice. Given its orbit and the tidal forces from Jupiter and Io, it was reasoned that there might well be active volcanoes at the bottom of Europa's ocean. In that case, there would also be hydrothermal vents, like those on Earth. It would not be surprising for unique life-forms to have arisen and evolved in that environment. Subsequent observations refined and adjusted this initial impression, and most scientists continued to believe that life might be present.

Of course, this view was based mostly on hope rather than fact. Angular mass data sent back by unmanned probes suggested that the depth of Europa's surface ice and the underlying ocean was around 150 kilometers. Long-term investigation using synthetic aperture radar and other technologies indicated that the depth of the ice layer, though irregular, averaged around ten kilometers. To investigate the possibility of life on Europa, a hole would have to be opened in the ice; however, mechanical drilling required a huge investment in equipment, time, and people. Of course, ice samples recovered during drilling would be of great scientific value—the few ice cores taken from the surface had already yielded telltale traces of life. But the cores told a limited story. Only access to the ocean beneath the ice would yield definitive answers.

Did this sheltered sea really harbor life? By chance an opportunity to test this hypothesis presented itself. Satellites detected icequakes caused by tidal forces and convective movements in the ice. These quakes created subsurface fissures where the ice was as thin as 250 meters.

Energy transmitted from the accretion disk via laser and microwave melted a hundred-meter access hole in the ice. This feat also helped prove that Kali's energy could be focused into a tight beam over millions of miles. To prevent a steam explosion, the ice was thinned gradually. After weeks of careful work the layer was breached.

The first ship assigned the mission to search for signs of life—

the submarine *Swordfish*—was quickly dispatched to Europa. Two things happened in quick succession: traces of life were discovered and the submarine disappeared for reasons unknown. Our mission was to confirm the existence of life on this moon and discover the whereabouts of the submarine.

—•◦•—

MY WEB showed a depth of 150 meters. We weren't even below the ice layer yet.

"Captain," said Kameda, "I think you should know that according to my web the influence of Mars and Uranus is very strong today."

"Kameda, this is a moon of Jupiter. How could the influence of Mars and Uranus be strong here? What do you think, Dr. Kurokawa?"

"I think the forecast might be right."

"Really? Why?" The captain seemed surprised that I'd suggest astrology could affect our fate.

"It's the reason we're here now, aboard *Remora*. Terraforming on Mars and Kali orbiting Uranus—that's how we ended up on Europa."

"See, Kameda? Pros don't actually believe in astrology."

"Did I say I believed in it? Fortune-telling is all about inter-pretation. You look at a lot of methods for telling the future and pick the one that suits you best. The important thing is to make the right choice."

The banter abruptly stopped. Both men peered carefully at their consoles. The ship's rate of descent slowed.

"Are we coming into a dangerous area?" I asked.

"Yes, soon now. But *Swordfish* got past it okay and *Remora* is a smaller ship. Nothing to worry about." The captain sent a 3-D profile of the access hole to my web. A simple tube a hundred meters in diameter extended deep into the ice. But for its last few tens of meters, the hole shrank from a cylinder to a long, narrow fissure. This section had been cleared by pumping high-pressure water into the hole. The inner surface was rough and irregular. To keep the hole from freezing from the bottom up while we were under the ice, powerful heat pumps around the edge circulated water from the surface into the depths. Only Kali's unlimited energy made this possible.

"Ready to fire her up, Cap'n?" said Kameda.

"You may proceed."

Kameda activated the sonar and the laser radar developed specifically for deep-sea use. Thousands of high-efficiency semiconductor laser devices, shielded by pressure-resistant glass, were arrayed along *Remora*'s hull. Within a limited range their wavelength could be tuned. Electronically switching the array made it possible to judge the density and composition of objects within a certain range of the hull.

At least that was the theory. In practice, making it work was extremely difficult. Deploying laser radar in the vacuum of space was one thing, trying to get it to work underwater was something different. AADD's Special Equipment Team had solved the problem by combining sonar and laser radar into one integrated system. *Remora*'s sonar was a parametric array able to measure the density of the water with precision. In effect, subtracting the sonar data from the radar data—handled by a specialized processing unit—yielded sharp, three-dimensional images of anything outside the hull. We could see fractures in the ice as clearly as if they had been optically imaged. It must have had something to do with the enhancement algorithms—I could even see the way the fractures were arranged in layers. I couldn't help but admire the sheer artistry of it. "The resolution on this radar is amazing."

"The team put a lot of time into it. I don't like to brag, but what can I say—they're the best in the solar system at this work." The captain's pride in his team's accomplishment was obvious. Others might not be as impressed, but as a scientist I envied their willingness to accept challenges. I started to wonder—what had I been doing for the last twenty years?

Suddenly the ice disappeared from the monitor. "We're in the clear," said Kameda. We were below 250 meters. Around us stretched an ocean the size of Earth's moon.

"Is this where *Swordfish* was lost?"

"If you believe the data from the ultrasonic relay buoy," said Kohara, "it was about twenty kilometers from here."

"How long before we arrive?"

"Oh, I'd say about four hours at our current speed. No point in getting anxious now. Hey, Kameda, I'm starting to feel cold. Maybe it's the depth. Make us some coffee."

"Aye aye, sir. Join us, Doctor? How do you take it?"

"With milk, if you've got any." The tension eased. Passing safely through the last section of the gateway seemed to have relieved my shipmates.

"Coffee's on." Kameda produced ceramic—in fact they were real porcelain—coffee cups seemingly out of nowhere and filled them with coffee, first mine, then the captain's. As he poured his own he asked casually, "That's right, Dr. Kurokawa—I was meaning to ask you. As a scientist, what do you think of all this talk about dragons on Europa?"

SWORDFISH had been built by AADD's spacecraft manufacturing group, the giant Ferry Nakaya Ltd., using a typical spacecraft design. The basic assumption was that a submarine was simply a spacecraft with a pressure hull. *Swordfish* was a shark-shaped vessel fifty meters long—in effect, a submersible spaceship—with propulsion via proton/antiproton annihilation, the same approach used in the latest AADD ships.

The accretion disk at the center of the Milky Way galaxy was known to produce vertical gas jets. Kali displayed the same phenomenon, and AADD succeeded in using these jets to mass-produce antiprotons. These particles were better suited to energy production than antimatter—that is, antihydrogen—though AADD could produce that as well. Of course, antiprotons were carefully rationed.

Output was still limited to a few grams a day.

The heat produced by the annihilation of protons and antiprotons drove a Sterling-type heat engine that in turn propelled *Swordfish* through the water. Even in their upper strata, Europa's waters were close to freezing. This cooling potential boosted the efficiency of the power plant.

But although *Swordfish* was advanced as a vehicle, Ferry Nakaya faced a difficult challenge when it came to the ship's sensing systems. FN's sensing technology was impressive, but it was designed for outer space, not the deep waters of an icebound ocean. FN was aware of its limitations. The system it developed for *Swordfish* was designed to function under conditions expected on Europa. Its engineers had access to more than enough data to make the required modifications—or so they thought.

But they had misjudged the scope of the challenge. The upper and lower layers of Europa's ocean turned out to have starkly different compositions and densities. The upper reaches were comparatively transparent; dissolved mineral content was low. Under these conditions *Swordfish* could easily carry out its mission. But as the ship went deeper, conditions quickly changed. The concentration of organic matter and minerals rose, and visibility diminished drastically.

Under these conditions, the radar that was supposed to serve as the ship's eyes couldn't function as designed. The ultrasonic link to the support team on the ice became *Swordfish's* only connection to the rest of the mission. Still, the crew continued their explorations. They wanted to collect enough data to upgrade the radar for the next mission.

And so *Swordfish* cruised farther from the gateway and deeper into the ocean. Its crew was able to use differential radar data to send low-resolution footage to the surface. However, the radar continued to perform erratically and the images were not very useful.

Twenty kilometers from the gateway something happened. The ship collided with something organic—and dense.

"It's after us! It's alive!"

"It's no use, we can't outrun it!"

"Evading—We can't get away from this thing! No! It's a *dragon!*"

That was the end of the transmission. The final radar image showed something enormous and snakelike, maw agape, immediately behind the submarine. Whatever it was, it did look like a dragon. Analysis verified that it was a real object, not a refraction artifact.

For AADD, the loss of *Swordfish* was eclipsed by a bigger danger: the crew's last transmission. "It's a *dragon!*"

Too much remained a mystery. Their cry for help suggested that Europa might harbor a huge life-form with some degree of intelligence. If this was true, it could turn into a huge headache. Those opposed to terraforming Mars could easily use a dragon on Europa as a weapon against AADD.

Terraforming was AADD's primary use for the boundless energy promised by the artificial accretion disk. But an energy distribution system spanning the solar system demanded a complex infrastructure. One element of this infrastructure was a positioning system driven by hundreds of satellites, equipped with atomic clocks and distributed throughout the solar system. Cesium ions, cooled to a Bose-Einstein condensate, gave the clocks unprecedented accuracy.

The positioning system was only one part of the infrastructure necessary to deliver energy with pinpoint accuracy from Kali to planets, moons, and low-cost long-haul spacecraft throughout the solar system. The development and construction of this infrastructure was enormously expensive. A major portion of the budget was covered by loans secured with future profits from terraformed land sales.

But many on Earth clung to the belief that microbes native to Mars would someday be discovered beneath its surface. If even a single amoeba came to light there would be urgent demands to halt all terraforming. Those holding this view were in the minority, but they were still a force to be reckoned with. If life was found on Europa, it would indirectly strengthen their position.

AADD was searching for life on Europa in order to demonstrate that it wasn't ignoring the possibility of life elsewhere in the solar system. Organic contamination from Earth was widespread throughout the solar system; all of the microbes found on Mars had been proven to have originated elsewhere. AADD hoped to encourage the view that humanity was the only intelligent life-form in the solar system. Proclaiming that Mars was "humanity's birthright," AADD wanted to present terraforming as an irreversible act of progress.

The ground would be cut from under this strategy if intelligent life was discovered on Europa. If its hostile environment could harbor such a creature, there might well be life hidden somewhere on Mars. Earth might call for a freeze on terraforming until the absence of such life could be proven—and nothing is more difficult to prove than a negative.

Terraforming Mars neither benefited nor harmed the people of Earth. The labor as well as the financial and technical resources had been provided almost exclusively by the Martians themselves. AADD could ignore Terran public opinion if it chose to do so, but only at the risk of a highly undesirable deterioration of its relations with Earth.

AADD hoped to dampen speculation regarding intelligent life on Europa. The probability of finding such life was indeed low, but if *Swordfish* had done it, AADD needed to establish that fact quickly in order to devise an effective damage control strategy.

And so, less than twenty-four hours after *Swordfish* disappeared, we were dispatched to Europa.

I SIPPED MY COFFEE. "I wouldn't say the odds of finding a creature like that in these waters are terribly high." I wasn't saying this because I hoped it was true. It was my opinion as a scientist. "As an exobiologist, I'd have to assume it's impossible for a creature big enough to swallow a submarine to be swimming around on Europa. Our geophysical simulations show that there are limits to the energy that a system of hydrothermal vents can put out. It's hard to believe that vents with enough energy to sustain a large life-form could exist anywhere on a body this size. If there were, we would've noticed them by now. But let's say they exist, just for argument's sake. How could a large life-form survive out here, so far from a thermal energy source?"

"You never know until you go." Kohara increased our speed by a small increment. "Kameda, how's Salmon?"

"All systems nominal."

"Dr. Kurokawa, are you sure that all we're obliged to do is release the robot once we reach the location where *Swordfish* was lost?"

"Yes, but it'll take more than two or three days for Salmon to have a look around. This is a pretty big ocean."

"And we have to remain on station till it's finished its survey?"

"Wasn't that covered in the contract?" I asked.

"I don't remember." At this, the three of us checked the agreement on our webs. It was foolish to read through a document when you could call it up whenever you needed it.

"It says here, 'The officer in charge is free to exercise discretion to preserve the safety of the vessel,'" I read. "It also says something about keeping me out of harm's way, but that's the same as preserving the safety of the ship, I guess."

"I just wanted to hear you say it," said Kohara.

I couldn't say I was one of AADD's most distinguished exobiologists, but I did develop Salmon, and that was the reason I was here dealing with a problem that could well blow up into something serious for AADD. In fact, I wasn't really a pure exobiologist. Rather, I specialized in the potential pitfalls of first contact with an alien civilization.

The debate over how humanity should respond to contact with an advanced nonhuman species stretched back to the twentieth century. Salmon's AI was designed as a first step toward a fully functional go-between for humanity in the event of such contact. The AI was equipped with cutting-edge learning algorithms to search for evidence of rule-based behavior—the "common sense" embodied in its programming. If the robot encountered an intelligent life-form, that life-form would become the focus of its learning. Given sufficient exposure to alien behavior, the AI was capable of acquiring the rules governing that behavior and could pass them on to its human handlers, making it possible for humans to acquire tacit alien knowledge, subject, of course, to the limitations of human-designed learning algorithms. The knowledge obtained would permit an estimate of the degree of danger—if any—posed by that alien civilization. The data transmitted by the AI would also make radio or laser communication far more efficient. To prevent the aliens from learning too much about humans, any attempt to dismantle the robot would cause the AI to self-destruct.

Although Salmon was barely past the basic concept stage, it was the only tool available to investigate whether an intelligent life-form was at large on Europa. Still, there was a reason why we weren't relying solely on Salmon but were also conducting manned investigations from aboard *Remora*. AADD had to prove that it was performing a good-faith, unbiased investigation.

<hr />

NOTHING OUT OF THE ORDINARY happened as we approached the site of *Swordfish*'s disappearance, but the moment we arrived things changed. Something scrambled *Remora*'s radar data; the next instant the display went dark. The same thing happened with Salmon's radar.

"Kameda, what did you do?" barked the captain.

"Nothing. Something's messing with the lasers."

Kohara disengaged the screw, left the cockpit, and came to the rear of the bridge where Kameda and I sat. With the radar out and *Remora* blind, proceeding any further would be risky. The idling of the diesel engine was barely audible; *Remora* continued to drift forward under her own inertia.

Kohara and I stood behind Kameda, peering at his console.

Kameda had isolated the radar's computer from the network, but it still wouldn't respond to his commands. He ran a detailed trace, showing each execution of the source code in time sequence. "Okay, here it is."

"What happened?" asked the captain.

"The sonar and radar are giving us conflicting data. That's why the computer couldn't process the image. The sonar says there's nothing ahead of us. The radar says we're facing some sort of huge wall."

"A wall?"

"That's what the radar's telling us, Captain."

At that moment we felt a slight increase in speed. None of us gave it a thought; it might have been some local current. "Do all the testing you want." I sighed. "Something always happens when you get the gear out into the field."

Kameda turned to look at the captain. "What next?"

"Reboot the radar. If that doesn't work, we'll have to try analyzing the error log."

Kameda rebooted Salmon's radar. Now it seemed to work in perfect sync with the sonar. The monitor showed nothing ahead of the ship. "Cap'n, what are the onboard sensors showing? I'm seeing a lot of organic matter. Wow, temperature's up too—it's five degrees outside."

I ran a diagnostics program I'd developed to analyze Salmon's sonar data on my web. "I think I know what caused the problem—and why the temperature's rising."

"What do you mean?" said Kohara.

"Are we moving forward, Captain?"

"Probably a bit, just our inertia. Why?"

"We had a wall of organic matter in front of us earlier. It wasn't returning any echoes because it was absorbing the sonar." I cursed myself for my carelessness as I rebooted Salmon's sensing systems. Now there was no disagreement with *Remora*'s sensors—the ocean ahead was empty. "We've gone through some kind of wall, Captain.

The radar saw it, but it absorbed the sonar. That's what confused the system. The acceleration we noticed just now was probably *Remora* penetrating the wall. Her inertia took us right through it. *Swordfish*'s dragon metaphor suggests that the object had the same surface characteristics as whatever it was we just passed through. I think we may be in the belly of the beast."

"We can't be inside a dragon. What nonsense," growled Kohara.

"Maybe 'inside' isn't the right word. We're within something connected with *Swordfish*'s disappearance. A gigantic egg, maybe, or a nest. Or something else entirely. But I'm certain we're within something."

"Then *Swordfish* should be here too," said Kameda.

The captain and I exchanged glances. Kameda was probably right; it would make sense. This might well be some kind of habitat or nest. Then again, it might be a huge collective organism. Maybe it spat *Swordfish* out, as it might shortly do to us as part of some immune reaction. At this point it was impossible to tell.

"Let's drop Salmon and get the hell out of here," said Kohara.

"Cap'n, we can't just—"

"—leave, Kameda? You mean without trying to find *Swordfish*? You're right, they may be here. But if they are, it means there's something else here that we need to steer clear of. I don't see anything we can do to help them. On the contrary—if this creature attacks us, no one can come to our aid. *Swordfish* and *Remora* are the only vessels in the solar system that can dive these waters."

"I agree with the captain," I said. "Let's release Salmon and clear out of here. Once we have a chance to analyze the data, we'll have a better idea of how to proceed."

Kohara seemed relieved to have gotten backup from a scientist. For my part I was glad to hear him talking sense. The last thing AADD needed right now was more fatalities. The danger to *Remora* was also a danger to AADD. Kameda didn't bother to argue the point further.

Kohara increased power to the engine. RPM should have risen immediately, but nothing happened. "What's the story? Why's she running so hot?"

"It looks like something's blocking the cooling intake. I'll increase power to the pump."

At first this seemed to help, but then the intake jammed again. At length, after alternately increasing and decreasing power to the pump, Kameda managed to clear the line and water started to flow again. The engine began to settle down, though it was still running a bit hot.

But a still bigger problem awaited us. When Kohara engaged the screw, nothing happened. We were dead in the water.

"Cap'n, the protection circuit just kicked in."

"I was half expecting that."

"What's happening?" I said.

"Something's tangled in the screw. If the load exceeds a certain level, a protection circuit cuts power to the motor. For some reason that just happened."

"Is it the same thing that blocked the cooling intake?" The radar showed nothing ahead of *Remora*—not even fish, much less a dragon.

"Dr. Kurokawa, we still have Salmon, right?"

"Yes, I haven't released the cable yet."

"Can you walk her around the ship and see what's out there?"

I routed Salmon's sensing data to their webs, so they could monitor its progress, and began to guide the robot toward the rear of the boat.

"What the hell is *that*?" Everyone froze. More than half the length of *Remora*, from the screw forward, had disappeared down the gullet of some giant creature. "Now we know why the screw won't turn."

It seemed to be the same as the creature captured by *Swordfish*'s radar, but not quite as large. The tail was quite a bit shorter and the body was more compressed. It reminded me of a hydra—not the nine-headed monster of Greek myth, but class Hydrozoa, family Hydridae, genus *Hydra*. On Earth these tiny water-dwellers had rubbery, tubular bodies they could compress or extend to swallow food larger than themselves. The thing that was busily trying to swallow *Remora* looked almost identical. Or maybe it was some jellyfish-like species?

Kohara grabbed the hydrophone to alert the support team, but the creature's body attenuated the ultrasound. Communication was now impossible. Up on the surface, they were probably already panicking.

"Why didn't we just send a robot in the first place and have done with it?" muttered Kohara. "Then we wouldn't be dropping like flies." This was directed at me. I wasn't in a position to disagree, but for AADD the right course consisted of demonstrating to the people of Earth that we would go to any length to investigate the possibility of extraterrestrial life. And now here we were.

"Come on, Captain," said Kameda. "This mission is too important to leave to robots. Hey, it's really hot. It's forty degrees!"

"Where's the air conditioning?"

"Hold on . . . Protection circuit again."

"What the hell for?"

"We can't vent the heat. The system won't run above a certain temperature."

Just then we were all struck by more or less the same thought. The water temperature was five degrees. Why would heat be building up in the boat?

I hurriedly switched Salmon's sensors to infrared. The surface of the creature's body was almost as cold as the surrounding environment. But by now the cooling water from *Remora* must be quite hot—which would make this coldness impossible unless the cells of the creature's body were highly insulating. This wouldn't be surprising if its only source of energy was heat from hydrothermal vents.

"Maybe we should take a sample with the manipulator," said Kameda.

"We don't have time to analyze it."

"It's not the sample, Captain. It's what happens when we take it. Maybe it'll spit us out."

"You're going to have a long life, Kameda."

"That was the general idea."

I wasn't sure the creature would respond to pain by spitting us out—or if it would even experience pain at all. But we decided to try. It might give us a clue as to how to escape. And if we were destined to die, we wanted to know something about what was to kill us.

Luckily *Remora*'s manipulator was mounted on the bow. It was a huge gripper, like the oversized claw of a fiddler crab, with separate, smaller arms extending to either side for precision work. Each appendage was equipped with a camera. The surface of the gripper was translucent and could emit light for illumination, eliminating the need to manipulate spotlights. The visibility outside was poor, but not so poor as to completely obscure the tip of the gripper.

I grasped the manipulator's joystick for the first time. Facility with the controls wasn't as important right now as familiarity with the thing that was about to be manipulated. And if I didn't handle this myself, I wouldn't be doing my part to help deal with the danger.

Remora's pressure hull was ultrapure specialty steel, the number of openings in it kept to a minimum. The manipulator and its cameras were controlled by a computer in a separate pressure hull; a single strand of optical fiber led to where I sat. Most of the manipulator's movements were AI-controlled, leaving only selection of objective and sequence of operations to the operator. I had a pseudosensation of touch through the glove, but no sense of force feedback.

I moved the gripper cautiously. The creature ignored it. The cameras showed more than half the ship engulfed in a gray-white mass. As if from a great distance, I heard someone's voice say nervously, "I'm taking a sample."

It occurred to me that the thing attempting to swallow *Remora* might be a different species from the one that had attacked *Swordfish*. I had a feeling the creature would not react. The gripper brushed against the creature. No reaction. I pinched a fold of tissue with the gripper. The surface rippled like jelly, but there was still no reaction.

"Dr. Kurokawa—look at the temperature."

The manipulator was tipped with a simple sensor array. The temperature under the creature's skin was close to forty degrees. I gingerly lifted a large section of tissue with the gripper. To my surprise it immediately tore away, the detached tissue quickly reforming itself into a sphere. No fluid leaked from the wound, which closed up in seconds.

"Is this thing indestructible?" marveled Kohara.

"Captain, it may be an alien life-form but I doubt it's indestructible." A theory was forming in my mind based on what we were seeing. The sphere of tissue drifted toward the manipulator like a ball in a zero-G game of water polo. I guided it into a collection cylinder on the hull with one of the smaller manipulator arms. *Remora* had six of these containers, each with a chamber—almost a miniature laboratory—equipped with a microscope, chemical sensors, manipulators, and other simple experimental apparatus. It was vital to ensure that no samples actually entered the ship, where the risk of contamination in either direction would be hard to control.

I sealed the collection cylinder, evacuated the water, and moved the sample into the testing chamber. I took a slice of tissue with the manipulator and examined it carefully with the microscope.

"Take a look, Captain. Here's your dragon." The monitor showed a confused jumble of cells of all sizes and shapes, some similar, some very distinctively different. Some cells were fibrous and long, others were organized into lumps of a single cell type. Everything was enveloped in some gelatinous, transparent substance, probably macromolecular.

"I don't see any real structure," said Kohara.

"It looks like chaos, but I think it's probably an organized chaos. These are cell colonies. We may be looking at an ecosystem."

"An ecosystem?"

"I won't be able to confirm it until we return to the base and I can run these tests on better equipment, but this gel-like substance is probably an insulator. This is probably how colonies store heat from hydrothermal vents. Those vents are going to be localized, their heat a precious resource. The whole ecosystem of cell colonies would be organized around this trapped heat. The interior contains warm water. The water outside the ecosystem is close to freezing. The thermal gradient could drive cellular metabolic activity."

"So that's why the piece you pulled off formed into a sphere, to retain the heat?"

"It's the most efficient shape for minimizing surface area relative to volume. The surface would include cells that are hypersensitive to changes in the temperature. This far from the ocean floor, waste heat from our cooling system would be a very attractive source of energy. And these cells here"—I zoomed in with the monitor—"are probably the source of this insulating substance."

The spherical cells on the monitor were by far the most numerous. Around three-quarters of their volume was a reservoir for that strange, transparent slime.

"So is this what got *Swordfish*?"

"The heat from *Remora*'s diesel is really pretty minimal. But *Swordfish* used proton/antiproton annihilation as a power source. That would create a huge heat wake. I don't think anything was actually chasing them—I think the 'dragon' they saw was cell colonies forming in their wake. The truth is as simple as that."

Kohara nodded. "And the faster they went, the more heat they put out and the faster the colonies formed behind them."

"Ultimately the entire ship would have been enveloped, blocking the cooling vents and bringing the ship to a halt. But without knowing what was happening, the crew would have continued applying power to try to escape. And that could have taken them below crush depth."

"But, Dr. Kurokawa, if you're right, there'd have to be billions of loose cells in every cubic centimeter of Europa's ocean. We haven't seen any evidence of that."

"*Swordfish* and *Remora* both encountered waters with much higher ambient cell concentrations—and in both cases, the concentrations skyrocketed without warning. My guess is that the wall we passed through is the outer surface of the real ecosystem."

"What do you mean by 'real'?"

"The usual form this ecosystem takes on Europa—a gigantic balloon coated with insulating gel. The balloon's volume increases by the cube of its radius, while the surface only increases by its square. So the bigger the better—a giant sphere is the most efficient way to exploit large amounts of trapped hydrothermal energy. Europa may harbor millions of these spherical ecosystems, hundreds or thousands of meters across. The trapped heat causes the colonies to rise. After they cool, they descend again to the seabed, to recharge around another vent or dissociate until the next thermal opportunity presents itself. That's why we only found traces of life—until we penetrated the wall."

"Look, Dr. Kurokawa. I'm not arguing for the sake of arguing, but if these ecosystems form as you say, what would they be doing at these shallow depths? If the heat the cell colonies need is on the seafloor, wouldn't venturing a hundred klicks away be suicidal? There's no heat source this far up, unless you're lucky enough to run into the occasional submarine."

"What do you mean, Cap'n? There's a great heat source up here."

"And what might that be?"

"The gateway. Energy from Kali is keeping it ice free."

Kameda's horoscope had been right. Our fate was completely under the influence of Mars and Uranus after all.

———◦⋯◦———

WE FINALLY BROKE FREE by venting a huge bubble of cold, compressed air from our ballast tanks. The sudden drop in temperature and the pressure of air gushing from *Remora* scattered the colonies into a rain of small spheres that sank out of sight.

To avoid emitting heat and attracting other colonies, we recovered Salmon and used its power supply to creep slowly back to the gateway. Those twenty kilometers were the worst part of the mission—the heating had to be shut down and the temperature in the boat dropped close to freezing. On the way, Kameda made some tepid coffee.

"This is great coffee, Kameda," said the captain.

"I didn't know you were capable of praise, Cap'n. This is quite a discovery."

Back at base, we resupplied and made some hurried modifications to reduce *Remora*'s heat signature. After we'd retraced our steps to the colony, we quickly located *Swordfish* with the help of infrared sensors and established contact with her crew. Following our instructions, they shut down their power plant and blew compressed air from their tanks to free themselves from the embrace of the "dragon," which fragmented into a number of huge spheres. We then guided *Swordfish* through the colony wall and safely back to the gateway. It had been four days since we had first dived into Europa's icy waters.

Before the day was out, AADD had announced to the solar system that there were no dragons on Europa. The captain of *Swordfish* told the media that the life-form they had encountered was similar to plankton. The discovery of extraterrestrial life preoccupied the media for weeks, and for weeks people on Earth were exposed to information about extraterrestrial "plankton." Eventually, talk of intelligent life on Europa ceased.

———— ●✦● ————

THREE MONTHS LATER Kohara and Kameda dropped by my lab at AADD's Jupiter Development Center on Mars. Their rescue of *Swordfish* had paid dividends: their team had recently been entrusted with development of all submarines for the exploration of Europa.

A base was under construction and both men were scheduled to depart soon for Jupiter. Before their departure they wanted to update themselves on my research, which was still confidential except to members of their team.

We stood before a large monitor with a view of the lab's giant aquarium. "We keep the light levels in the tank close to darkness to simulate conditions on Europa. Everything that goes on is monitored with night-vision cameras."

The monitor showed a CG-enhanced view of Salmon threading its way through a forest of gelatinous shapes anchored to the bed of the tank.

"What are those, anemones?" asked Kameda.

"They were cloned from that sample we took on Europa. I like to call them Hydra."

"But the colonies on Europa are spherical!"

"Blame it on Salmon. Its AI is designed to learn from its environment. The cell colonies respond to changes in their environment. We wouldn't mistake that for intelligence, but Salmon's AI doesn't understand that these are just colonies of different cell types. The colonies responded to Salmon's heat emissions. The AI thought that was intelligent behavior and paid them closer attention. This cycle kept repeating until the colonies assumed the anemone shape you see here. Now there's a stable equilibrium between the AI and the colonies."

"So are these creatures actually intelligent, Dr. Kurokawa?"

Were they? It was a simple question, after all. In pursuit of answers to such questions, I'd given up structural engineering to become a scientist studying intelligence. But during my twenty years of research, I had uncovered only progressively deeper levels of the same question—and no answers.

"Are either of you familiar with the story of how Ouroboros, the ring around Kali, was nearly destroyed twenty-some years ago through miscommunication with an AI?"

"I heard about it, but I don't know the details," said Kameda.

"I witnessed the whole incident. It's why I decided to devote myself to this research."

"So you've been working on this question for that long? And what conclusions have you come to?"

"Simply put? None." That was the best answer I could give. Given the opportunity I could talk about the subject for hours, I had that much to say. But if I had to boil everything down to a conclusion, "none" was the only answer I could give.

Sometimes this thought crossed my mind:

If I had to prove I was intelligent, could I do it?

PROGRESS IN TOOL MAKING probably triggered the blossoming of human cognition. Tools can reveal that which lies beyond cognition, and tools enabled humans to discover that apparently accidental events had their proper causes.

For example, most astronomical events—the fall of a meteor or the passing of a comet—were first believed to be omens or portents. But by calculating orbits, humankind learned to predict these events.

As technology progressed, humanity advanced into space, growing more intelligent still. Humans cannot sense infrared radiation, much less electromagnetic or gravity waves. But they learned to build devices to detect these phenomena, and these devices expanded their cognitive capacity. They came to understand that things once thought inexplicable were inevitable.

Thanks to superb observational technology, humanity was about to unlock the mystery behind the sudden appearance of a tiny black hole in the solar system. But not all cognitive abilities can be extended by machines. Sometimes cognition can only be expanded by the greatest mystery of all—human action.

THE VOICE OF EINGANA
A.D. 2163

1

NINETY ASTRONOMICAL UNITS from the Sun, space reclaims its true darkness. At three times the distance from the Sun to Uranus—twelve hours at the speed of light—sunlight attenuates to nearly one-tenth of one percent of its intensity on Earth. The Sun is still the brightest object in the heavens by far—magnitude minus seventeen, far brighter than Sirius. Still, at this distance it is just another star in the sky.

This sun-star hung over Shocho Kanda as she stood on the hull of *Shantak II*. To determine her position with respect to the outer planets, the first thing she did was look for the Sun.

First she adjusted the opacity setting of her helmet's visor to bring the Sun's brightness to an index value. This yielded her exact distance from the Sun. The position of Sirius or Canopus would then tell her where she was relative to the rest of the solar system. None of this was necessary, of course. The solar system was dotted with positioning satellites to guide space traffic, and these could give Shocho her position to within a few meters' accuracy. But whenever she EVA'd, she confirmed her location herself. It was a kind of ritual. Machines can fail; that was more than reason enough.

Even in the Sun's dim light, the amplification circuits in Shocho's visor let her find her way along the hull of *Shantak II*. The space around her was hung with mirrors tens of kilometers across, polished discs shimmering with starlight. There were more than twenty-five thousand of them in this region of space. Though invisible from where she stood, there was also a laser interferometer for measuring gravity waves, tens of kilometers long. The crew of *Shantak II* controlled the devices, analyzing the information they gathered and carrying out occasional repairs.

After confirming her location, Shocho turned to the task at hand: inspecting *Shantak II*'s communications module. Most of the ship's communications were laser based. The main comm unit floated above the hull, cradled in a magnetic field to isolate it from vibration. It looked like the compound eye of an insect, its small lenses tracking sun and stars to maintain its orientation. In its center was a huge optical module housing a laser transmitter. Although the unit looked like a huge eye, it functioned more as an ear and mouth.

"Do you really think we'll find something amiss with the transmitter?"

EVA was always carried out with a partner. Chaa was looking at Shocho, waiting for an answer. Shocho couldn't read his expression; the suit visors were electroplated with reflective gold. But it was clear from Chaa's voice that he didn't think this EVA would turn up anything.

"It's odd. If someone deliberately disabled the comm system, they'd have to physically access the optical module."

"They'd still need the access codes. I doubt our Terran guests are that sophisticated, which means the blackout must be real. No one's transmitting." In other words, they should be looking for answers inside the ship, not out here on the hull.

"Chaa, you realize we're in a difficult situation right now?"

"I was going to ask you the same question."

The conversation was taking place between agent programs. Web implants extended their users' sensorium and facilitated communication. While agent programs didn't guarantee perfect mutual understanding, Shocho and Chaa had accumulated hundreds of hours working together. Each had an accurate grasp of the other's capabilities. Still, at this moment neither understood what the other was thinking.

"We should be doing something more productive than checking the comm unit," Chaa persisted. "We might be at war with Earth already."

"There isn't going to be any war. They don't have a fraction of the ships we do, even without the energy supplies Kali gives us. Even if there's actual fighting, it won't last beyond a few limited engagements. That's hardly a war."

"You don't really believe that, do you? It's no secret the Terrans are building armed spacecraft capable of reaching the outer planets."

"And how are they going to reach Mars without being detected, much less Jupiter? There are hundreds of unmanned ships shuttling around the solar system with energy transmitted from the accretion disk. We can track those ships to within a few meters. Do you really think an armed Terran spacecraft could conduct offensive operations in that environment?"

"If they're sufficiently determined there's no telling what an enemy is capable of."

Chaa's use of the term *enemy* was revealing. He seemed to have already made up his mind. Shocho wished she could see his expression.

"So you think they'll start a war they can't win?" They were arguing past each other. She was focused on capabilities; he cared only about intent.

"Your ancestors were Japanese, Shocho. You should know humans don't always make rational decisions. Organizations can run amok and behave in irrational ways. It's clear from your history. Japan's military started the Pacific War even though they knew they didn't have a chance of winning it. And when it was clear they'd be defeated, it took them two years to summon up the will to end it. What's rational about a kamikaze attack? History hasn't ended, and history will always include people who are prepared to start wars they can't win."

Chaa was a scholar with a deep understanding of humanity's past. His insights had frequently proven useful. But his example from Japanese history extended back more than two centuries. Shocho's ancestral ties to Earth had ended a century ago.

"*We* learned from the people who preceded us into space. Are you saying Terrans can't learn from their own history?"

"It's not a matter of their capacity to be rational. The problem is simple: they hate us."

◆•┃•◆

SHANTAK II was a self-propelled observation platform nearly three times farther from the Sun than Neptune. The reason for its placement here, half a light-day from the Sun, was to carry out precise observations of the dwarf galaxy Eingana. The Terran research vessel *Discovery* had been deployed opposite *Shantak II* in the same circumsolar orbit. Separated by a full light-day, the two ships would soon begin to share differential data, acting as a titanic laser interferometer.

Dwarf galaxy Eingana was a tiny agglomeration of objects. The Eingana of Australian aboriginal legend was a snake goddess, a creator whose appearance nonetheless often foretold calamity. The dwarf galaxy christened with this name hovered just above the plane of the Milky Way, almost touching it. For its mass, Eingana was inexplicably dark. No existing theory or model fit its observed characteristics, and thus the recently discovered galaxy threatened to upset the prevailing models of stellar and planetary evolution. Astronomers feared and welcomed Eingana as a potential destroyer of paradigms.

Shantak II was two huge spars, five hundred meters long and fifty meters wide, joined at right angles to form a trussed cross. The spars themselves were capable of acting as a laser gravity-wave interferometer. Trusses seventy meters from the apex formed a platform a hundred meters square. At the center was the main power module—a hybrid fusion reactor with fusion pellets ignited by the heat from proton/antiproton annihilation—and another module containing communications and life-support systems. At the corners of the square, perched on the spars, were habitat modules and work spaces for the crew.

Shantak II was a spacecraft, an observatory, and even a factory, as well as being home to fifty AADD crew. Its mission was a joint project with Earth; there were ten Terran scientists aboard. There were no AADD crew on *Discovery*, reflecting the fact that the project wasn't truly collaborative. AADD didn't make an issue of this. There was little of interest they could learn from embedding people on a Terran spacecraft.

At first, the observations went smoothly. But then something happened that changed everything: a man-made communications blackout.

Even at the speed of light, round-trip communication with the inner solar system took a full day—not ideal for an exchange of urgent messages. Most communication was via laser, complicating line-of-sight transmissions passing close to the Sun. The solution was to route most comm traffic through relay stations on the Trojan asteroids. This was how *Shantak II* and *Discovery* communicated. The Trojans were also the relay for other research installations throughout the solar system.

The early stages of the project had been marked by tensions between AADD and Earth. But the unprecedented scale and shared scientific promise of the project had gradually dampened any mutual suspicion—not least because as soon as observation commenced it became clear that Eingana was a scientific enigma.

Until the day when transmissions from the rest of the solar system ceased, Shocho had seen for herself how the project was fostering a sense of solidarity that overcame differences between AADD and Earth. That was why the day when the message arrived remained so clear in her memory. She had been with the project leader, Dr. Atwood, in the central lounge. Atwood had a hard time organizing his theories without someone to act as a sounding board.

"Commander Kanda, do you know what our solar system looks like from a distance?"

"No, I can't say I do. We're not far out enough for that."

"Right. Well, you would think that from a distance any planetary system—not just our own—would appear to have a central star orbited by planetary bodies in empty space. But the truth is rather different. In infrared, clouds of asteroids and minor chunks of matter would shine far more brightly than the planets. The solar system, seen from the proper distance, would appear as a series of brightly shining rings surrounding the Sun, with spaces between the rings swept clean by the planets. The interaction of the star with the dust that orbits it creates this sort of phenomenon.

"Given its near-total lack of luminosity, our dwarf galaxy could theoretically be a group of brown dwarfs. But in that case we should be seeing circumstellar dust rings emitting in the infrared. We're already very familiar with this type of star from observations in our own galaxy. Since Eingana is already colliding with our own galaxy, we should be able to confirm the presence of brown dwarfs—if, in fact, there are any."

"Maybe there's no dust?" said Shocho. "That would explain the prevalence of brown dwarfs. Not enough material for bigger stars to form."

"Good guess, but that doesn't get us off the hook. Eingana's interstellar material is emitting photons in response to light coming from our galaxy. There does, in fact, seem to be a fair amount of such material present. But our theories of star formation suggest that there's more than enough material for the formation of larger, brighter stars. Our simulations point to the same conclusion."

"Then maybe you don't have brown dwarfs after all. Something smaller?" Shocho was speaking from intuition now. "Black holes or something else that can't easily be observed. If you're seeing X-rays as well as gravity waves, that would clinch it."

"We *are* seeing X-rays. You're right. Our observations are preliminary, but taking the data at face value, Eingana doesn't contain a single star. It's composed entirely of black holes with stellar masses."

Shocho was no astronomer, but she did have a general knowledge of the subject, and she knew that what Atwood was proposing flew in the face of established theory. No galaxy like the one he was describing had ever been observed.

"A galaxy of black holes?"

"It's the best-fit conclusion for the data. Hard to believe, though."

Just then the message came through, addressed to Atwood and Shocho as the senior AADD crewmembers aboard *Shantak II:*

In view of possible armed conflict with Earth, further comm traffic will be restricted to scientific data, effective immediately.

With this, transmissions to *Shantak II* from other parts of the solar system ceased completely. The Trojan relay stations ignored Shocho's requests for confirmation.

It was unsettling. The message was properly formatted and looked genuine. It was sent by the Guardian steering committee, but sending it only to Atwood and Shocho was unusual. A message like this would normally have been copied to all AADD personnel. Shocho had to retransmit the message to the rest of the crew herself.

Even more unsettling, the ten Terran crewmembers did not receive a similar message from Earth. This left them even more anxious than the rest. What would their status be if war broke out?

The Terrans quickly split into two factions. The moderates centered around Dr. Whitley, their African Japanese senior representative. His deputy, Japanese American Maria Teranishi, was the leader of the hard-liners: "AADD must immediately disclose all information in its possession. As U.S. representative on *Shantak II,* I demand an explanation!"

In fact, Shocho had received nothing more than the one short message from the Guardians. But the Terrans were not convinced.

———◦•◦•◦———

THE DAYS PASSED and the blackout continued. Oddly, *Shantak II* continued receiving routine observational data from *Discovery*.

In other words, the relay stations were functioning. The blackout wasn't due to some technical issue.

Of course, the AADD crew didn't simply wait passively for matters to be resolved. Using the backup comm system, they attempted to contact both Mars and the Chandrasekhar Space Station in orbit around Uranus in case something was amiss with their main system. The position of the planets in their orbits put Uranus, Saturn, Mars, and Jupiter in the same relatively narrow angle, making direct transmission possible. But the result was the same for each planet—no response. As might have been expected, the Terran crew had insisted on bringing along their own comm system but were unable to establish contact with Earth, which seemed to baffle them. Apparently the blackout extended throughout solar system.

Dr. Whitley and the other moderates did their best to restrain the hard-liners, but they possessed no inside information to help them make their case. And Dr. Whitley didn't have the influence of Teranishi, who was also the U.S. representative aboard *Shantak II*. As time went on, her influence only seemed to grow stronger.

Moderate/hard-line conflicts were not confined to the Terran crew. Opinion was split among the AADD crew for the same reason—the lack of further situation updates. Even the Guardians responsible for shipboard security were divided. The AADD hard-line faction was also gradually gaining influence. Still, however much the hard-line factions on both sides might want to take action, they had no concrete ideas about what sort of action to take. Isolated as they were from the rest of the solar system, there was nothing they could do except continue their observations. This only aggravated their frustrations.

The only person aboard *Shantak II* who seemed unconcerned was Dr. Atwood, the project leader. Atwood was also the youngest crewmember and one of AADD's group of emerging stars. Though barely out of his teens, he was a genius. His generation knew of the solar system only as a wealthy place. Partially due to this, his sunny outlook didn't have much impact on the older people around him.

The atmosphere aboard ship was beginning to resemble the twentieth century's Cold War—all because of one cryptic transmission.

"THERE'S NO SIGN the system has been tampered with. We ought to get back," said Chaa, without much expectation that Shocho would agree. But she had no objection. If the system hadn't been tampered with there was no reason for them to be out here.

"Any sabotage that's not immediately visible," said Shocho, "would have to have been committed by someone who knows the system in detail."

"Or maybe there really is a war going on and they've blocked all transmissions."

Without further discussion, they decided to end their EVA. But even before they reached the air lock they had news. The Terrans had barricaded themselves in their quarters.

2

SHOCHO AND CHAA felt the tension emanating from the central lounge as soon as they were out of their suits. The entrance to the west and south modules had been blocked by a webwork of synthetic netting, usually used on space stations to provide hand- and footholds for astronauts during EVA. The Terrans had used it to erect a barricade.

Three of the exits from the central lounge gave access to the modules at the corners of the platform. The east module, which housed the AADD crew, and the north module, which held the observational equipment, had their own entrances. The west module, where the Terrans lived, and the south module, used as a workshop, shared a single entrance leading to separate corridors at right angles. The lounge was used for meetings and events; because there was almost no equipment there, the walls were covered with vegetation adapted to zero G. Each wall was covered with different types and colors of vegetation, offering a floating astronaut many different decorative details to admire.

The Terrans' barricade stretched across the entrance to the west and south modules. It was anchored to the netting behind the plants, making it difficult to gain access from the side. In the center of the netting was a circular metal hoop, apparently to allow movement in and out. But now it was tightly closed. The message was brutally clear.

"Where the hell did they get this?"

"They must've put it together in the workshop during off-hours."

One of the crew webbed this message to Shocho and Chaa. The Terrans didn't use these devices. Their society rejected the minor physical alterations needed for a user to make the most of the web's potential. The result was that most communication with Terrans had to be carried out verbally. This made it hard to know what they were doing aboard ship when they were out of earshot.

"Does this mean they've occupied the west and south modules?" asked Shocho.

"They say they've appropriated the west module—anyway, those are their assigned living quarters. The south module is supposedly under protective occupation."

Shocho was momentarily stumped. She had to check the meaning of *appropriation* and *protective occupation*. There was also a short message that appeared to be a declaration of some sort from a Terran representative. Shocho wasn't surprised to see that it had been signed by Maria Teranishi, the Terran number two. In addition to being a scientist and the U.S. representative aboard *Shantak II,* she held the rank of colonel in the UN Marines, at least according to the signature on the message.

This was the first Shocho and the rest of the AADD crew had

heard of Teranishi's military background. Because of the comm blackout her record couldn't be confirmed, but there was little reason for Teranishi to make false statements, so it was likely true. Her multiple roles—soldier, scientist, and representative for her country's interests—were not such an unusual combination on Earth.

Teranishi's declaration was straightforward. "Any assembly of Terran citizens, no matter how small, has the right to protect its lives and property. AADD must respect these rights for all crew on *Shantak II*. Unfortunately, in the present circumstances AADD has given no credible assurance that such rights will be protected. Furthermore, AADD has provided neither an explanation of this abnormal situation nor any apology. Consequently, and in order to secure for ourselves the minimum degree of basic human rights, we hereby appropriate the west module of *Shantak II*."

In effect, Teranishi's declaration meant that any orders coming from the senior administrator—in this case, Dr. Atwood—would be ignored as far as they applied to the west module and its occupants. Of course, this also meant that no one from the AADD crew would be allowed inside.

The south and west modules of *Shantak II* were connected to the central lounge by a single hatch; the other two modules were connected to each other only via the central lounge. Airtight hatches were distributed throughout the ship, making it a simple matter to occupy any part of *Shantak II* by dogging down a single hatch.

The lounge was already accumulating off-duty AADD scientists and Guardians waiting to see how things would develop. The walls of the lounge were studded with handholds for the weightless environment. The waiting AADD crewmembers were clustered around the Terran barricade. If the Terrans were to open the door at their end of the corridor, they would probably be reminded of a circle of vultures staring down a well.

"Well, Commander? Shall we go in and retake the module?"

There were only six Guardians aboard ship including Shocho, but ten more of the crew had trained for support operations under

Shocho's direction, giving her up to fifteen people to handle security. There were also enough nonlethal weapons aboard to equip all of them.

Chaa's proposal would mean going in with weapons and full protective gear and forcibly restoring access to the module. The use of force was, in his opinion, the easiest thing for the Terrans to understand.

"What if this is provocation?" asked Shocho.

Although Chaa seemed to understand instantly what Shocho meant, she was shocked that he hadn't already thought of something so obvious. Normally Chaa would have considered such a possibility immediately. Shocho's closest associate was losing his objectivity. This was a far greater problem than trying to decide whether to storm the Terrans' barricade.

"Remember, Chaa, we don't know exactly why there's a blackout. We have no evidence that there's a war on. The Terrans have holed up in their quarters, that's all. If we respond with force, they can notify Earth with their own gear. All that does is give Earth an excuse to strike back at AADD. And anyway, what would we do with them after we turfed them out of there? The only place we could confine them would be in their quarters."

Chaa's proposal hadn't been well-considered. Although he had already sent a message to the others telling them to prepare for an assault, Shocho downgraded that order to a standby alert. Chaa seemed dissatisfied but didn't argue. He merely said, "Shocho, whose side are you on, really?"

For the moment, Shocho had averted the hard-line push to assault the Terran quarters. The next step, again at her initiative, was to communicate with the Terrans.

Luckily or not, Shocho was a senior Guardian, and the Terrans were under the impression that her security responsibilities effectively put her in command of the ship. This was a misinterpretation of AADD's organizational structure, but apparently the Terrans were incapable, given their obsession with rank and hierarchy, of seeing things differently. Shocho hadn't been completely comfortable leaving this misinterpretation in place, but if it would help solve the crisis now, she was willing to use it to maximum advantage.

The Terrans seemed slightly mollified to be approached by the ship's "captain" herself. Apparently the moderate faction was still intact, though it had been temporarily overruled by the hard-liners. It was Dr. Whitley, not Maria Teranishi, who responded to Shocho's invitation to talk.

Although physical modification was taboo on Earth, people still needed personal data devices. Thus each Terran was equipped with a PDA. Given her need to communicate frequently with the Terrans, Shocho had one too. She could easily have used her web to interface with the Terrans' PDAs, but they disliked that—in fact, they seemed insulted by it—so Shocho used the PDA when not speaking directly to them.

Dr. Whitley's face filled the tiny screen. He seemed to be in the west module's mess area. Meetings usually ended up taking place in these areas; it looked to Shocho as if she had interrupted one in progress.

"Dr. Whitley, I think you know why I've contacted you."

"We're willing to concede that the barricade was going too far. But we have no intention of apologizing."

"We're not interested in an apology."

Shocho was an experienced Guardian and certainly no stranger to Terran customs, but this obsession with apologies was something she'd never quite been able to grasp. Apologizing for creating a problem—that made sense, but there was no guarantee that an apology would help get to the root of the problem, much less solve it.

"Not interested in an apology! Well, fine, then. We'll go along with your customs in this case. We will remove the safety net immediately."

"On whose authority?"

At the word "authority," Whitley's face darkened, though he understood the need for confirmation on this particular point. It was clear even from the PDA's tiny screen that he was speaking under the watchful eyes of his team. Shocho's agent had already filtered the audio to confirm the presence of ten distinct breathing patterns in the room.

"On my authority, of course," said Whitley at length. "As senior representative of Earth."

"Not on the authority of Colonel Maria Teranishi?"

A murmur of astonishment rose around Whitley. The agent confirmed the presence of Teranishi's voice print in the audio. It wasn't possible to make out what she was saying, but the frequencies pointed to profanity with a high level of certainty.

"Not her authority. Mine." Whitley's voice print showed marked indications of stress. Likely the moderate faction was barely holding the hard-liners at bay. Some generous concessions seemed called for, as the hard-liners were likely to regain the upper hand. Still, Shocho wasn't going to mince words. Terran culture seemed to place far more emphasis on the way things were said rather than on the content. But *Shantak II* was ninety AUs from Earth, and such niceties were a waste of time.

"Remove the barricade and we're willing to recognize your exclusive control over the west module, but only for the duration of the blackout. We should avoid any unnecessary trouble that might interfere with observation work."

Whitley seemed surprised. Evidently so were the others standing outside the PDA's field of view. Teranishi could be heard exclaiming with surprise.

"You guarantee those terms on your authority, Commander Kanda?"

"Of course. It's my job."

The Terrans couldn't conceal their astonishment. This was obvious from the PDA's audio even without an analysis from the agent.

"All right, understood. We will remove the barricade, and you will recognize our exclusive occupation rights to the west module."

"Only until the blackout ends. And we'll need unrestricted access to the south module."

"Agreed. We thank you for a wise decision."

The screen went black; almost simultaneously Shocho's agent showed her mailbox filling with comments from her team. The agent selected the first message—from Chaa—and Shocho forwarded it to everyone before reading it.

What do you mean by allowing them to occupy the west module?

"The Terrans are split into moderate and hard-line factions—just as we are, in fact. We can support their moderates by making concessions now. That's the surest way to avoid further trouble. Is there a problem with that?"

You've given up too much ground. Moderate or not, they're still Terrans. Who knows what they might do? They'll probably push for more concessions. Today the west wing, tomorrow the south wing. The next thing we know they'll have the whole ship.

"You're not thinking, Chaa. Aside from the fact that we outnumber them five to one, there's no reason we have to give them the whole ship."

You're letting them off too easily, Commander. Everyone knows the Terrans are trying to take over our accretion disk. This whole incident could be part of a plot. There's no limit to their greed.

Control over the artificial accretion disk had recently become a point of contention with Earth. The Terrans argued that AADD's sole control of Kali was illegal and that representatives from Earth should take part in the operation and management of the disk on an equal basis with AADD. Naturally AADD had no intention of agreeing to that.

"Chaa, the one has nothing to do with the other. I'm not going easy on the Terrans—you've just lost your objectivity."

But Shocho knew the situation didn't allow for much optimism. Her web agent had already informed her that a bare majority of her fifteen-person team agreed with her—and some were wavering.

Among the six actual Guardians, there was only one other moderate. Chaa was sitting on the fence but was against further concessions. Shocho's biggest problem was the fact that he'd let his emotions get the better of him.

Such things did happen, of course. Before AADD was created, the challenges faced by the first Martian settlers had seemed insurmountable and Earth had had no scruples when it came to exporting its social problems to the red planet. In that sense Chaa's resentment was natural. It didn't take a leap of imagination to conclude that Earth might be secretly planning to dismember AADD and take over the accretion disk, and it would be hard to view the Terran action aboard *Shantak II* with anything but similar apprehension.

But for Shocho, these were additional reasons for preventing emotions from taking over. Passion would just make it harder to see what was in front of them. From a crisis management standpoint, that would be extremely dangerous.

"I think the Terrans would be happy to see us arguing like this," said Shocho. Chaa was generally not one to let his emotions get the better of him, and he knew that nothing was achieved by letting the rest of the team see him arguing with Shocho over fundamental matters like this.

All right, I'll trust in your command and see how things develop. But if you continue to make concessions to the Terrans and I determine it's putting the rest of us in danger, I'll proceed on my own authority. Do you agree?

"Of course. That is our way."

Shocho's agent signaled that the rest of the team was now behind Chaa.

3

THE BARRICADE blocking the entrance to the south and west modules was immediately removed, just as Whitley had promised. For the time being, observation of Eingana progressed. Data continued to accumulate. But as the days passed there were still no transmissions from within the solar system, with the exception of data coming from *Discovery,* one light-day away.

"*Discovery* continues to ignore our requests for information, Commander." Shocho heard this on a daily basis. The only thing coming from *Discovery* was numerical data. As a Terran ship, they must have had some information from Earth on the general situation, but if they did they weren't disclosing it. *Discovery* might as well have been an unmanned satellite as far as *Shantak II* was concerned.

"I wonder what's going on with their crew," ventured Chaa.

"Well, whatever they're doing, there aren't any AADD crew aboard to witness it. At least they don't have to worry about the kind of friction we're having. Still, it's a bit worrying."

"What is?"

"Why haven't they asked *us* what's going on? At least they should've sent some information to Dr. Whitley, don't you think?"

In fact, Shocho knew that Whitley *had* received confidential transmissions from *Discovery* but apparently hadn't learned much from them. Of course, Whitley had kept the content of the messages to himself. But he had sent repeated queries to *Discovery* and received little by way of reply.

Shantak II continued to wait, starved for information. Perhaps AADD and Earth were at war this very moment. No one could say.

OTHER THAN during their observation work, the Terrans and
the AADD crew had no contact. Almost mysteriously, there was
no friction, but the situation couldn't be called peaceful. It was as
though a tremendous load of energy were accumulating ahead of
a huge explosion. The slightest disturbance might release it.

Shocho, who was responsible for crisis management, soon grew
isolated from the other Guardians. She had begun to lose the support of her team.

Who could replace her? It was a decision that conferred responsibility on the people making it. Supporting Chaa would entail the
same responsibility as supporting Shocho; Shocho herself had no
intention of making a fuss about losing her team's support. Her
stoicism was part of their culture.

It would be unusual for a team leader in one of the cities of Mars
or Uranus to lose the support of her team over a disagreement, since
diversity of opinion was the norm. But there were only five other
Guardians on *Shantak II.* Shocho was truly isolated.

In point of fact, Chaa was under even more pressure. If the other
Guardians adopted his outlook, it would mean using force. This
would expose the squad to physical danger. Chaa knew this, and it
made him slightly more cautious than before. Shocho reciprocated
by steering clear of Chaa, partly from a desire to allow him to grow
through figuring things out on his own, partly because she wanted
to give him a taste of his own medicine.

Still, further problems would have to present themselves for
a process of education or punishment—whichever it ultimately
was—to be effective. Sure enough, soon after the barricade came
down, the next problem came up.

"*Hastur*? In this quadrant? You've got to be joking."

Chaa had taken Shocho into an empty meeting room to give
her the news out of earshot of the rest of the crew.

"I'm just guessing it's *Hastur.* I assumed that war would mean a
lot of ship traffic, so I carried out some observations."

Both Guardians knew the significance of Chaa's taking such a step without consulting Shocho, but both pretended not to notice it. This was not the time to test the limits of Shocho's weakened position.

"How did you find her?"

"With the spare optical telescope. No one's on it these days. I wrote a program to scan for signs of traffic."

"And what makes you think this is *Hastur*?"

"Process of elimination. Very few spacecraft—even for us—have the legs to do a round-trip all the way out here. Luckily she was decelerating when I saw her. The plasma spectrum was a match."

Hastur's antiproton propulsion system could kick the ship up to five percent light speed for voyages to the Kuiper belt and the Oort Cloud—prospecting missions to the swarms of comets in those regions. Its mission had nothing to do with servicing *Shantak II*. Normally the ship wouldn't even be in this part of the solar system.

"Did you hail her?"

"Not yet. I wanted to clear it with you."

"All right." Shocho quickly drafted a short message outlining their situation and webbed it to Chaa. He signed off on it and they sent the message using the optical telescope's laser sighting system to ensure that it wouldn't be detected by others on the ship. The sighting laser wasn't designed for communication, so the message had to be sent using Morse code.

"When can we expect an answer?"

"With no change in course, about three hours." Chaa was a hard-liner, but he was as anxious as Shocho for the news from *Hastur* to be favorable—that war had not broken out.

They spent the next three hours huddled with the rest of the security team, weighing options. Should they try to determine how all communication from the rest of the solar system could possibly be blocked if a state of war did not exist? And if war had been declared—what then?

"Receiving transmission!" The response came slightly later than expected. Maybe *Hastur*'s crew had guessed the situation on *Shantak II;* in any case, the reply was also in Morse code.

A-A-D-D t-h-i-s i-s D-e-e-p S-p-a-c-e C-r-u-i-s-e-r H-a-s-t-u-r—

The message appeared character by character. The transmission speed seemed unaccountably slow, even allowing for the use of Morse. Perhaps whoever was sending the message wanted it read off directly by the receiver.

"I was right," said Chaa. "It's *Hastur.*"

"Come on, tell us why you're here," Shocho muttered to herself.

The six Guardians assembled in the tiny room peered intently at their webs, but there was nothing further. Then, unbelievably, *Hastur* disappeared from the display. The coordinates were correct, but the display was empty, the airwaves silent.

"Something hit them! It's war after all!" shouted Chaa.

"Calm down," snapped Shocho. "Why would anyone attack *Hastur*? Is she strategically important? Are we?"

"Well . . . of course not. Then what do you think it was?"

"Maybe something harder to deal with than news of war."

"How could anything be harder than that?"

"Because the transmission was inconclusive. *Hastur* is gone. For some reason it's disappeared. If we tell the rest of the crew—and the Terrans—all we'll do is make everyone aboard even more paranoid. If we conceal what we've just seen, the Terrans are likely to find out anyway. Then there'll be hell to pay because we didn't tell them."

"But what else can we do?"

"We can't let the Terrans know we sent *Hastur* a message. I want everyone in this room to consider themselves under a gag order. The existence of the gag order is under gag order too."

Shocho's agent transmitted a summary to each team member's web for confirmation. Not even Atwood was to know what had just happened. It looked like things were going to get much worse before they got better.

IN FACT, it wasn't long before Atwood contacted Shocho, asking for a meeting. Since Atwood was the project leader, Shocho assumed that he wanted to discuss the comm blackout and the tension between the two crews. As it turned out, she wasn't wrong, but Atwood clearly saw things in an optimistic light.

"I can't imagine there'll be a war. Even if there was, the Terrans don't have a hope of winning. We've got the energy, the technology, and the economic power. If they're not fools, they won't use force. But say there's a war—what's the impact on this station? We're ninety AUs out. The Terrans can't just reach out and grab us. I don't see what all the fuss is about."

Shocho and Atwood were in one of the east module lounges. The AADD crew module was the largest on *Shantak II,* and in addition to the large mess area there were three smaller meeting lounges. When the ship was accelerating, there was enough space in the compartment to set up a small table.

In freefall the table was stored and handholds extended from the four walls, the floor, and the ceiling. The handholds were coded in six colors so the astronauts could orient themselves with respect to the rest of the ship.

Atwood lightly grasped a handhold to stabilize himself. Shocho floated facing him, in the posture that signaled a desire to talk.

Atwood's generation—he was about ten years younger than Shocho—had no doubt that AADD's society had surpassed that of Earth. They had never known AADD as anything other than a far-flung, relatively wealthy society. Occasionally, they might feel that the Terrans deserved pity, but they would never regard them as a threat.

"What did you want to speak to me about, Dr. Atwood?"

"Well, I'm sure you've noticed that the atmosphere aboard this ship isn't exactly conducive to good research work. My own staff seems to be smoldering. It's completely unnecessary, really."

Atwood apparently didn't regard the situation as all that serious. It wouldn't be surprising, thought Shocho, if the data he was obtaining on the dwarf galaxy was far more fascinating and important to him than an outbreak of garden-variety cultural chauvinism.

Atwood always seemed to be smiling; he was smiling now. Shocho couldn't personally testify to his reputed genius, but she had no doubt that he was exceptional in ways that counted at least as much.

"So I wanted to ask you: do you think we could arrange an assembly of both crews?"

"*Both* crews?"

"I'm becoming convinced that Eingana is far stranger than we could have imagined—and not only because it's populated by black holes. The question is, where did they come from? How did they form? Why is this one galaxy comprised of black holes and not other types of stars? I think the observational data we've been getting has put me onto the trail of the boggart behind it all."

"Boggart? What do you mean?"

For a moment Atwood didn't seem to understand the question. Then his face reddened and he quickly looked away. "Oh, it's nothing. Just a label I use for something only I know. A boggart is a malevolent fairy, a creature that creates strange phenomena. Somewhere there's one that holds the key to the mysterious composition of this dwarf galaxy. I think I've got this particular boggart by the tail."

Shocho felt as if a drought had ended with torrents of rain. A meeting of the whole crew might well be the only way to break the impasse between the two camps. Of course, the immediate cause of the tensions was the comm blackout, which had plunged both crews into a state of anxiety and remained unexplained. The only solution was for everyone to begin exchanging information to erase the perception that one side knew more about the situation than the other. Some sort of pretext was needed to bring everyone together, but so far Shocho had been unable to come up with something suitable. If things weren't handled the right way—if the meeting turned hostile—the Terrans would naturally end up feeling even more isolated. This would force them to harden their position.

Shocho needed something out of left field. A presentation of data wasn't likely to spark conflict between the two camps. It was the perfect pretext for a general meeting.

Ultimately, Shocho was convinced that human reason was the only answer. If problems like this were not solved with reason, they would be resolved by violence. Perhaps that was what it meant to be human. But she wasn't willing to let instinct overwhelm reason just because communication with the rest of the solar system had suddenly been interrupted.

"Dr. Atwood, how long would it take you to prepare a presentation on your theory?"

"A day? I'm pretty busy, there's a lot going on. Say two days."

"Then I'll make the arrangements."

"That'll help a great deal. We need to redirect the negative energy aboard this ship toward the mission's real purpose."

4

THE EAST MODULE MESS AREA was cleared for the meeting. In zero G, volume rather than floor space determines how many people a compartment can accommodate and the mess area was already outfitted with holographic projection equipment. This equipment was mostly for the benefit of the webless Terrans.

Atwood appeared after everyone had taken up spots along the walls of the room. His team acknowledged his entrance with the customary signal of respect, but the Terrans applauded. The applause of fewer than ten people in the group of nearly sixty sounded slightly forlorn. Shocho was not surprised to see Dr. Whitley applaud Atwood enthusiastically, but she was startled that Maria Teranishi also applauded without apparent irony. Shocho felt it was a good omen.

Oddly, Chaa and the rest of Shocho's team were nowhere to be seen. Had they decided to skip the meeting? Their agent programs hadn't even acknowledged the invitation, which was very odd. Shocho was unsettled by this, as she couldn't imagine what Chaa and the others might be up to. In any case, if the meeting ended in success the danger of a clash would be greatly reduced for the time being.

Yet success might be temporary, because the explosive truth about *Hastur*'s disappearance was still under wraps. Even though it wasn't clear what exactly had happened to the ship, the fact that the Guardians were concealing the incident was likely to light another fire sooner or later.

Shocho could feel the weight of responsibility pressing down on her. She began to wonder if keeping *Hastur* a secret had been the right decision. But it was too late to change that now. The meeting was about to begin.

"Now then. I'd like to present the results of our observations so far."

Atwood raised his hand. A holographic representation of the Milky Way and the dwarf galaxy Eingana floated in the middle of the room. The hologram reminded Shocho of an arrow that had struck a target off center. Eingana was colliding with the Milky Way at about the same distance from the galactic center as the solar system, but on the opposite side. Eingana comprised perhaps a hundred thousand objects sharing the same velocity components—compared to the Milky Way's billions—and was as slender as an arrow.

"Here you see the spatial relationship between Eingana and our galaxy, derived from gravity wave data. Eingana began its collision with the Milky Way relatively recently, probably a few tens of thousands of years ago. Given the short time span, our galaxy hasn't had time to exert much gravitational influence on Eingana. In view of the distance, this is how it looked a few tens of thousands of years ago. Still, the current situation is probably more or less as you see it here."

Suddenly Eingana disappeared from the hologram. Atwood's agent did not indicate why. Apparently he intended to deliver the whole presentation verbally for the benefit of the Terrans. They wouldn't notice this act of kindness, of course.

"Eingana has enough interstellar material to create stars. And, in fact, we know that Eingana had been giving birth to stars over a long period. So why has this dwarf galaxy never before been optically detected? The simplest explanation is that all of Eingana's stars became black holes.

"Well, none of this is news. The next question is, what could have created such an assemblage of celestial objects? Our data is primarily based on gravity waves, but we've also been running detailed radio emissions studies. We've detected some very strange emissions from Eingana, specifically from the most distant cluster of objects within that galaxy. Since we know the time it's taken the emissions to reach us, we can calculate the actual time of occurrence of the event that caused those emissions."

The hologram changed to show Eingana alone, an ordinary stellar system. Radiation pressure from the stars formed the interstellar material into spheres.

The hologram changed again. The stars shrank rapidly, becoming black holes. As the stars winked out and their gravitational relationships became chaotic, runaway accretion pulled the remaining interstellar material into the black holes. Now the black holes were surrounded by thin, faintly shining accretion disks. Eingana's radio emissions were coming from excited atoms in the spiraling disks. Some of the radio sources were rapid bursters—black holes with disks of interstellar matter undergoing sudden, violent phase transitions as they cascaded toward infinity.

"I think this hologram says it more eloquently than I could. But to summarize, until very recently—no more than a hundred thousand years ago at the most—Eingana was an unremarkable dwarf galaxy. Then, over a period of about ten millennia—the blink of an eye in astronomical terms—Eingana's stars became black holes.

"Why would normal stars suddenly behave this way? Based on the data, we can rule out supernovae. The most logical explanation would be that each of these stars encountered a small black hole with roughly the mass of a planet."

One of the Terran scientists raised his hand. "How can you be sure it was a small black hole?" This was the moment Shocho had been waiting for.

"It's the only conclusion that doesn't contradict the data," replied Atwood. "Our gravity wave observations suggest that there was a negligible change in Eingana's total mass after this transition occurred. If the stars had collided with black holes of similar mass, Eingana's velocity components would have been drastically altered."

Shocho found this theory hard to accept. At the same time, she realized her earlier discussion with Atwood had influenced his approach to this presentation.

"The idea of a star being swallowed by a black hole is naturally an oversimplification. Before that can happen, the star undergoes a dramatic structural transformation. There may be small novae caused by disruptions to the star's internal pressure and gravity after a large amount of mass had been siphoned off.

"But for most of these stars, collapsing into a black hole wouldn't have caused a change in mass—which would have allowed them to retain their planets, even though the collapse may have exerted a major effect on those planets."

Dr. Whitley raised his hand. "Dr. Atwood, assuming your theory is correct, what's your explanation for the origin of these planetary-mass black holes that supposedly initiated this process—your so-called boggarts?"

Whitley's question was obvious, but it seemed to take Atwood by surprise. "That's a question I can't answer at this time. I don't see any *natural* mechanism by which this could happen."

The room erupted with excitement. Atwood motioned for silence, but the clamor took some time to die down. The tension between the two camps had vanished in the astonishment over Atwood's conclusion. It occurred to Shocho that Atwood had suggested this presentation in order to achieve just this effect. Although he gave the impression of not paying much attention to shipboard politics, he had actually been well aware of them. Shocho began to reassess her opinion of this young man. This was certainly the first Shocho had heard of the possibility that planets had been somehow transformed into micro black holes.

So this presentation was Atwood's strategy for restoring harmony. Before the commotion had died down, he dropped yet another unexpected bomb.

"We've noticed something extremely interesting in our gravity wave data. We'd like to gather more data just to be sure, but apparently a highly directional beam of gravity waves is emanating from one region of Eingana. Not only is the beam tightly focused, it's also highly coherent—almost a kind of gravity wave laser.

"Laserlike phenomena sometimes occur in nature, though of course these are very rare. I'd like to regard this as a new, very interesting natural phenomenon, but there's a stumbling block to that explanation: the beam is obviously modulated. We don't have any idea what this might mean. There's no evidence that the modulation follows a meaningful pattern, at least not with the existing data. But what we are seeing follows a consistent modulation protocol. In other words, this looks like formatted data."

Now there was pandemonium. Shocho was sorry that the other Guardians were missing this moment, clearly a turning point in the history of the human species.

"So how should we interpret these data?" asked Atwood.

Shocho deeply admired Atwood's competence. He had merely implied that the signal was from an intelligent nonhuman source. Still, if that was the case, then a confrontation between AADD and the Terrans would seem truly absurd. And yet, Atwood had said none of this directly. He wanted his listeners to come to that conclusion on their own.

Shocho was basking in relief that things were going so well when Maria Teranishi spoke up. "The meaning of this discovery is clear. A gravity wave laser proves the existence of a nonhuman civilization. It's the only natural conclusion. But why is Eingana composed only of black holes? I'm probably the only astronomer here with a military background, and when I apply Occam's razor, what it tells me—the simplest, cleanest explanation—is that this dwarf galaxy is evidence of a victory by one civilization over another. It's a relic of war."

"War? Dr. Teranishi, do you actually believe that this is evidence of a conflict between two alien civilizations?" asked Atwood.

"It's the most logical explanation. There was a war. One side wielded small black holes as weapons and fired them into the stars of their enemies. The other side responded with similar weapons. If there is one constant in human history, it's that monopolies on military technology don't last forever."

Again the room was filled with the din of voices. The sense of species solidarity from a moment before had evaporated at Teranishi's suggestion of interstellar warfare. At least for the Terrans, the concept of a clash of civilizations was fresh and immediate.

"Listen, everyone," said Teranishi. "Eingana's civilization did not perish. It triumphed. If that gravity wave laser is sending meaningful signals from an intelligent life-form, then its civilization lives on. At least one of those civilizations survived an ancient conflict. The laser proves it."

"What makes you say that, Dr. Teranishi?" Atwood was trying to contain the damage, but he was only displaying his ignorance of military theory. The gap in competence between Atwood and Teranishi was obvious.

"Dr. Atwood, do I have to spell it out for you? The beam follows a consistent modulation format."

"Are you saying this civilization has one language? That an advanced civilization—a victorious civilization—will ultimately use one language?"

"Defeated civilizations adopt the language of their conquerors. Based on human history, that's not a daring interpretation. We also know something else that applies to humanity and will also apply to alien civilization—the coexistence of two civilizations means that one dominates the other."

Shocho was starting to think she had underestimated this Terran. Teranishi was every bit as formidable as her background suggested, something Shocho had at first been reluctant to accept. She was about to contact Atwood on her web to brainstorm a way to limit further damage when she received an alert signal from Chaa. "Where have you guys been?" she replied.

"In the south module. You need to get over here right now. We've discovered something serious—guns."

5

"IS THIS WHY you missed the meeting, to search the module?"

"I'd say it was worth it, seeing what we've found," said Chaa as he sent one of the weapons floating toward Shocho. Its ponderous inertial push as she caught it seemed to signal the defeat of everything she'd been working to achieve.

The south module held a full range of equipment needed to repair and modify the ship's observation devices and other infrastructure. Apparently the Terrans had found an innovative use for the equipment.

There were three weapons, all identical, constructed from cooling pipe and designed to function as mini mass drivers, using electricity to fire metal slugs. The weapons' stocks were sturdily built, suggesting heavy recoil.

"What do you intend to do?" asked Shocho. Her question implied that she was ready to hand leadership of the team to Chaa, but he refused to take the bait.

"I'm afraid you're going to have to ask yourself that, Commander."

"All right. I want all the numerical control data from the lathes backed up as evidence. Then delete the data from the machines. We'll need to secure these weapons. The question is how we should deal with the Terrans."

"I'll assume responsibility for that."

It was Dr. Whitley. He had appeared out of nowhere; he must have noticed Shocho leave the meeting. Perhaps he had been anticipating this development, though he was in no position to admit it.

"Responsibility? In this situation? We guarantee your safety and security, and you thank us by secretly fabricating weapons? What exactly were you planning to do with them?"

"I regret this, Dr. Kanda. I didn't realize Colonel Teranishi was so lacking in judgment. I'm afraid I've miscounted my cards."

Shocho felt a wave of anger at the way the Terrans had repaid her. They could hardly expect to get off with a slap on the wrist now. But losing her temper would only make the thin-skinned Terrans harder to deal with. That was something she could do without.

"All right then. As AADD's representative aboard *Shantak II*, I hereby notify you, as the senior Terran representative, of my decision. One: those responsible for fabricating weapons on board this ship are to be penalized by you, in accordance with Terran law. Two: until I am satisfied that it's no longer necessary, you and your team are strictly prohibited from setting foot in this module. Do you understand?"

Dr. Whitley seemed surprised. Perhaps he was expecting something much more aggressive. "Then no apology will be required?"

"What would I do with an apology? It won't improve the situation." Shocho spoke without considering that her words would amount to a slap in the face for a Terran. Dr. Whitley was shaking with anger. Under the circumstances, there was little he could say.

ATWOOD'S PRESENTATION—and the discovery of the guns—had made things worse, not better. Teranishi insisted that the guns were merely a ploy by AADD to illegally search their module. And naturally the AADD crew was now more suspicious of the Terrans than ever.

Observations continued on a very limited basis, done only by Atwood and a few other AADD crew. The Terrans created another barricade, sealing off the corridor leading to their module. Ironically, the rest of the crew welcomed this—it kept the Terrans in as well as keeping the AADD crew out.

The day after Chaa's discovery, leadership of the Guardians passed to him. Shocho's attempt to control the situation had ended in complete failure. Chaa knew this wasn't entirely her responsibility, but both of them agreed a change of leadership was necessary.

The trigger was the Terrans' reaction. They dismissed Whitley as their senior representative and replaced him with Maria Teranishi, who promptly refused to penalize any of her crew for the production of the guns. Chaa posted a Guardian in the south module, armed with a nonlethal weapon. This kept the Terrans from producing any more ranged weapons.

Under the circumstances, *Shantak II* no longer functioned as a joint observation platform. Shocho considered the entire effort a failure, but that was only because she was certain the situation couldn't possibly get worse. She was wrong.

⸺

"I SEEM to have underestimated them," said Shocho with a sigh.

"No," said Chaa, "this one is my fault."

"I don't think there's much point in arguing about it."

Chaa's confidence in his competence as leader was starting to waver. Shocho wanted to help him find a solution, not dissect his competence. "No one could have guessed they'd be able to assemble their own telescope."

Ignoring the possibility that the Terrans would discover *Hastur* on their own had been a miscalculation. If the approaching ship couldn't be located with *Shantak II*'s equipment, there should have been no way for the Terrans to learn of its existence. But the communications blackout had caused the Terrans intense anxiety, and so they had assembled a homemade optical telescope to allow them to monitor events in the solar system without the knowledge of the rest of the crew—another indication of the deep mistrust they harbored toward their offworld cousins.

The scope's construction was another of Teranishi's initiatives. Numerical data from one of the workshop machines indicated that they had carefully polished a section of sheet metal into a mirror to make a small reflecting telescope, apparently without Dr. Whitley's knowledge. Teranishi had also kept the observational data a secret from Whitley. Using the scope, they had sighted a large spacecraft approaching *Shantak II*. No Terran vessel matched its size. Though the scope's resolution was limited, they were able to calculate that the ship was heading directly toward them. This only served to harden their attitude further.

Confronted with the data, Chaa confirmed that the ship was *Hastur*. This infuriated the Terrans even more, since AADD had clearly been concealing facts. If Chaa knew the vessel's name, there must be other information he wasn't revealing. In fact, the Terrans weren't the only ones who found Chaa's explanation suspicious. The other crewmembers—those who hadn't been let in on the secret— also found it hard to believe he was being candid with them. Chaa found himself losing the trust of his own people.

Odder still was the fact that *Hastur* was again visible on *Shantak II*'s backup telescope. The ship was definitely inbound. Though it was still somewhat distant, it was clearly *Hastur*.

In a bid to regain the crew's confidence, Chaa attempted to contact the approaching ship while they watched. *Hastur*'s cylindrical form, visible on the monitor in the AADD mess area, was at a distance from which a reply should have returned within a few minutes.

But *Hastur* maintained radio silence. The minutes passed with no response, not even in Morse code.

With a spacecraft rapidly approaching *Shantak II* yet refusing to respond to hailing signals, the Terrans reacted with disbelief. Disbelief became deep anxiety and anxiety gradually turned to anger—anger mixed with fear. It was this fear that finally prompted them to act.

———

"WE'D BETTER REINFORCE the south module before this pot boils over," said Shocho. The entire team, including Chaa, responded via web with signals of agreement. Two more Guardians armed with nonlethal weapons immediately took up positions in the south module. Shocho and Chaa remained in the central lounge to monitor the situation. From here they could see anyone emerging from the Terran area of the ship.

"Maybe we shouldn't have tried to contact *Hastur* again," ventured Chaa.

"I can't say it made things better. But I would've done the same thing. How could anyone anticipate that the ship would disappear and then reappear? More to the point, what's your plan?"

"*Hastur* will be here soon. All we can do is hold on and wait. I don't know who she's carrying, but in any case we'll know a lot more about what's going on after they get here. What we do then depends on what we find out."

"I think you're right."

Suddenly the hatch to the Terrans' barrier popped open. Several crew rushed out, headed for the south module. As they went they yelled, "Out! AADD off our territory!"

Shocho did not hesitate. She told the Guardians in the south module, "Permission to fire." Scattered popping was quickly audible from the south module. The Guardian's weapons, powered by compressed air, fired projectiles that opened into nets of viscous acrylic fibers. Anything in the way would instantly be entangled and immobilized.

One of the Guardians fired her weapon, immobilizing the first two Terrans through the door. But it had been a feint. The third Terran was armed. His rail gun fired its metal slug with a flash of purple light and a metallic clang. This weapon was cruder than the ones Shocho had confiscated, probably a prototype.

The shot went wild, tearing into a ceiling beam, which erupted in a flurry of acrylic flakes. The Guardians tried to suppress the fire, but the shooter was behind cover. Their acrylic nets were no match for lethal metal slugs, so the Guardians turned their weapons on the equipment. At least the coating of sticky netting would prevent the Terrans from making immediate use of the machines. But the Terran's rate of fire increased. The air was pungent with ozone generated by the weapon's discharge. Seconds later the Guardians made a desperate run for it. The south module was now in Terran hands. Miraculously, no one had been hurt.

"AADD policy or not, the Guardians should have been issued lethal weapons." Shocho was seething with anger, but not merely because of this latest ploy. All it had taken was a comm blackout to reduce *Shantak II* to two warring camps. Instinct's triumph over reason had reduced her to speechless rage. She could not accept the idea that she had no influence at all over what was unfolding.

As soon as the Guardians left the south module, the Terrans welded shut the hinges on the central lounge's access hatch, making it impossible for anyone to enter their domain. Since they hadn't tried to seize the rest of the ship, they probably had just the one weapon.

The situation had reverted to what it had been earlier—except now the Terrans were armed. Shocho knew she couldn't afford to wait them out. They would produce additional guns as soon as they got the equipment back in operation. In a few more days they might be capable of killing everyone on board.

"What do you think they're up to?" Shocho turned to Chaa.

"It's been quiet since they sealed the hatch, but I'd bet they're getting ready to turn out more weapons. It won't take them long to input the control data for those rail guns. Killing machines are the one thing Terrans know how to make."

"That's just speculation. What do you intend to do?"

"Go in before they can finish what they started."

"That sounds rash to me." Seeing his look of surprise, she added—with a self-deprecating smile, yet still as an order—"Shut down the power and O_2 to the south module. You'll need to shut down the power in the west module too. Let's leave them with O_2 in their quarters. We're not barbarians. But bring the heat down, say, one degree every fifteen minutes. They'll surrender once the cold and the CO_2 levels get to them. There's no point in forcing our way in and taking casualties."

"All right. I'll take care of it."

Shocho was again in charge. Everyone on the team signaled their agreement, as if her status had never changed. Her mastery of the situation spoke for itself.

FORTY HOURS HAD PASSED since power and heat had been cut in the west module. AADD had taken the south module a few hours after the oxygen had been switched off.

"It's five degrees in the west module," said Chaa. "Should we keep going? We don't want to endanger their lives."

"If they don't want to die, they can surrender. Anyway, even with the heat shut down I doubt it'll get to freezing in there. If they stay in the same room, they can keep each other warm. They'll just have to deal with the CO_2."

"Do you think they'll do anything other than surrender?"

"Not if they're rational. We'll know soon enough. Conditions in their quarters must be pretty rough right about now."

Just as Shocho finished speaking, they heard a sharp *bang!* from behind the wall of the west module. The rail gun. The Guardians in the central lounge gripped their weapons, but there were no further sounds from the Terrans' side of the wall.

A few minutes later, they heard the sound of an acetylene torch being used behind the hatch. Then it opened and a white flag was pushed through the gap.

"Dr. Whitley?" Shocho called out. For a moment she wasn't sure, the tall figure beyond the open hatch was so pale and disheveled.

"Colonel Teranishi has met with an unfortunate accident. She is dead. We . . . we ask that you guarantee our safety."

"Medic!" Shocho shouted. "Hurry!"

The lights came on in the west module. In the mess area the medics nearly collided with floating body parts. The rail gun's slug had ripped Maria Teranishi to pieces. The mess was filled with thousands of floating globules of blood.

6

HASTUR STOOD BY to take the Terrans aboard and return them to Earth. AADD had urgently dispatched *Hastur* after all contact with *Shantak II* had been lost. Soon after Maria Teranishi's "accident," the laser transmitter had suddenly begun functioning normally again. The following day contact was reestablished with the Trojan relay stations.

The message that came from the Trojans indicated business as usual throughout the solar system. AADD and Earth were not at war. The message received by Shocho and Atwood about a communications blackout—"in view of possible armed conflict"—had never been sent.

What Shocho's guests from Earth thought of this news wasn't known with much certainty. The astronomers on the Terran crew seemed inclined to believe that the entire episode had been a plot hatched by Colonel Teranishi. The initiative to manufacture guns had certainly come from her.

The UN refused to comment in much detail and the truth was never made public. The official position was clear: *Shantak II*'s comm system had simply failed and Maria Teranishi's death had been accidental. But as instigator of the disturbance aboard ship, she was posthumously demoted to major, instead of receiving the customary two-rank promotion to major general. But then, the dead have always had to shoulder responsibility for the living.

Hastur's three-hundred-meter cylindrical bulk was dwarfed by *Shantak II*. To avoid interfering with the gravity wave observation work, *Hastur* waited a few hundred kilometers away and used a small shuttle to transfer the Terran crew.

"To be honest," Dr. Whitley told Atwood and Shocho as he was about to board the shuttle, "I still don't feel comfortable in this society of yours. I don't understand it. But I'm very honored to have worked with you, Dr. Atwood. As an astronomer, I found my time here intellectually stimulating, though our stay ended in an unfortunate manner."

Whitley extended his right hand. For a brief moment Atwood clearly didn't remember the meaning of this Earth custom; then, recalling his Terran cultural briefing, he awkwardly extended his hand. Nervous at this first zero-G handshake attempt, he almost sent himself into a backward spin. Whitley smiled and turned to Shocho.

"Commander Kanda, I'm afraid I may have put you to considerable trouble. I just want you to know that was not my intention. Don't misunderstand—I'm not apologizing. You and I live under different skies. I hope you'll understand that."

"I don't know about different skies, but we certainly stand on different ground." Shocho extended her hand. Whitley seemed slightly startled, then grasped it firmly. His hand was soft and warm. For some reason Shocho was surprised.

"By the way, I have a hypothesis about our findings, Dr. Whitley," said Atwood. "Please accept it as my parting gift."

Whitley couldn't conceal his surprise at the young scientist's sudden declaration. "A hypothesis? Would that be about your boggart?"

"Yes, concerning its identity. At my presentation, Colonel Terani-shi interpreted the conversion of Eingana's stars to black holes as evidence of a war between two interstellar civilizations. But I think another interpretation is possible. If one civilization in Eingana conquered another and took over the galaxy, why attempt to send a message using gravity waves? Gravity waves travel no faster than light waves or electromagnetic waves. Communication between different parts of the 'empire' could much more easily be accomplished with electromagnetic waves. It's far simpler technically. Nevertheless, whoever's sending the signal is using gravity waves."

"Gravity waves are far more effective for long-distance communication. Are you suggesting that the civilization, assuming there is one, is attempting some kind of intergalactic communication?"

"Surely you remember Project Ozma from your study of history?" said Atwood. "If humans considered it possible to send a message to alien civilizations, why shouldn't some other species have the same idea?"

"You're not suggesting that merely attempting to communicate indicates peaceful intent? That would be a logical leap."

"True. There's just as much chance that these hypothetical aliens are warlike. The important point is not whether they're pacifists or cruel conquerors. One would assume they're essentially different from humans. Perhaps we wouldn't even be able to communicate with them. But even if we can't communicate with them, the question remains: can we live in harmony with them? The answer depends on what we do here, in our own system. If members of the same human species cannot peacefully coexist, the chances of our coexisting with an alien civilization are vanishingly small indeed. Wouldn't you agree?"

"This sounds like a polemic disguised as scientific theory. What's your point?"

"I'll send it to your web—along with the supporting data."

Whitley's jaw dropped. For a moment Shocho didn't understand why. Then it hit her.

"Dr. Whitley? Are you using a web?"

"Certainly he is," said Atwood. "Of course, the specifications un-doubtedly differ from ours in many ways. That's how he monitored and analyzed the signals on our network. It's also how he was able to disable our laser transmitter remotely."

Shocho cursed her stupidity. Yes, Terrans loathed the devices. But they had the technology to implant them.

"Then the blackout . . . Wait, that doesn't make sense. Hacking the comm system is impossible even with the most advanced web. The system uses strong encryption. The key is changed every three days."

"I thought of that," said Atwood. "But then I realized the Terrans had their own communication equipment—and sending encrypted access keys to *Discovery* wouldn't attract any attention. *Discovery*'s own signal analysis capabilities could be reconfigured for code breaking. We were looking for a fault in our system, when all this time *Discovery* was working hard to break into it. All Whitley had to do was send our access keys to the far side of Sol System and wait for the answer. It would have been a lot of work, but it still probably only took a day or two to decrypt a new key. The Terrans were involved in configuring *Shantak II*'s signal processing software. They could've added a back door for their own use."

"You inferred all of that . . ." Whitley seemed staggered—not only that this young man had deduced his actions, but that he seemed to regard them as having little importance.

"Why did you do it?" asked Shocho, but Whitley's answer indi-cated a different interpretation of the question.

"I'm not prepared to explain it to you. Let's just say that in order to be treated like human beings, African Japanese have to handle dirty jobs from time to time."

"Let me guess then," said Atwood. "This entire exercise was meant to study how AADD's society and organization functions under extreme conditions. If we had used force against you, that would've been a good excuse to return the favor in some form. The experiment went well up to a point. Beyond that you had a problem—your own people were having more trouble withstanding the stress than we were. Ultimately they went so far as to fabricate weapons, and a life was lost. That's why the experiment ended. You ended it."

"Is that true, Dr. Whitley?" Shocho asked.

Instead of answering her, Whitley turned to Atwood. "You're every bit the genius they say you are, Atwood. But—how?"

"I formed my suspicions quite a while ago. Occam's razor, as Colonel Teranishi would have said. But I wasn't certain until the day I made my presentation. You used the term 'boggart.' Neither of you know this, but the only person I ever told about my use of that term was Commander Kanda here, and the only time I ever used it with her was in a subconversation between her agent and mine, via web. The fact that you were aware of it could only mean that you were tapping our web system with a web of your own. I have to admit, I wasn't ready to believe that a Terran web could handle something as sophisticated as breaking into our system."

"It wasn't a very sophisticated break-in," said Whitley philosophically. "All we did was alter the coordinates for the laser transmitter's servo mechanism slightly. *Discovery* knew about this, of course, and made the necessary adjustments. It was a simple matter to place a relay satellite near the Trojans to pick up your transmissions. With the laser pointing in the wrong direction, you obviously couldn't get in touch with anyone. But why didn't you say something? Why didn't you accuse me?"

"Why accuse you of anything? I have my responsibilities to AADD, you have yours to Earth. That's all. You lost control of your situation, but in the end you handled matters wisely."

Whitley turned and entered the air lock. Shocho thought she glimpsed the shadow of defeat darken his face. But Atwood was upbeat. Perhaps he didn't realize that this outcome represented defeat for Whitley. Or maybe he didn't even understand that for Whitley this had been a competition.

"I have my position to consider," said Whitley. "I can't put myself in opposition to it. But before I arrived here, I had always assumed that a clash between different civilizations was inevitable. Now I'm beginning to suspect that may have been a mistake. If we had nothing in common, there'd be no possibility of conflict."

The air lock closed. The only indication of the shuttle's departure was the changing lights on the console. The vacuum of space separated the shuttle from *Shantak II*.

"Well, they're gone." Shocho had completely missed the possibility that the Terrans might be using webs. This was something she'd need to consider at length and in private. She changed the subject. "Ninety AUs to Earth. What an enormous distance."

"Not at all, Commander. Nothing in the universe is truly far away. We have a ringside seat for events happening tens of thousands of light-years from here. Think about it the right way, and a hundred thousand light-years is just around the corner. In a different situation ten centimeters might be an unbridgeable distance. It all depends on how you look at it."

Atwood smiled. Somehow Shocho envied him.

EDUCATION EXTENDS human cognitive capacity. Learning is simply the cultivation of empathy. Education transmits far more than just knowledge.

AADD focused on the individual and emphasized education. The prodigies collectively known as Dr. Agnes's Mafia symbolized that emphasis. Ultimately they were all students of the genius named Agnes, but educating the "mafia" wasn't solely her responsibility. Hundreds of others devoted themselves to training these students, and the method used to educate them had an ancient pedigree. Promising young people from around the solar system were brought together to live in close proximity with the best minds in AADD. In these environments, their abilities blossomed in accordance with their potential.

They did not always receive instruction directly from Agnes. The program was conducted throughout the solar system and one could be a member of Agnes's Mafia without ever having met her. But a small number of students lived with her; in the process at least some degree of mutual empathy and understanding was acquired. Empathy was not something Agnes taught. It was a product of close proximity.

But education does not unfold the same way for each person. Even those who were supposed to have developed mutual empathy found the process difficult to understand. Ultimately, the structure of human consciousness remained a mystery.

THE WINGS OF CALIBAN
A.D. 2146-2171

2146
Port Shiva, Titania

"HEADS ... HEADS ... HEADS ..."

There was barely more than a whisper of gravity in the park. Shi'en flipped the coin over and over, her interest never flagging. If she did it just right the coin tumbled slowly upward, then just as slowly fell back down. When it dropped into her palm, it came up heads.

"The experiment's about to start. Look, don't you care?" Dr. Agnes was sitting on a bench, a bank of augmented-reality display monitors suspended in front of her. The setting was parklike, but this location was also one of the control nodes for the experiment. Agnes had done her work already. Now there was nothing to do but wait.

"My job is to protect you, that's all," said Shi'en.

"Is coin flipping part of your job?"

"Yes. It keeps me focused. Makes me a better bodyguard." Shi'en kept the coin moving. Protecting a seventeen-year-old girl seemed to hold little interest for her. This vibe made Agnes feel like a child, which made her angry. She felt the urge to pick a fight, but there wasn't time for that, so she decided to ignore her bodyguard. There'd always be time for a fight later, especially with Shi'en. Agnes alerted her agent program.

"Enhance."

She didn't actually need to speak to inform the agent what she wanted. But when Shi'en was around, she felt a need to fill up the time. The agent responded automatically. A sphere resembling a titanic birdcage grew larger on the center monitor. This was the AAD, the artificial accretion disk. Her experiment was about to take place inside that enormous shell.

The AAD was essentially a small Dyson sphere. The structure of the cage enclosing the black hole was supported by a rapidly rotating stream of heavy functional liquid. Heat-absorbing fins extended from the inner surface of the cage. The cage was 4,050 kilometers across. Tilted at a sixty-degree angle to the cage's rotation was the outer ring, 6,540 kilometers in diameter—roughly the size of Mars. A mesh structure extended downward from the ring toward the cage. This was the AAD's heat dispersion structure.

Agnes could see Titania, the largest moon of Uranus, floating in the distance beyond the lattice of the cage. Titania was over fifteen hundred kilometers in diameter. Cutting across its surface was a titanic gorge, seventy-five kilometers wide and almost as long as the moon's diameter. The gorge held huge deposits of nickel and iron.

Port Shiva, Titania's only city, was the hub of development on Titania. It had begun as a mining center for construction of the AAD. A ten-by-ten-kilometer section of the gorge had been roofed over, creating a gigantic pressurized living space two kilometers deep.

Once Kali was nudged into its final orbit around Uranus, Port Shiva expanded rapidly. Construction, maintenance, and management of the AAD required large numbers of people. The roof and its enclosed living space were designed to house these people.

Titania's gravity was a tiny 0.04 G. Within the habitat one could actually fly, with the help of simple equipment. This freedom to fly was a major factor in the design of the structures beneath the roof. At the bottom of the gorge, giant mines knifed deep into Titania's crust, while most of the habitats were built on platforms suspended from the roof, like castles in the air. The platforms also supported parks planted with trees, like the one Agnes and Shi'en were in now.

"Like hanging around here flipping a coin?"

"Can't say I care. Knowing the details of your experiment won't help me do my job."

Shi'en was right, but it irritated Agnes. It had taken a huge amount of effort just to get approval for this experiment. If her theory was right, this would be a historic moment in the history of science.

Dr. Agnes was, in clinical terms, a genius. Her parents and sisters were unremarkable; only Agnes was different. Her intelligence bordered on the freakish. For better or worse, AADD focused more on a person's gifts than on age or experience. From early on, Agnes had been granted authority—and burdened with responsibilities— that other children couldn't possibly imagine.

Being treated as an adult while still a child had both advantages and disadvantages for Agnes. Whether there was a net benefit, she couldn't say. One thing was certain: her real family had no place for her. Her sisters—even her parents—had no idea how to relate to her. To some extent her intelligence simply made them aware of their own limited abilities.

The drab duck that gives birth to a beautiful swan must drive the swan from the nest to preserve its self-image. Agnes had never felt a sense of belonging, not anywhere.

"This experiment will go down in history. Aren't you at all interested?"

"Sorry. Whatever it is, it won't affect my life."

It really was time for some bullying. "I'd like your honest opinion. Does Shiran have it in for me?" said Agnes.

"Commander Kanda regards you very highly, Doctor. That's the reason she sent me. The only reason, actually."

"She regards me highly? Have you forgotten what you tried to do to me?"

"I tried to assassinate you. It was much harder than I expected. That's why you're still alive." Behind Shi'en's deadpan expression was discomfort with this assignment. But that was something Agnes couldn't know.

A year before, at sixteen, Agnes had been the target of an assassination attempt. At the time Shi'en had still been using the name Rahmya and had been a top-class contract killer. That she failed to kill Agnes was, as far as Shi'en was concerned, merely due to certain unforeseen factors. It had just been business, but Agnes had a hard time seeing it that way.

"I tried my best to kill you. Just doing my job. Now I'm protecting you, which is also my job. There's no conflict."

"Would you really protect me if something happened?"

"Of course. That's why we're here. It's easier to protect you."

"But is it really safe? I mean, if it was safe, I wouldn't need a former ninja assassin to watch over me."

"I doubt there's anyone alive who can stop a professional hit better than I can. I assume that's why they sent me. I just follow the orders I'm given."

Agnes suddenly realized what Shiran Kanda was aiming at. Shi'en was being tested. They'd sent her to kill Agnes, then covertly prevented her from succeeding. Now she had to show she could play the other side if ordered. This caution made sense. Rahmya had come closer than anyone else to besting Shiran.

Even Agnes didn't know the full story behind Shi'en's joining the Guardians. The fact that she had once killed on behalf of a Terran mining cartel was itself highly classified. Agnes knew of this only because Shiran had told her personally—and verbally. "Her background as a professional assassin will help us protect you. Of course, we have full backup."

Now the countdown had begun and Agnes and Shi'en were alone in the park. This must explain the "full backup." Shi'en could not kill Agnes here. If she did, she too would be dead in seconds.

"Well, now I know one thing at least," said Agnes.

"And that would be?"

"Your boss holds some pretty heavy-duty grudges."

"I'm starting to get that feeling too."

AADD HAD DEPLOYED two orbital platforms for the experiment—spacecraft, in a sense, but really multipurpose facilities for research in space. They had been built purely for functionality, with bulky habitat modules and exposed propulsion systems attached to skeletal framework. Different components could be added or removed to service particular experiments. Now the platforms orbited Kali within the cage at a distance of two thousand kilometers.

AADD had dubbed the platforms Rosencrantz and Guildenstern. All of the moons of Uranus were named after characters in Shakespeare's plays; the custom had been extended to the orbital platforms.

Agnes was about to fire a stream of nanomachines toward Kali.

Kali was a rotating black hole with an electric charge. Unlike a static Schwarzschild black hole, Kali was surrounded by an ergosphere, an oblate region of space surrounding a black hole's event horizon. Via the Penrose process, objects could transit safely across an ergosphere given the correct course and velocity. An object entering the black hole's rotation could exit the ergosphere and extract energy and mass from the black hole in the process. Kali and its ergosphere were only a few millimeters across, but objects the size of Agnes's nanomachines should be able to pass through the ergosphere without being ripped apart by violent tidal forces.

Platform Rosencrantz carried a magnetic accelerator that would fire beams of nanomachines toward Kali with exquisite precision. There were five types of machine, each the same size and mass. They weren't particularly complicated; their simple structure was almost undeserving of the term *machine*.

The accelerator fired equal-sized groups of machines toward the ergosphere at nanosecond intervals. Thousands of groups firing in succession made a single swarm. The number of machines in each group and swarm was the same, but the proportion of each type differed from swarm to swarm, and the order of each type in the queue was randomized.

Each machine swarm exiting Kali's ergosphere would be detected by sensors on Guildenstern, which orbited Kali opposite Rosencrantz. Consistent with the Penrose process, there was no guarantee that a swarm would exit in the same sequence by which it entered. But noting the proportions of machine types in a single swarm allowed the swarm to be identified.

Kali's tidal forces were immense. Small deviations in the accelerator beam's accuracy could send some machines to their destruction, so Agnes planned to fire a trillion swarms into the ergosphere. Five hundred trillion machines comprised a swarm, yet the total mass of these five hundred trillion trillion objects was less than a gram.

"BEGINNING EXPERIMENT," whispered Agnes's agent. The center display began streaming data. Firing nanosized objects at nanosecond intervals wasn't a process humans could control, except in halting the experiment in an emergency.

Data streaming in from Rosencrantz confirmed that the experiment was proceeding normally, but so far Guildenstern had little information to offer. Although the nanomachines would pass through the ergosphere and reach its sensors almost instantaneously, before any insights could be provided an enormous amount of data had to be analyzed.

Guildenstern's sensors were equipped with data buffers and processing capabilities to deal with enormous amounts of information. Analysis would start only after all data was in; even then, data wouldn't be displayed until Guildenstern's analysis was complete.

Because of the danger to a human crew from nanomachines traveling at near light speed, Guildenstern was unmanned. Agnes had to be satisfied with the AI's confirmation that all systems were nominal.

From the frame of reference of Agnes's space-time, the experiment took less than an hour. If Agnes had been able to experience events from the nanomachines' point of view, she would have witnessed an unbelievable drama. But Guildenstern remained silent as to the nature of that drama; before it could offer any results it had to take an enormous trove of data and convert it into something human beings could grasp.

Agnes could only wait, alone with Shi'en and a coin in constant motion.

⸺◆⸺

THE OUTCOME OF THE EXPERIMENT was startling. Based on its results, Agnes insisted on a need to rerun the experiment, but her request was denied. The AAD was too important to place at the disposal of a single individual.

When Agnes realized that a second experiment would never be approved, she acted unilaterally.

She didn't understand the significance of her actions until later. Only then was she able to reflect calmly on them. When Shi'en appeared at her quarters in Port Shiva, she knew the game was up.

"I used to think you were the angel of death," said Agnes. "Now I know you're just a jinx."

"May I come in?"

"Why not? I can't refuse."

Shi'en entered Agnes's quarters without answering. Titania's slight gravity gave the room a floor and a ceiling, with finely controlled air circulation eliminating the need for most furniture. The room's AI noted Shi'en's heat signature and adjusted the airflow to lift her into a sitting position above the floor. On Titania circulating air supported everything from eating utensils to people.

Agnes floated in front of Shi'en. It didn't look like refreshments were going to be on offer.

"So? What are you going to do with me?"

"Actually I don't know," said Shi'en. "That's up to Commander Kanda. In the course of my work I discovered that you'd hacked the Distribution Management System and the Sol System Universal

Network. That's the extent of my involvement on this one."

"That's all? You didn't come here to arrest me?"

"I have a new assignment. They're transferring me to Mars. I don't know how they plan to deal with you. You'll probably find out tomorrow. Maybe the next day."

"Then why go to the trouble of coming here? Not just to say goodbye, I'm sure."

"Partially that. But there's another reason. That experiment, shooting nanomachines past Kali. What did the data tell you?"

"I thought it didn't interest you."

"Not at the time. I'm interested now. I know you haven't released your formal report, but you sent the abstract to a few people. I did some digging. Anyway, after reading your abstract, the commander had me monitor your activities. You did exactly what she was afraid you'd do."

"Is that why you want to know what the experiment showed?"

"Maybe I'm just not used to AADD's way of doing things, but I don't like the idea of being shipped off to Mars without knowing the reason. What are they so afraid of?"

"I guess I was a fool to think you might've developed an interest in science. All right, I'll tell you. Just don't blame me if you find it impossible to believe. Agreed?"

"Agreed. If I can't follow you, that'll be my problem."

Dr. Agnes commanded her agent with a gesture. A hologram in the shape of a squashed donut materialized in the space between Agnes and Shi'en. It was a representation of the ergosphere; countless tiny points of light wriggled inside it.

"Those moving points are nanomachines. Just staring at them won't tell you anything. The key to understanding their movement lies in the space that surrounds them."

"What did you discover?"

"Kali emits X-rays that are anomalous for this class of black hole. I suspected that some sort of substance might be trapped in the ergosphere. My experiment confirmed it. The ergosphere contains a substance in plasma form. My analysis shows that the plasma exhibits a coherent structure. Firing the machines through the ergosphere created local disruptions in that plasma—disruptions it promptly repaired on its own."

"Meaning there's some sort of entity inside Kali?"

"Common sense suggests that what we're seeing is a self-organizing reaction triggered by the nanomachines, something like the Belousov-Zhabotinsky reaction in a test tube. But you're right. We can't rule out the possibility that there's some sort of life-form concealed in the ergosphere. Perhaps it's something we can't detect directly, and what we saw during the experiment was a kind of shadow cast within the ergosphere, a shadow from some other dimension. All we can do is infer the presence of an entity from what we see.

"If you'll excuse the poetic license, there's a mystery unique to the space-time within that black hole. If this is a life-form, we may be forced to rethink our definitions of life from the ground up. But it's just a hypothesis. All we know from that one experiment is that a structure exists. Further investigation is clearly needed. We should run another experiment."

"You proposed it, they rejected it. So you broke into the distribution system looking for assets to run your experiment. I don't get it. Is this important enough to run those kinds of risks?"

Agnes gestured again. The hologram disappeared. "If there's a life-form beyond our imagination inside Kali, I suspect it's there for a reason. Of course, that hypothesis stands on pretty thin evidence, which is why I haven't told anyone about it until now. You're the first."

"Honored, I'm sure."

Dr. Agnes proceeded to lay out an astounding hypothesis. Some might say it was ludicrous. But her experiment—and her criminal actions—grew from that hypothesis.

Soon thereafter, Shi'en took her leave. She had learned what she had come to find out.

YOU'LL EITHER BE a weapon or a threat. We'll have to find out which.

Shiran's words echoed in Shi'en's memory. When she'd first heard them, she'd thought they were justified. She had been Shiran's enemy.

Joining AADD had taught Shi'en how harsh space could be. The environment sometimes turned people into fiends. This was a risk humanity faced as it tried to make a home in space. Yet the pressure exerted by this harsh environment also worked to steadily expand human potential. A species capable of conquering such an environment need fear nothing.

On Shiran's orders, Shi'en had maintained her surveillance of Dr. Agnes after the experiment—and discovered her attempt to hack into AADD's distribution system. When she reported this to Shiran, the result was a new assignment with no explanation.

Why had Shiran thought it necessary to put Agnes under surveillance? Shi'en suspected she knew the answer. Shiran had boundless confidence in humanity's potential, but she also feared its potential for stupidity.

Shi'en paused to ponder how she felt about this herself. AADD had offered her a place in its society. Compared to her life on Earth, it was a far more desirable situation. Still, the feeling of being an outsider had never really left her. Perhaps she'd feel differently one day, but for now she was on the outside.

Shi'en felt neither optimism nor pessimism about humanity's future. She wouldn't deny the possibility that the species might propagate throughout the solar system until the sun burned out. Or perhaps humankind would reach some sort of dead end, an impasse that would force the birth of a completely new phase of human potential.

But what did all this mean for her? She had never felt fear. She had never been overconfident. It might be satisfying to continue observing AADD as an outsider. Maybe there was space within AADD for a path of her own, a path with a third-person point of view. The prospect pleased her. Outsiders had their own way of doing things.

Someday, someone may go into space to make contact with that entity—an intelligent entity living inside a black hole, she thought. *If it happens, I'd like to be there with Agnes to see it.*

Shi'en felt a sudden conviction that the day would come.

2151
In Orbit Around Titania

AADD's orbital platforms could be linked to create larger structures. Compound Orbital Platform Cecily Neville was just such a structure. Cecily Neville linked Rosencrantz and Guildenstern in a squared-off U, forming a giant space dock in orbit above Titania. Within the dock's embrace, work to complete humanity's first unmanned interstellar probe was entering its final stages.

Agnes was nonplussed. "What was important enough to get you and Shiran to come all the way from Mars?"

The lattice framework of Cecily Neville was pierced by a huge cylinder that included crew quarters; the progress of work in the dock could be monitored from anywhere inside this cylinder. Agnes, Shi'en, and Aguri presently floated in a glassed-in lounge at one end of it.

Aguri Kanda was Shiran's daughter. Soon she would be five years old. The little girl and her rangy Guardian bodyguard made a strange pair.

"Guardians take vacations too, you know," said Shi'en. "Commander Kanda came to Uranus for sightseeing. She wanted her daughter to see the accretion disk. It's by far the biggest thing we've ever built, as big as Mars."

"All right—but why are *you* here?"

"The commander wants to enjoy some of the sights on her own, but she can't unless someone looks after Aguri."

"Maybe her 'vacation' with her daughter is just cover for a top-secret investigation with her trusted subordinate?"

"What kind of investigation?"

"How should I know? It's top secret."

"Listen, we didn't come all the way to Uranus for any secret investigation. I'm just here to babysit the kid," said Shi'en.

"It's just that a badass ninja riding shotgun for a four-year-old makes less sense than a secret investigation."

"Children should be protected. They're not like adults."

"So you thought I was a child at seventeen?" Agnes said.

"I thought you were an adult at sixteen."

Shi'en had caught the reference a little too quickly. Agnes hadn't really meant to dig up the past. It had been six years since Shi'en's failed attempt to assassinate Agnes. Since then, Agnes had faced danger and brushes with death several times in space. The incident with Shi'en was over and done with as far as she was concerned.

But Shi'en didn't see it that way. Since joining AADD, she had also faced many dangers, far more than Agnes. Still, she had never been able to put the assassination attempt behind her.

On the whole, the relationship between the two women was positive, but Agnes would hesitate to call it equal. "I'm sorry," she said. "I didn't mean it that way."

"Don't apologize. Sometimes you do things you can't go back and change, that's all. It's in my nature to let things go, like water under the bridge. But I don't think people should forget who they are."

"You're pretty hard on yourself."

"I'm an adult."

"Sorry about that."

Aguri stared out the window at the work proceeding on *Richard III*, oblivious to their conversation. Not that she was so interested in the ship itself. Anything taking place in zero gravity seemed to enchant her.

Christening humanity's first unmanned interstellar probe *Richard III* might have seemed somewhat inauspicious, but the use of names from Shakespeare's plays was an established tradition for Uranus. Unfortunately, most of the names with positive associations had already been taken, leaving only villains and tragic figures. More obscure names like Cecily Neville were suitable for orbital platforms, but an interstellar probe deserved something memorable. *Richard III* certainly met that requirement. This was another reason why the platform where the probe was under construction had been named Cecily Neville: Cecily Neville, the fifteenth-century Duchess of York, had been Richard III's mother.

The probe's design was straightforward, although it looked more like a cargo shipment than a spacecraft. A cluster of fuel tanks, a powerful main engine using matter-antimatter annihilation for propulsion, the engine's heat sink, and a bulky nose shield designed to protect the probe from interstellar dust—functional beauty it might have, but compared with the refined designs of interplanetary spacecraft, *Richard III* looked more like a warrior preparing to face the battlefield. This was no accident. In the wastes of interstellar space, the probe would be beyond human help or intervention.

"Listen," said Shi'en. "You're not bitter about the way we handled your case five years ago, are you?"

"Why not use the correct term? 'Criminal activity,' maybe?"

"All right. How's this: are you still bitter about the measures we took after your criminal activity five years ago?"

"Did you travel all the way here to pick a fight with me?"

"I told you, we're here for sightseeing."

"There's another possibility," Agnes said. "Let's see . . . Dr. Agnes is running the interstellar probe project, so she might be plotting more criminal activity. Maybe we'd better get out there and investigate her. Does that sound familiar? This project gives me access to tons of antimatter."

"Why should you still be under suspicion for a childish prank committed five years ago? Children deserve protection, as I just told you. In fact, the commander is grateful for what you did."

"Grateful? I have a hard time believing that."

"You created a phony research project and tried to procure supplies for it. Thanks to you, security for the Distribution Management System and the Sol System Universal Network was redesigned from the ground up. It's far more reliable now. At least no one's hacked into it since you managed to. We've plugged the holes."

"Meaning there's no one more dangerous to you than me."

"For you to be a threat you'd need capacity and intent. You've got the capacity to commit a crime but not the intent. Therefore you're not a threat. Your involvement in this project proves it," said Shi'en.

"How can you be sure I've given up on that experiment?"

"I'm not. All I need to be sure of is that you've given up breaking the law. You've changed since then. You're an adult. Right?"

"I'm an adult. But I haven't changed."

Shi'en floated over to where Aguri peered out the window, fascinated by the views of Titania. Shi'en wasn't cutting the conversation short; rather, she wanted to explain to Aguri what she was seeing. Agnes reluctantly joined them.

Cecily Neville was just passing over Port Shiva. Five years ago, only one percent of the fifteen-hundred-kilometer gorge had been occupied. Now the AAD was fully operational and Port Shiva sprawled across ten percent of the gorge's length.

The Old City, as the earliest sections were called, had been given over to forest. Trees had been allowed to grow without culling and the resultant natural forest had become an attraction for the inhabitants. In the newer districts of the city, genetically modified dawn redwoods had been planted at regular intervals. The trees were thriving; in a few decades they would be big enough to support habitat platforms.

"Haven't you seen trees before?" Agnes asked the little girl. In zero gravity she could easily position herself at Aguri's level. "There are forests on Mars."

"But on Mars trees don't go underneath me," said Aguri. She was riveted by the fascinating sights flowing past. Beyond Port Shiva and the gorge, Titania was blanketed with devices for relaying energy from Kali to the rest of the solar system. This offered a very different view from anything one could see on Mars.

When Kali became a satellite of Uranus, its moons were inevitably affected. The greatest impact fell on Uranus's largest moon, Titania.

Kali's orbital insertion was the culmination of two decades of effort. For the first time, humanity had altered the orbit of a celestial body with significant mass. Efforts to change the orbit of the next object—Titania—began immediately. Its distance to Uranus was around 436,000 kilometers. Kali, with a mass close to that of Mars, orbited Uranus at only 550,000 kilometers. Naturally Titania's orbit would be greatly perturbed by proximity to such a large body.

Kali's influence threw Titania out of its original orbit and into an elliptical one beyond Oberon, one with a perihelion of 660,000 kilometers and an aphelion of 30,000,000 kilometers. But for Titania to act as a relay station for energy transmission throughout the solar system, this orbit needed further adjustment. Gigantic propulsion devices were built along its equator. Every time Titania reached aphelion the devices would fire, using Kali's energy to gradually nudge the moon into a circular orbit thirty million kilometers from Uranus. This orbital adjustment had been in progress for several years.

"Are you saying you haven't given up on that experiment with Kali after all?" Shi'en continued looking down at the surface. "That probe is going to the stars, not into a black hole."

"Ever heard the expression 'kill the rider by shooting the horse'? One of this project's main goals is to search for extraterrestrial life. That's why we're not going to just fly by different planetary systems. We're going to slow down, stop, and investigate thoroughly. That's why I need so much antimatter."

"Wouldn't flybys be technically simpler?"

"Of course. But to spend nearly a decade getting somewhere just to have a few hours for observation isn't good enough for this mission," Agnes said. "By carrying enough fuel to decelerate, we can observe continuously over several years. If we run into problems, we can still do flybys."

"Still . . . the nearest system is Alpha Centauri, and that's a triple system. Proxima Centauri has planets, but it's a flare star. I doubt life could survive under those conditions."

"You know me—I'm convinced there might be life in the most unlikely places."

"I knew you lacked common sense even before you ran that experiment with Kali. Still, if the hypothesis you told me about five years ago is correct, this probe might be a way to verify it. Seems like a very slow way, though."

"Of course, we may not find life, not even life outside our theories of what life is. But even finding nothing would tell us something valuable. The search for life doesn't have to have positive results to be worthwhile. I can't ignore the nearest star if that's the fastest way to test the probe's capabilities," Agnes said.

"I see. Well, that makes sense."

"Now are you convinced that I'm not plotting anything?"

"Pretty touchy, aren't we? I already told you why we're here."

Shi'en noticed that Aguri had drifted over to a different spot along the window. From there she could see the entire length of *Richard III.*

"Why doesn't that ship have windows?" Aguri asked Agnes.

"Because nobody's going to ride in it." Agnes floated down to Aguri's level again. The little girl's eyes widened in surprise. She pointed to the probe accusingly.

"Nobody rides in it? How can it go without people?"

"It has an advanced AI . . . The ship can think, just like you. That's why it can go all by itself."

"Won't it be lonely with no people?"

"No, it'll be fine. It's going to look for friends who understand what it wants."

By the time Aguri would be old enough to understand Agnes's real meaning—to understand the concept of extraterrestrial civilizations and intelligent nonhuman entities—the probe would be making its first transmissions from a distant star. Agnes gazed at the little girl, lost in thought. The time required to reach even the closest stars was a significant fraction of the human life span. What could Agnes accomplish in the time left to her?

Agnes and Aguri gazed down at *Richard III*. Shi'en wordlessly activated her agent. "Professor? White. Just as I expected ... Nothing suspicious on your end? I'm not surprised. This probe is what it appears to be. I don't think this investigation is worth more of our time. You'll be heading back, then? Yes, that's a good idea. I can be ready immediately ... What? What do you mean, look after Aguri? Why should we stay another week? No, that's not what I'd call a special vacation. Professor? Professor!"

Shi'en's agent signaled that the call had been terminated. Shiran's trust in Shi'en must have been boundless. Either that or Shiran didn't care much about her daughter.

Shi'en had served under Shiran Kanda for five years without ever quite figuring out what sort of person her boss was. As soon as she thought she understood, Shiran pulled something off the wall—like this. Someone else might assume this meant Shiran trusted her. But Shi'en knew the truth. Shiran would simply never accept that Shi'en—or anyone else who worked for her—was an outsider. From the moment you met Shiran, you were an insider in her eyes.

"Auntie!" Aguri sailed toward Shi'en, heedless of her own inertia. Shi'en caught her carefully, as if the girl were an egg that might break. "Momma told me to stay and play with you."

Parents often gave their toddlers small webs that could be worn on the wrist. It seemed that Shiran had also given her daughter her own agent program. It would let Shiran stay in touch with Aguri even when Shiran was sleeping.

"Amazing. The badass is also 'Auntie'?" marveled Agnes.

"Mm-hmm. Momma said she likes to be called that," the girl said.

"I guess children really are innocent. Right, Shi'en?"

2164
Port Shiva, Titania

Thirteen years had passed since *Richard III* had departed for Alpha Centauri. In the years that followed, humanity launched one probe after another toward the nearby stars. By 2164 the total had risen to fifteen.

Each probe was functioning as designed, sending data back to the solar system. Of course, a large portion of this data was routine system status information. But as the images of Alpha Centauri became more detailed, scientists began monitoring the data on a daily basis.

Still, thirteen years is a long time for human beings. Most of the original program participants had been reassigned to other departments and were looking after other projects now, their places taken by new people.

Agnes and Aguri were on a dish-shaped structure twenty meters wide. Benches and vegetation gave the area a gardenlike atmosphere. In the center of the dish was a round, roofless brick structure. The structure contained a number of data-processing devices, most of them embedded in the walls.

The dish hung suspended from a dawn redwood, the trees having been incorporated into the structure of Port Shiva itself. This particular dish was one of the control points for the interstellar probe program.

Agnes had upgraded the probes since *Richard III* had been launched. There were three generations of probes now; the third and newest sported a more efficient matter-antimatter propulsion system and was faster than the previous generations. Because of this, data from second-generation probe *Desdemona*, bound for Epsilon Eridani, would reach Agnes later than data from third-generation probes like *Apemantus* and *Beatris*, launched toward the more distant 61 Cygni and Epsilon Indi.

"Are all fifteen probes telling us this?" asked Agnes.

"No, we're only getting data from the first ten. The last five haven't reached maximum velocity yet."

"If our five newest probes aren't traveling fast enough to gather this data, it's going to be less precise than I hoped. Charon, Triton, and *Shantak II* are corroborating the probe data. But those facilities were built to detect specific phenomena. They're not broad-spectrum observation sites."

"True, they're not," Aguri said. "The big interferometers on Charon and Triton look for gravity wave sources by comparing time differentials across data. But the interferometers themselves aren't specialized. It's their data-processing infrastructure. They're doing narrow-band analysis geared to what they're looking for. But the newest processors can handle a much wider range of frequencies."

"So you used those processors to go back and review the data to verify your hypothesis?"

All interstellar probes, beginning with *Richard III*, were equipped with an advanced AI. For the first few years of their missions, the AIs could be monitored and, within limits, upgraded remotely, especially if the AI encountered a problem beyond its capacity. *Richard III*'s AI was upgraded not far from the solar system. The data from each probe was applied to the next, making each one more "experienced" than the last.

This increasing sophistication had led to an unexpected discovery. The newest probes were capable of accelerating to around thirty percent of light speed. At this speed, starbow effects—relativistic Doppler shifting of starlight—were not yet pronounced. They could only be detected with specialized sensors. Confirmation of the starbow effect was an important goal of all interstellar probes, beginning with *Richard III*. Astronomers hoped that relativistic Doppler effects would open up new methods of observation.

The ability to upgrade AIs after launch played an important role in the effort to gather starbow data. Now Aguri had discovered that the effect applied to gravity waves as well as electromagnetic waves.

Unfortunately, the need to shield the fast-moving probes against interstellar dust prevented them from serving as long-range laser interferometers. Instead, the probes observed minute frequency shifts in starlight caused by gravity. Careful analysis of the data confirmed that starbow effects applied to gravity waves.

Aguri had boosted the accuracy of the probes' sensors by networking them. The results were confirmed by the large interferometer arrays on Triton and Charon and by *Shantak II*, the gravity-wave observation platform half a light-day from the Sun. Collating all this data would eventually lead to new ways of utilizing gravity waves in astronomical research.

"And this tells you that gravity wave transmissions are going to other points in the galaxy?" said Agnes.

"That's what the data suggests. That implies the existence of nonhuman intelligences."

"Atwood said the same thing. During the standoff on *Shantak II*, he never stopped observing. He's completely sold on the idea of nonhuman civilizations. Has the bug bitten you too?"

"Atwood is a strange bird, but he's a first-rate scientist. The trouble we had with the Terrans put an end to the ultra-long-baseline gravity-wave observation project. But Atwood's data and his hypothesis seem solid to me."

Agnes peered at the girl with narrowed eyes. She had practically raised both Aguri and Atwood. They were the first members of Agnes's Mafia, which had led some parents to joke that giving one's child a name beginning with *A* was essential for a future as a first-rate scientist.

"I'll concede that the data points in the direction you say. But don't you think it's premature to pin extraterrestrial intelligence on coherent gravity waves? After all, why use gravity waves? They penetrate interstellar dust and gas better than radio waves, but on the whole they're too weak. Radio waves are technically far better for communication.

"So we seem to have detected gravity wave transmissions. What about two centuries of monitoring for intelligent signals in the electromagnetic spectrum? We've found nothing. And even if we assume this is an intelligent signal, how do you account for the complete absence of similar electromagnetic signals? Of course, we're not in a position to guess how an alien civilization would choose to communicate, but still . . ."

"Maybe it's more natural for them to use gravity waves. Maybe their biology makes it easier. You can't rule that out."

"What kind of life-form would find it natural to use gravity waves?"

"Well, for example, a life-form like the one you speculated about, once upon a time."

"How in the world did you find out about that?"

"Your paper on the nanomachine experiment is in the public domain."

"But there must be as many AADD experimental papers as there are stars in the galaxy," Dr. Agnes said.

"Yes, but the revolutionary ones are as scarce as the number of moons in our system. I didn't find the math that hard to follow. Well, okay, I had to pay careful attention to some sections."

The relationship between the two women was more like that of an older sister and a younger sister than research advisor and student— sisters bound by shared outlook and vision instead of blood. They still lived in the same complex in Port Shiva, though Agnes traveled so often now that Aguri only saw her rarely. AADD's family units often followed this pattern; Agnes's Mafia was no different.

Still, Agnes wouldn't have expected Aguri to read all of her old papers. It certainly wasn't essential for her work. But she understood why Aguri had made the effort—she wanted to know as much about Agnes as she could. Perhaps Aguri idolized her. Agnes had nursed similar feelings toward some of her teachers.

"To be honest, something else made me remember that report just now," said Aguri. "If the galaxy is filled with gravity wave transmissions, there must be evidence in Sol System. Gravity wave observation doesn't have the history that radio astronomy does, but we do have lots of data."

"But Atwood is the only one reporting signals that seem to be coming from an extraterrestrial civilization. Application of the gravity-wave Doppler shift to observational technique is still in its infancy. You may have trouble getting repeatable results."

"Agnes, there's corroboration. I found it in an old paper from 2123, right after they started work on the AAD."

"2123 . . ." Agnes caught her breath. The year was engraved in her memory. Everything started in 2123.

"It was before Chandrasekhar Station was complete, when all they had was the ring around Kali—Ouroboros. You know the story. The ring's AI was convinced it had detected gravity waves. The result was nearly a catastrophe," Aguri said.

Catherine Sinclaire had been Agnes's instructor, and she had been on Ouroboros when it happened. Catherine had been young at the time—almost a child, really. Agnes knew her report of the incident by heart. Catherine and her partner Tatsuya had told her the story many times; reliving it together had become a kind of family tradition.

"Yes, I know about that incident," said Agnes.

"Do you know what I thought when I read your paper on the experiment?" Agnes didn't answer, but she could guess what Aguri was about to say. "Aiming a gravity wave transmission at a black hole implies a receiving entity. That's why you fired nanomachines toward Kali, isn't it? To find that entity?"

Agnes's hunch had been correct. "I was your age when I did that experiment. Maybe your examination of the existing data is the next logical step."

"But why didn't you confirm it with another experiment? Maybe they wouldn't let you then, but you could do it now."

The question awakened painful memories for Agnes. "I have

to think about others now," she said at length. "About what's best for AADD."

Aguri clearly didn't understand. Agnes felt she was looking into a mirror. At Aguri's age, she hadn't been able to grasp the concept of personal responsibility either.

"That incident has always been attributed to AI failure," said Aguri. "But the gravity wave transmission the AI detected was identical to Atwood's signal. At least, the format is the same."

"There's another interpretation. Maybe Atwood's signals and the Ouroboros signal both come from regular, human-induced structural perturbations."

"But *Shantak II*'s detectors are suspended in a magnetic field, isolated from the ship and from external vibrations. You know that as well as I do. We can rule out a false reading. The only other possibility, given the identical signal formats, is that the Ouroboros AI really was picking up a gravity wave transmission like the one we're seeing now."

"Then why haven't there been any transmissions aimed at the AAD since then?" Dr. Agnes asked.

Aguri stared, baffled. Agnes was a scientist. Even now she must be convinced that Kali harbored an unknown life-form. Why look for objections to data that might point to the reality of an extraterrestrial civilization?

"Agnes, listen to me. We changed Kali's orbit. If the Ouroboros signal was originally intended for Kali, the black hole isn't in the right location to receive it anymore, because we moved it. These transmissions appear to be very tightly focused."

"Appear to be, yes. But that's just an assumption. Focus presupposes intention, and there may be no intention at all behind these signals. It's all speculation. We have very little reliable data. How are you going to get around that?"

"There is a way—manned interstellar missions. If the signals beamed at our system are being transmitted to other stars in the galaxy, we should be able to verify that. And that calls for sending humans, not just probes!"

"Manned spacecraft have to be far more reliable than probes, you know."

"I think it would be worth it," Aguri said.

"Is that why you came to see me personally?"

"Is that a problem?"

"Talking to me personally isn't going to move things forward. If you really think manned interstellar missions are necessary, submit a formal proposal. If you convince the steering committee, then in ten years your first spacecraft might be departing on its mission."

"*My* spacecraft?"

"Of course. Once you propose it, it's your baby." Agnes felt a twinge of déjà vu. Eighteen years ago, when Agnes had described her idea for an experiment to fire nanomachines through Kali's ergosphere, Catherine had said the same thing to her.

Eighteen years from now, Aguri would say these words to someone else. Who would it be?

2171
Port Shiva, Titania

Agnes hurried over to the console where Shi'en was standing. "What do you mean she's in no condition to leave port? What's going on?"

Shi'en returned her gaze calmly, as if she'd been expecting this reaction. "*Titus Andronicus* is a military spacecraft, and she's not going anywhere right now."

"I got that. I want to know why."

"Because she's in dock for a major refit."

"What refit? No one told me."

"I'm not surprised. This is a Guardian project. We're upgrading her fire control systems. All of her weapons have to be dismounted. At this moment she's useless as a warship."

"How long will the refit take?"

"Agnes, could you calm down a little? A dismount/remount for a battery of laser ordinance and ultra-long-range pulse cannons can't be hurried. It certainly won't be finished in time to do anything about *Caliban*."

"Can't you send it out without weapons?" Agnes asked.

"*Titus Andronicus* was built to deal with armed incursions from Earth, not internal security problems. It's going to take weeks to refit. Anyway, if the stalemate's still unresolved by the time *Andronicus* is ready to leave dock, you'll really have problems."

"Damn it . . . Yes, you're right, of course." Agnes kicked the floor of the shop in irritation, launching herself upward fifty meters. She reversed her trajectory, pushing off from the underside of the next level to float back down in the microgravity; she landed on her feet in front of a holographic projection of a sharply tapered silver cylinder. The ship it represented was three and a half kilometers long, shaped like a huge tusk.

This was humanity's first interstellar spacecraft, *Caliban*. The base of the cylinder was encircled by twenty-four chemical boosters. These boosters—burning first methane, then hydrogen—would accelerate the spacecraft to the optimum speed for ignition of its antimatter engines. They would also ensure that the ship was at a safe distance from Titania and its hundred million inhabitants before the ship's antimatter engines began spewing huge amounts of radiation.

Titania was at aphelion, the best position for *Caliban* to begin its journey. The problem was simple: the ship was carrying 160,000 tons of stolen antimatter.

"What do you intend to do, Shi'en?"

"Nothing. Wait. See what Aguri does. The antimatter on that ship—and the radiation it will release if it fires its anti-m drive—has made hostages of Port Shiva and one hundred million people."

"Is that why you don't want to use *Titus Andronicus,* even for a demonstration?"

"I can't. I wouldn't even if I could. We don't solve problems like this with force. *Andronicus* and her sisters were built as symbols of deterrence. Terrans understand such symbols. They were developed to project power, not to use it. Unless there's no other option. You have to understand that."

But Agnes already seemed to have abandoned the idea of trying to put a scare into Aguri. She absently poked a finger into the hologram in the vicinity of the crew quarters. "Has Aguri really commandeered the ship?"

"You're a scientist, Agnes. You may not want to accept the situation, but I need you to open your eyes. She's taken control of *Caliban*."

Caliban had been constructed to investigate the source of the anomalous gravity waves, the existence of which had been confirmed by multiple unmanned probes. While a few scientists still insisted that the transmissions were a natural phenomenon, most believed the data proved the existence of an extraterrestrial civilization. Both camps agreed on the need to devote more resources to observation.

Furthermore, *Shantak II* had just completed observations, unprecedented in scale and detail, of the dwarf galaxy Eingana—observations that confirmed the presence of phase-modulated gravity waves. This added fuel to the arguments favoring stepped-up investigation. It also reinforced the confidence of the team working to develop manned interstellar spacecraft, since the main goal of such vessels was the search for extraterrestrial intelligence.

Initially Agnes had managed the program; later Aguri had taken over. Development had proceeded smoothly. Through close team collaboration, it had taken only seven years to complete the prototype spacecraft instead of the decade or more projected by the plan.

The original plan hadn't included sending *Caliban* to the stars. Instead, the ship's design and operating systems would be tested in visits to the Kuiper belt and the Oort cloud. Such distances were great enough for shakedown voyages, but not too great for high-speed rescue craft if problems were encountered.

Caliban's operating trials were set to continue for five years. After that, construction would begin on additional spacecraft, and after another five years, a manned interstellar probe would depart for the stars every year. The first data was expected to reach the solar system around the year 2200.

Evidently Aguri hadn't been willing to wait ten years for the first spacecraft to launch. In theory, *Caliban* was fully capable of interstellar travel; however, because of the project plan it hadn't been fueled to capacity with antimatter.

Aguri's reaction to the cautious rollout plan was vehement. "We have the ship and all the fuel she needs. The only problem is our lack of will! The evidence is staring us in the face. An extraterrestrial civilization is sending out signals. What are we waiting for?"

But she had forgotten one reality: AADD encompassed a wide range of outlooks and values. Older steering committee members understood the importance of manned interstellar exploration, but they saw Earth as an unfriendly presence—the incidents on *Shantak II* had only served to confirm that—and were more concerned with husbanding resources for possible conflict with Earth.

The younger generation of AADD officers didn't see Earth as a significant threat. For them, the search for nonhuman civilizations was far more important and any surplus resources should be funneled into those efforts. The generations talked past each other—and Dr. Agnes was with the older members. The last time they'd met, Aguri had listened impassively to Agnes's arguments against plunging ahead without further preparation. Now Agnes sensed that her urgings had probably struck the younger woman as betrayal, though on the surface Aguri had seemed to accept them.

But Aguri had hacked into AADD's Distribution Management System and arranged for stockpiled antimatter to be transferred to *Caliban* under false pretenses. She and a crew of like-minded confederates had been just hours from launching *Caliban* toward the source of the transmissions when the Guardians had discovered her intrusion. The entire interstellar exploration project had been frozen, Aguri's crew summarily dissolved.

Why couldn't she wait ten years? This was a mystery to Agnes, but with 160,000 tons of antimatter in orbit around Titania, it was a mystery of decidedly secondary importance.

Agnes had been staggered to learn of Aguri's crime. When she discovered that Aguri had seized *Caliban*—and threatened to fire its antimatter engines if the Guardians attempted to board—she had been overwhelmed by a sense of helplessness.

For her part, Shi'en was mystified to discover this side of Agnes. Back when Agnes first assumed her place on AADD's highest steering committee, relations with Earth had entered an extremely difficult and dangerous phase. AADD's growth and culture were perceived by the Terrans as threats to their societal norms. Even when the Terrans had begun to assemble an armada, threatening to seize the artificial accretion disk by force, Agnes's calm hadn't wavered. Why would she be seized by panic at the rebellion of a mere student?

Shi'en knew that Aguri was one of the few people in the solar system who really understood Agnes—and that this understanding was mutual. Shi'en knew, too, that the steely personalities of these two women had also been responsible for much misunderstanding, both between themselves and with others. In a sense, both women had wasted a good portion of their lives correcting the mistaken impressions of others, impressions they themselves had been responsible for creating. That made it all the more important for each woman to have the other, to have someone who was family.

For Agnes and Aguri, trust didn't mean licking each other's wounds. Understanding might mean acceptance, but neither of them would ever allow self or other to become dependent. Although they held each other to standards that sometimes left scars, their shared bond of trust was too deep for mere pain to cause either to run away. That confidence was probably the reason their relationship had endured for so many years.

But Shi'en had always walked alone, and she frankly didn't understand why it was necessary for two people with such grounds for conflict to sustain a relationship. If mutual wounding was a prerequisite for building deep trust—and mutual dependence was ruled out—then why not choose rejection? Not, of course, that it made any difference to her.

Still, it seemed to Shi'en that ultimately this mutual understanding had proven a mirage. Although Dr. Agnes and Aguri knew far more about artificial intelligence than the average scientist, Shi'en had a hunch that both of them found two-way empathy with another individual an especially difficult challenge. Such minds might do better to seek trust from an AI.

But perhaps their tragedy was that they expected understanding from another person—a person as close to family as anyone they'd ever had. And now Agnes was panicking in a way Shi'en had never seen.

"She's still ignoring our attempts to contact her. That's not all." Shi'en shook her head and webbed her agent program's latest data to Agnes.

"What is this? She's erased her personal data from the network!"

"Are you really surprised? You hacked the system once yourself. If Aguri can slip a hundred and sixty kilotons of antimatter past us, purging her system data wouldn't be much of a challenge."

"How can you be so calm about this, Shi'en?"

"Getting excited doesn't generate results. If Aguri has demands, she'll make them. Then again, she may not have any."

"What does that mean?"

"Maybe she already has what she wants. If so, she's no threat to us, at least as long as we don't interfere. Port Shiva is in no danger."

"You mean . . . ?"

"Aguri isn't holed up on *Caliban*. She's preparing for departure. The ship's configured to be pilotable by a single individual if necessary. Aguri was the chief system designer. If anyone can do it, she can, even without universal network support."

"But it will take her fifteen years to reach her destination. How can she . . . Oh, this is just absurd!"

"Agnes, listen to me. Twenty-six years ago, when Shiran captured me, she gave me two choices: join the Guardians on the spot or try to make it back to Kobe City alone on foot—ten days in the desert with no survival gear and barely any supplies. I'd already decided to join her, but I wasn't going to do it her way. She had to see that I was choosing the Guardians my way. Sometimes how you face life is more important than life itself. Now Aguri is facing the same decision—and she has more than enough provisions for the trip."

That was when it happened. Shi'en's last few words were drowned out by the roar of rocket boosters. Aguri had made her decision. In a moment, *Caliban* became a fiery beacon against the blackness of space, then a bright but dwindling star. Agnes stared in disbelief. The spacecraft was already invisible to the naked eye, but the monitor showed twenty-four boosters falling symmetrically away, like flower petals. Finally, *Caliban*'s eighteen AE-20 antimatter engines roared to life.

Even at this distance, Titania was directly in the path of the radiation stream. But Port Shiva faced away from *Caliban* now, and the bulk of the planet acted as its shield.

"So she escaped from the solar system," Agnes said. "No, she escaped from me." Agnes felt overwhelmed by the loss. "I don't know what she could have done to reject me more absolutely."

"You underestimate her, Agnes. Aguri is Shiran's daughter, your disciple. Look at what she's become. She's not escaping anything. She's just gone ahead of you."

"I don't know what that means."

"*Caliban* is a prototype. Aguri may travel to the stars, but I doubt she can make it all the way back on her own—unless more ships are built to follow her. Now she's made certain that will happen. New spacecraft will have to be designed, plus the infrastructure to support them."

"Shi'en, were you expecting this? The distribution system... How did Aguri...?"

"You want to know the truth? Ask her yourself. You were the

first to carry the search for unknown life to the stars. Or have you forgotten?"

Caliban still showed faintly on the monitor. The light from its engines reminded Agnes of a newborn star.

And for Shi'en, that fading gleam was herself in another life—a solitary figure trekking slowly across a desert, carving a new destiny through the badlands of Mars.

THUS HUMANKIND took their first steps toward the stars. Was it accident or necessity? There is more than one way to answer this question. After all, we are not omniscient.

We can say this much: these first steps enabled humans to encounter nonhuman intelligences. Without these steps, humanity would never have been able to achieve empathy with entities such as ourselves. Contact with humans has taught us that there are more ways to perceive the universe than via mass and gravity waves alone. We now perceive light and sound, just as humans perceive gravity waves.

Of course, many complications, many twists and turns were required to reach this point. Differences in the structure of consciousness brought AADD and the inhabitants of Earth to the brink of violence, despite the fact that they were members of the same species. And ironically, the same differences allowed humans and nonhumans to communicate successfully. That success will become the necessity of the future.

We know this—that happenstance is necessity in disguise.

AFTERWORD

I FIRST CONCEIVED THE IDEA of an artificial accretion disk on March 14, 1988. But it was eleven years before the first story, "The Dragons of Europa," appeared in *SF Magazine*, and fourteen years before this book was published—a very long gestation period, even for me.

I can pinpoint the date with accuracy for a simple reason. I recorded it in the book that inspired the idea: Jun Fukue's *Kōchaku Enban heno Shōtai* (Introduction to Accretion Disks, Kodansha, 1988). As I turned the pages, I experienced a wave of intellectual excitement. After I finished it, I was almost a different person, and the impression it made is still fresh in my memory.

And the idea of an artificial accretion disk was born.

Naturally, my original concept was quite different from the stories that finally became this book. This included the construction of the artificial accretion disk as well as the organization and culture of AADD. Possibly the only ideas that survived unchanged were the concept of creating an artificial accretion disk around a small black hole, of using it to terraform Mars and create an energy transmission system on the scale of the solar system.

In fact, there is one other element that remained unchanged, but I will set that aside for now. One hint, though, would be that this linked series of short stories is a history of the development of the solar system, and at the same time is planned as a work of First

Contact SF. Ultimately, humanity will probably reach the center of the galaxy by one means or another. The story will probably take me several years more to write. If the reader would be kind enough to accompany me on the journey, I will be extremely gratified.

In any event, this world of short stories about AADD was inspired by a single scientific text. While I have not conducted a survey and cannot speak in quantitative terms, I think most ideas for so-called "hard science fiction" are inspired by actual contact with the front lines of science. The inspiration might come from a book or might arise out of a conversation with a practicing researcher. Of course, a work of hard SF is neither scientific analysis nor educational text. It is strictly fiction.

Still, basing the core of a novel on a scientific idea takes it beyond the boundaries of the concept story. Different authors will probably derive different meanings from the same idea. It may be that the act of writing hard SF is itself a search for meaning. In my case, that search will probably occupy the rest of my life.

In closing, I would like to thank Atsushi Noda, Naru Hirata, Masao Hirota, Tomohiro Araki, Jun Fukue, and Masahiro Maeno, as well as the members of the Minor Body Exploration Forum (http://www.as-exploration.com/mef/index.html), for their invaluable suggestions and guidance. I would also like to thank the members of the Osaka Chapter of the Space Authors Club, especially Housuke Nojiri and Yasumi Kobayashi, for many stimulating discussions.

In "Hydra's Ice," I dubbed the Mars orbital elevator Tsutenkaku, after the landmark tower in Osaka. As far as I know, the first writer to apply this name to an orbital elevator was Sakyo Komatsu, in his short story *Tsūtenkaku Hakkutsu* (The Excavation of Tsutenkaku) in the January 11, 1965, edition of *Sankei Sports* newspaper. (The author refers to the orbital elevator as a "space bridge.") I obtained Komatsu's kind permission to do the same in this work.

From the appearance of the various stories in magazines to their publication here, I was the grateful recipient of unfailingly spot-on counsel from Yoshihiro Shiozawa, editor-in-chief of *SF Magazine*. In a sense, this book is a Hayashi/Shiozawa collaboration. I acknowledge my debt to him and the other individuals mentioned herein.

Finally, I would like to thank my wife for all her help during the writing of these stories.

—Jyouji Hayashi
July 2002

ABOUT THE AUTHOR

Born in Hokkaido in 1962. Having worked as a clinical laboratory technician, Jyouji Hayashi debuted as a writer in 1995 with his co-written *Dai Nihon Teikoku Oushu Dengeki Sakusen*. His popularity grew with the *Shonetsu no Hatou* series and the *Heitai Gensui Oushu Senki* series—both military fiction backed by real historical perspectives. Beginning in 2000, he consecutively released *Kioku Osen*, *Shinryakusha no Heiwa*, and *Ankoku Taiyo no Mezame*, stories that combine scientific speculation and sociological investigations. He continues to write and act as a flag-bearer for a new generation of hard SF.

HAIKASORU
THE FUTURE IS JAPANESE

SUMMER, FIREWORKS, AND MY CORPSE BY OTSUICHI

Two short novels by the Shirley Jackson Award–nominated author, including the title story and *Black Fairy Tale*, plus a bonus short story. *Summer* is a simple story of a nine-year-old girl who dies while on summer vacation. While her youthful killers try to hide her body, she tells us the story—from the point of view of her dead body—of the children's attempt to get away with murder. *Black Fairy Tale* is classic J-horror: a young girl loses an eye in an accident, but receives a transplant. Now she can see again, but what she sees out of her new left eye is the experiences and memories of its previous owner. Its previous *deceased* owner.

ROCKET GIRLS BY HOUSUKE NOJIRI

Yukari Morita is a high school girl on a quest to find her missing father. While searching for him in the Solomon Islands, she receives the offer of a lifetime—she'll get the help she needs to find her father, and all she need do in return is become the world's youngest, lightest astronaut. Yukari and her sister Matsuri, both petite, are the perfect crew for the Solomon Space Association's launches, or will be once they complete their rigorous and sometimes dangerous training.

DRAGON SWORD AND WIND CHILD BY NORIKO OGIWARA

The forces of the God of Light and the Goddess of Darkness have waged a ruthless war across the land of Toyoashihara for generations. But for fifteen-year-old Saya, the war is far away and unimportant—until the day she discovers that she is the reincarnation of the Water Maiden and a princess of the Children of the Dark. Raised to love the Light and detest the Dark, Saya must come to terms with her heritage even as she tumbles into the very heart of the conflict that is destroying her country. The armies of the Light and Dark both seek to claim her, for she is the only mortal who can awaken the legendary Dragon Sword, the fearsome weapon destined to bring an end to the war.

THE OUROBOROS WAVE BY JYOUJI HAYASHI

Ninety years from now, a satellite detects a nearby black hole scientists dub Kali for the Hindu goddess of destruction. As human society expands to Mars and beyond, the generations-long project to harness the power of the black hole pits the retrograde humans of Earth against the imminently rational men and women of the Artificial Accretion Disk Development association. While conflicts simmer, a mystery within Kali itself tests the limits of intelligence—that of both human and machine.